MIDNIGHT EXPOSURE

ALSO BY MELINDA LEIGH

SHE CAN RUN

MIDNIGHT EXPOSURE

BY MELINDA LEIGH

Montlake
Romance

Text copyright ©2012 by Melinda Leigh
All rights reserved.

Printed in the United States of America.

Published by Montlake Romance
P.O. Box 400818
Las Vegas, NV 89140

ISBN-13: 9781612184753
ISBN-10: 1612184758

This book is dedicated to my family.

To my husband and kids, for believing I could be a success long before I did; my mom, for wallpapering the state of New Jersey in bookmarks; my dad, for buying copies of my book for everyone he knows; my grandmother, for teaching me early in life that a good story begins with murder; and my grandfather, for *encouraging* the local librarians to stock my books.

Your support means more to me than I can possibly express.

CHAPTER ONE

October 31

"Dude, I swear I'll get us out of this."

"It's OK." John bit back the whine hovering on the tip of his tongue. Camping sucked. And being lost for two days in the middle of the Maine woods sucked even more. He sniffed. Frozen air stung his nostrils. Wood smoke cut through the heavy scent of pine. "I smell smoke."

"Yeah, me too. Cool." In front of him, his roommate, Zack, hefted his pack higher on his narrow shoulders. "Going in the right direction then."

"I guess." Doubt laced John's voice. A scant half inch of snow dusted the game trail like powdered sugar. How had his roomie talked him into spending their fall break camping? "Long as it's not a forest fire."

"Not this time of year." Zack shook his head. "Gotta be a campsite close by."

John's gaze swept the shadowed, desolate forest surrounding them. Bare tree limbs pointed to the overcast sky like skeletal fingers. "That's what you said an hour ago. You sure you don't want to stop here?"

Zack stopped and turned around. "Tell you what, city boy. If we don't run into campers in the next half hour, we'll pitch our tent and start a fire."

1

"Man, it ain't the cold that bothers me. Chicago isn't exactly the tropics. It's just so freakin' quiet." *And dark.* No streetlights, no headlights, no neon signs. John pulled his fleece hat lower over his ears and stamped his feet. Inside his boots, his toes stung.

Zack sucked in an audible breath and blew out a puff of steam. "It's peaceful."

"Creepy," John corrected and sent a silent prayer skyward that his transfer application to the Art Institute of Chicago had been accepted. "Dude, I don't blame you for losing the trail. Everything looks the same out here. But you're crazy if you think this is fun." John's parents had thought he'd be safer attending college out here. Not. Didn't they know Stephen King was from Maine?

The trail curved around an outcropping of boulders. An erratic, pulsing glow shimmered ahead as faint murmurs carried over the crackling of fire. Hope flared warm in John's chest. "Do you hear that? It's people!"

"I told you everything'd be OK." Zack slapped John's shoulder as he hurried forward. Ice and dead pine needles cracked underfoot. "Hello?"

Instead of the expected greeting, the voices ceased, cut off suddenly like somebody'd pressed the Pause button. A shudder started at the base of John's spine and quivered up to his nape. He stopped.

Zack moved ahead. "What the fuck?" His voice dropped to a puzzled whisper as he stepped through a patch of underbrush.

John pushed aside an evergreen bough. "What?"

The tree limb snapped back and John ducked under it. Straightening, he faced a clearing the size of a half basketball court. A circle of upright wooden posts, thick as telephone poles and tall as men, ringed the space. Five shorter poles formed a half-moon in the middle. In the center of their arc, next to a large flat-topped stone, tall flames rose from a shallow pit. The tingle on the back of his neck surged into an electric charge. The wilderness might be foreign to him, but John recognized creepy shit when he saw it, and this whole place had a disturbing woo-woo feel.

John scanned the clearing. *Where are the people?* He'd heard voices. He knew it. Heat from the fire reached out to his frozen fingers, tempting him to step closer.

But he didn't.

"Hello?" Zack called out again before John could stop him.

"Shhh." John's harsh whisper echoed. "Something's not right."

This place was giving off nasty vibes. Zack was the expert on trees and animals and crap, but the street smarts that had saved John's ass from those gangbangers last spring wanted him to beat feet.

John's gaze dropped to the ground. Just inside the ring of posts, a dark line cut through the thin glaze of frost, as if someone had poured liquid in a giant circle, marking it for something.

John reached for Zack's arm to pull him back into the trees, but Zack was already moving forward.

Into the circle.

"What are you doing here?" A man stepped out from behind one of the posts. Silhouetted, with the fire to his back, he was featureless.

John's arm dropped to his side. Firelight gleamed off a dark hooded robe that draped the stranger's frame and pooled on the ground around his feet. John's weirdo-meter went ape shit.

"We're lost." The enthusiasm drained from Zack's voice.

The man took three steps. The expansive hood obscured his face like the Emperor's from *Star Wars*. He was close enough to touch Zack now. "You crossed the line."

John knew he should step forward with his friend, but his legs wouldn't budge. His feet refused to cross into the circle. There was something critical about that line. John could sense it.

The robed man shifted. A blade flashed silver in the moonlight, flicked at the white skin of Zack's neck. A gurgling gasp issued from his lips. Shock choked John like a hand clamped around his neck. His friend's body crumpled to the frozen earth. Zack's head hit last, bouncing twice on the frozen ground. One final breath clouded the night air as dark liquid gushed from the wound onto the frost in a wet streak, like the first brushstroke on a blank, white canvas.

Steam rose from the pooling blood in a lazy swirl. Staring, numb with nightmarish disbelief, John's empty stomach turned. He blinked and ripped his gaze from his dead friend to the shadowed figure. The man's head swiveled toward him. One hand clenched the knife by his thigh. A thick drop of Zack's blood dripped from the point and stained the snow next to the man's boot.

Horror paralyzed John's brain, but primitive instinct guided his feet. He turned away from the warmth of the fire, away from the man he'd thought was going to save them, and fled toward the darkness of the surrounding forest in a dead and panicked run. The rubber treads on his boots slipped on the slick ground. He crashed through a curtain of pine boughs. His gaze darted ahead. Which way? He paused and listened, disoriented by the monotony of the landscape. Footsteps rustled through the underbrush behind him, unhurried, as if his pursuer had no reason to rush.

John stumbled away from the sound. His legs pumped awkwardly, like pistons in need of lubrication. Branches whipped his face. Pine needles sliced his frostbitten cheeks like razors. He ducked behind the wide trunk of a towering tree and clamped a shaking hand over his mouth to quiet his breaths. His panting echoed over the rush of blood in his ears, the sound of futility.

The man was going to hear him.

He was going to find him.

He was going to hunt him down and kill him as if he were a well-fleshed buck.

Branches creaked over his head as the wind blew powder from the tree's limbs. The crisp night air closed in on him, caressed his sweat-coated skin. A hollow at the tree's base tempted him to curl up and hide like an exhausted rabbit.

Like prey.

A twig snapped to his left. He pushed away from the tree trunk and staggered forward—into a solid, robed chest. John bounced backward and lost his footing. A hand snagged the front of his coat, righting him, hauling him closer, up onto his toes. John's heart plummeted as he raised his gaze. Icy blue eyes stared back at him from the narrow slit of a black balaclava.

A huge fist slammed into John's temple. Pain exploded behind his eyes. His senses faded.

That's it, then. At least it can't get any worse than this.

But as blackness closed in on him, his last thought was that he could be wrong.

CHAPTER TWO

December 16

"You have arrived at your destination," the smooth, feminine voice of the GPS announced.

Jayne eased off the gas and squinted through her windshield at a whole lot of nothing. She glanced down at the palm-sized screen Velcro'd to her dashboard. Number twenty-seven, Route Six was supposed to be right in front of her. But on both sides of the two-lane road, a thin veneer of snow glazed an endless forest. No driveway. No mailbox. No sign of civilization.

Now what? The pale dusk of an overcast sky bleached the landscape, as stark and lonely as an Ansel Adams black-and-white. As much as Jayne appreciated the aesthetic beauty of the wilderness around her, she did not want to still be appreciating it in the dark, especially with her gas gauge nosing into the red.

Wait. What was that?

She guided the Jeep onto the shoulder in front of a narrow opening in the woods. Cleverly tucked behind a stand of pines, a black wrought-iron gate blocked the entrance. In the center of some simple scrollwork, right under the Private sign, was the number *27* in gold script. A narrow lane curved away from the gate. Beyond the bend, the corner of a house peered through the winter-bare branches. Cedar and glass. Modernish.

Odd house for an eccentric wood-carving hermit. She'd expected some sort of log cabin. Maybe a fenced compound complete with razor wire.

She drummed her fingertips on the steering wheel. Decisions, decisions.

To the left of the drive sat a stone pillar with a brass call button. Her first option was to ring it and pretend to be lost. Hope to get invited up to the house. Option number two: She could play it safe and head back to the nearby small town, where she had a reservation at a bed-and-breakfast. She could check in and grab dinner. Polite inquiries could be made. Someone was bound to know R. S. Morgan, if he truly lived here. But would the locals blab about one of their own? Probably not.

Number one was her best chance of getting the shot she needed, but that plan required her to lie. Tabloid photographers—and she'd better get used to the label—didn't get warm and fuzzy welcomes from the subjects they stalked. R. S. Morgan could have rottweilers or a shotgun handy. Number two was the most sensible choice. But safe didn't pay the bills. Jason, her creep of an editor, had given her one week to get the first-ever pictures of the reclusive sculptor. Juicy details warranted a bonus corresponding to the degree of juiciness. One week. Then Jason was sending another photographer. Her younger brother's medical care hadn't come cheap. Her family needed that money. Big-time.

She zipped up her jacket, palmed her smallest camera, and slipped out of the Jeep, shuddering at a blast of arctic wind on the exposed skin of her face. Quiet settled over her like a shroud. Under it, the protestations of her conscience were loud and clear.

You have sunk to a new low.

Ice crunched beneath her furry boots as she approached the gate. All she had to do was snap one picture of an old wood-carver and be on her way. No biggie, right?

She patted her pockets for gloves but came up empty. Her naked and freezing finger depressed the call button. Nothing. She tried again, but the speaker remained stubbornly silent. Which opened up option number three: sneak up to the house for a look-see.

Except for the iron barrier, the property wasn't fenced. There was plenty of room to slip around the gate post. But she'd never violated anyone's privacy like this. She'd never admit this to her editor, but those other celebrity pics she'd sold him were freak occurrences, taken while she was shooting pictures of Philadelphia for a travel brochure the same month a major motion picture was being filmed in the Old City section. One actress had literally fallen at Jayne's feet—and hurled on her shoes. There was a big difference between snapping some drunken Hollywood tartlet's picture outside a club and spying on someone's home.

Didn't matter that Danny's hospital bills were dragging her family under. Didn't matter that Jayne and her three brothers were going to lose the family tavern because of said bills. Didn't even matter that this artist's privacy was going to be violated whether it was Jayne or another photographer who snapped the pictures. Her feet wouldn't budge. This was not gonna happen.

Danny was getting better. That's what really mattered. He was adjusting to the limited use of his hand, and his post-traumatic stress was improving. The whole robbing-Pete-to-pay-off-Paulie thing wasn't exactly a new experience for her family. They'd always squeaked by in the past. But this time, Jayne wanted to be instrumental in getting her family out of a jam. Her brothers had been dragging her deadwood around for long enough.

She slipped the camera into her pocket. New plan. She'd go to town and attempt to contact the elusive sculptor legitimately. She'd explain that his anonymity was compromised and try to talk him into a picture taken on his terms. Morals were such a pain in the butt.

"Can I help you?"

Jayne spun around at the deep voice behind her. She splayed a hand over her thumping heart. A tall, lean man was climbing out of a giant red SUV. Jayne had been so engrossed in her personal debate she hadn't even heard it approach.

Her mental head smack was cut short as he stepped into full view. Power radiated from a broad, parka-encased chest and long, jeans-clad legs. The winter tan and muscular throat told her he spent time out of doors, even in this climate. Jayne's gaze slid higher, over a strong-boned face and shadowed, square jaw that begged her to snap his profile in black-and-white. Military-short, dark brown hair topped green eyes as clear as polished emeralds.

Oh. My. If this was R. S. Morgan, she would have to change her opinion on eccentric artists.

"I'm sorry. I'm blocking your driveway. I'm lost." *Liar, liar, pants on fire.* "My cell won't work and I'm really low on gas." She shushed her conscience. Those other things were true. "I'm on my way to the Black Bear Inn in Huntsville."

"You missed the turnoff for County Line Road. It's about ten miles back." A Southern accent laced his voice, smooth as warm caramel.

"Oh."

He stepped closer. Despite her five feet ten inches, Jayne looked up at him. *Nice.*

"It's another ten miles into town from the turn," he said. "Will your Jeep make it that far?"

It would, but just driving off wouldn't give her any more infor-mation. "I'm not sure." Sheesh. The next time she went to confes-sion, she was going to be saying Hail Marys for a week straight.

"I'll get you a gallon of gas." No offer to accompany him to the house. *Drat.* And he was being awfully, inconveniently nice. Her job would be a lot easier if he were as rude as the puking diva.

"Thanks so much." She offered her hand and a grateful smile. "I'm Jayne Sullivan."

He hesitated, staring down at her extended hand for a few seconds before accepting. His long, elegant fingers were marred by numerous small scars, and his callused grasp was burning hot as it engulfed Jayne's frozen fingers. She felt like something inside her was softening, slowly melting like an M&M on her tongue.

"I'm Reed Kimball. If you'll just move your Jeep, I'll get that gas." He tugged his hand free, and Jayne realized how hard she'd been holding it.

"Oh, right. Sorry." Face hot, Jayne hurried back to her vehicle and pulled forward. The gate opened and Reed Kimball drove through. A few minutes later, the truck reappeared. He tilted the nozzle of a fuel can into her Jeep without a word.

Jayne bounced on her toes, forcing blood into her frozen feet. "Nice piece of property."

"Mm." He made a vague sound of agreement and focused on the gas can.

"Have you lived here long?"

"A while."

"You don't sound like a Maine native." Jayne pressed on. "Where are you from originally?"

He removed the can and screwed on the fuel cap. "There you go. That should get you to town."

A sudden gust of wind ripped through the pines at her back. Needles trembled. His polite dismissal made her suddenly aware of her remote surroundings and of the size of the quiet man standing so close to her. Despite all her self-defense training, he looked like he could overpower her in seconds. She didn't get a threatening vibe from him, but their isolation felt acute. As did her vulnerability.

Relax. If he had sinister intentions, he wouldn't send you away. But her subconscious ignored reason, and a familiar ache sprung into her well-knitted jawbone. She forced a smile and hoped he attributed the slight trembling of her voice to the cold. "Thanks again."

He stepped back as she opened her door. "Big storm headed this way. Be careful."

"I will. You have a Merry Christmas." Jayne glanced over her shoulder. Those clear green eyes dropped to the ground. Was that a blush? Had he been checking her out? A quick flush of warmth spread through her belly, a surprise and a sharp contrast to her icy hands and feet. She reached for the camera in her pocket. Could she snap a quick, unobtrusive picture of him? His gaze was level again, sharp and clear and not missing a thing. Probably not. He stepped back into a shadow, and her chance was gone.

She cranked the heat to full blast before executing a tight U-turn. Jayne watched the gate close in her rearview mirror. Kimball stood behind the iron barrier, still as the forest around him. As he faded into the twilight, her fingertips traced the circular scar on her cheek.

She jerked her hand down and gripped the steering wheel hard.

Reed Kimball had nothing to do with the threat she'd left behind in Philadelphia. If she allowed herself to be afraid of every man she met, she was still a victim. Not acceptable. She didn't drag her sorry butt to all those years of counseling for nothing. She was moving forward, becoming a productive member of society. Besides, her brothers had been there when *she* needed *them*. Now it was her turn to help her family. She had the opportunity to get them all out from under the debt Danny's Iraq War injuries had rung up. Time to woman up and get the job done.

But whispered lies repeated in her head as if caught in an endless loop. Her throat tightened. The imaginary forearm pressed against her windpipe felt real as it had that summer night.

If you're quiet, I won't hurt you.

— — —

Standing behind the closed gate, Reed unzipped his parka and watched the woman drive away. The bitter wind was a welcome snap-out-of-it slap.

Now *that* was a woman. A warrior goddess. Tall and curvy, with legs up to her chin and curly red hair down to her butt. All she needed was a flowing emerald robe and a jeweled broadsword. Despite her urban fashionable clothing, he'd had the most ridiculous urge to kneel at her feet. The odd scar on her face didn't detract from her beauty, but Reed couldn't help speculating about its origin.

With a shake of his head he drove to the house and parked. A strange woman's scar was none of his business. Their Siberian husky mix, Sheba, raced across the front yard and circled his legs with a happy bark. He leaned down to greet the dog. His son was at the open front door, all long and lean and seventeen. Green Day, cranked to maximum volume, pulsed from the doorway. "Who was that?"

"Just a lost motorist." Reed stepped down to the frozen ground. The modern design of his house looked bare, just straight lines and glass. Normally he liked its minimalist design, but right now it looked colorless and, well, blah. He should've put some Christmas lights on the shrubs or something. "I could use some help with this wood."

"Sure." Scott ducked back into the house and emerged a minute later in boots and a jacket. He closed the door behind him, but the bass-drum vibrations seeped through. "What was she doing up here?"

"I didn't ask." Reed opened the rear of the Yukon. "I gave her directions and some gas, and she went on her way."

"Where was she going?"

"She said Huntsville." Reed grasped the long section of tree trunk and pulled it toward him.

"Really?" Scott grabbed the other end as soon as it was within reach. "Why?"

"I've no idea." A dull ache gathered in Reed's temple. He could've asked, but Miss Sullivan had had enough questions for both of them. Reed didn't like personal conversations any more than he liked strangers.

"Odd, though, don't you think?" Scott asked.

"No." *A little.* "And none of our business." Keeping to himself was a long-ingrained habit that kept Reed and his son firmly under anyone's radar. Just where they needed to stay. He would never allow his son to suffer another media barrage.

"Has to be visiting someone. You can count the number of cars that drive down this road a day on one hand."

"She just missed the turnoff for town, Scott. End of story."

Scott had a point, though. Just what was Jayne Sullivan doing in the middle of nowhere? Huntsville didn't attract winter tourists.

Together, he and Scott carried the hunk of white birch into his workshop, through the front room and into the specially designed space in the rear half of the building. Large skylights and adjustable track lighting allowed him to keep the blinds tightly closed. They heaved the wood onto the worktable. Sheba followed at their heels.

Scott patted a dark bulge in the trunk. "Nice burl."

"Yeah." Reed stroked the large knot that protruded from one side. This spot would have a unique grain, intricate swirls, once stripped of its flaking bark.

"You need any more help?"

"No. I'm good. Thanks."

"I'm going back to the house, then. Got some homework to finish up." Scott headed for the doorway. "Oh, you got two calls. Mae needs something fixed, and Chief Bailey wants you to stop by the station tomorrow."

Reed's headache spiked. "Christ, I've turned him down a hundred times—"

Scott held out both hands in mock surrender. "He said to tell you it isn't about the job. He just wants to pick your brain."

"Oh. Sorry." *What could the police chief want?* Reed pressed two fingers to his temple. Had to be police business, or Hugh would've just stopped by.

"Dad?"

Reed looked up. Scott studied the floorboards.

"You ever think about dating Brandon's mom?"

Shit. "Mrs. Griffin's a nice lady, Scott, but there's just no chemistry between us." Scott's best friend, Brandon, had a very attractive mother, but Reed had zero interest in Becca Griffin.

Scott scuffed a toe on the cement. "You mean you don't like her *that* way."

"Exactly."

"Do you ever like anybody that way?"

Jayne Sullivan's gorgeous turquoise eyes popped into Reed's head before he could stop the vision, but he shook his head at Scott. He just couldn't afford to let anyone get close. No sane woman would date him if she knew the whole truth anyway. "No. Not really."

"It's been a long time." Scott hesitated at the threshold, staring at his boots. Wet and frayed, the untied laces trailed on the floor. "It'd be OK if you found someone else."

"I know." But they both knew he wouldn't even try.

"Whatever."

As soon as the door closed behind Scott and the dog, Reed pulled a piece of scrap paper from his pocket and scribbled Miss Sullivan's Pennsylvania license plate number on it. He wondered if whatever favor the police chief was going to ask was worth the price of a background check. Either Reed was paranoid or she'd been overly friendly and nervous.

Just wary of a stranger, or something else?

Probably he was letting his son's overactive imagination get to him. But he couldn't be too careful. Not with his past.

From the minifridge in the corner he grabbed a Diet Coke, then walked in a slow circle around the bench. Quiet settled over him, instant as winter nightfall.

So like his mother, Scott liked blaring music, noise, and people. Reed craved solitude. In an attempt to purge his thoughts of his wife's death and Chief Hugh Bailey, he perched on a stool and sipped his drink. He watched the wood, willing it to speak, but the trunk stared back at him in defiant silence. Usually he saw something in the raw material immediately. A shape, at least. Details could come later. But as he waited for the wood to tell him what it wanted to be, the only image that came to mind was a gorgeous redhead with eyes the color of the clear Caribbean Sea.

How pathetic would it be if he drove into town to see what Mae, who happened to own the Black Bear Inn where a certain lost motorist was headed, needed him to fix?

Too pathetic. Bordering on desperate. He'd wait until morning.

Reed reached for a utility knife and began to score birch bark. Later he'd rough out the piece with a carving saw, but in the conception stage, he needed his hands on the wood to get the feel, the shape, the grain inside his head. Maybe he'd find what he was looking for when the log was stripped bare. His blade caught midstroke. Its razor-sharp edge slipped, slicing the pad of his finger painlessly. He moved to the sink and ran cold water over the wound. Blood swirled pink before eddying down the drain.

As the soap stung the wound, a twinge in his gut warned him something had changed. Something out of his control and unavoidable. He glanced back at the wood. Life was full of hidden knots that deflected the sure stroke of his blade. And left him bleeding.

CHAPTER THREE

Jayne steered through the turn for Huntsville. Insistent memories flashed. She could feel the arm at her throat, the burning knife-point slicing through her cheek, hot breath against her temple, smelling of expensive scotch. The mental movie clip had to be stopped. Work. She needed to work.

The display on her phone showed three bars. She hooked her Bluetooth earpiece over her ear and punched in her editor's number.

"Jason Preston's office." Tanya, Jason's administrative assistant, picked up his line.

"It's Jayne Sullivan. Can I talk to Jason?"

"I'm sorry, honey. He's not here."

"I need to ask him something. The information he gave me isn't playing out." Jayne didn't mention details. Jason guarded his office like the gates of Hell, assuming Cerberus was a three-headed mini pinscher. If she wanted to keep working for the skinny little bastard, she couldn't risk letting anything slip, even to the seemingly honest Tanya.

"He's never wrong."

"There's a first time for everything." Jayne wanted him to be wrong. She wanted the real R. S. Morgan to live in Taos or maybe even a foreign county. Peru would be good. She didn't want sexy, Southern Reed Kimball to be involved.

Tanya *tsk-tsked*. "Well, something's going on. You know Jason can sniff out a scandal like nobody's business."

Wasn't that the understatement of the decade? Jayne's fingers tightened on the steering wheel. "I know."

"You better do some diggin', girlfriend. He's chomping at the bit to get whatever it is. He said to tell you the clock's ticking."

"He's evil."

"No kidding. But don't worry, honey. The devil will come to collect his soul eventually." The line clicked, signaling another call on Tayna's end. "Gotta go. You take care."

Jayne tossed her cell onto the passenger seat and fished a roll of Tums out of her purse. Working with Jason made her feel like *she'd* made a deal at the crossroads. Whatever. As a bartender and accounting clerk for the family tavern, she didn't have any other way of making the kind of money Jason paid her. Her efforts with legitimate photography were the professional equivalent of running on a giant hamster wheel.

One thing was clear. She didn't have time to wait for R. S. Morgan to find *her*.

Five minutes later, the town appeared as Jayne rounded a gentle bend in the road. A rustic wooden sign announced Jayne was entering Huntsville, Maine, population 1,067.

Hills rose on either side of the town, creating a small valley. Beyond the gentle knolls, jagged mountains loomed over the town. After driving by a smattering of homes, spaced closer and closer together as she encroached upon the main drag, Jayne sighted a combination gas station and convenience store. She pulled up to the pump and turned off the engine with a relieved sigh. Her arthritic Jeep complained with a cough, rattle, and shudder before shutting down. The car door bounced open with a hard shove and Jayne stepped out into the empty lot.

Wind whipped across the pavement, nearly pulling the door from her grip. As she slammed it shut, the back of her neck began to tingle. Having been stalked once before, she knew that feeling, and she sure as hell wasn't going to ignore her primitive alarm system this time.

Someone was watching her.

She scanned the surrounding area. Nothing. Through the glass of the Quickie Mart she could see an old man working the register, but he was concentrating on something behind the counter, not looking at her.

She turned around. Behind the lot, a small snow-covered field separated her from a thick band of woods. Something moved in the trees, something tall and dark. Her camera was in her hand before she could think, sweeping across the forest's edge, snapping a quick burst of shots. She didn't have the telephoto lens attached, but with fourteen megapixels of resolution, she'd be able to zoom in on the dark shape later on her laptop.

Had to be an animal. But why did she still feel like she was being watched? Maybe the animal was a predator. Bears hibernated, right?

She shook it off. Paranoia was getting the best of her.

Gas tank full, Jayne followed the directions she'd printed from the B and B's website. A few minutes later, after a brief stop at a pizza joint for slices to go, she pulled up in front of the Black Bear Inn, a huge white clapboard house trimmed with glossy black shutters. A tiny electric candle glowed in the center of each windowsill, right above a red-bowed swag of greenery.

"Can I help you?" The middle-aged innkeeper was short and stout, with auburn hair that hovered somewhere between mahogany and magenta. Tinsel and holly dripped from the antique furniture, and Bing Crosby crooned "Silent Night" softly in the background. "I'm Mae Brown, the owner."

"Jayne Sullivan. I have a reservation." Jayne slid her credit card across the old-fashioned registration desk.

Mae consulted her laptop. "I have you down for three nights. You know there's a storm coming right in the middle of your stay?"

"Yes, I do."

"OK, then. What brings you to our town, Miss Sullivan?"

"Jayne, please. I'm a photographer."

"Oh. That's nice. Lots of pretty things to take pictures of around here." Mae handed Jayne a room key—a real metal key, not one of those plastic cards. Mae shouted over her shoulder. "Bill, come out and help this lady with her bag."

A large man shuffled in, head bent, shoulders stooped. In his late twenties, he looked like his bones were too big for his body. He gave Jayne's feet a quick sideways glance. His pale blue eyes were vague, his expression lost and timid as a child's on the first day of kindergarten.

Jayne tried a smile. "Nice to meet you, Bill."

Under a shock of sandy hair, his ruddy complexion flushed deeper. He whirled around and disappeared through a swinging door.

"I'm sorry." Mae sighed. "My son is a little shy."

"No problem. I only have the one bag." Following directions, Jayne grabbed her duffel and trooped up the steps.

The room was larger than she'd anticipated. The double bed, armoire, and writing desk were stained a warm cherry; the comforter looked thick and inviting. After changing into sweats, Jayne settled at the desk with her pizza and laptop. At Jason's insistence, her departure had been immediate, with no time for any research on her subject other than grabbing the Arts & Leisure section of *The New York Times* from the recycling bin. Inside, along with the review of Morgan's latest work, a columnist had speculated that the artist's mysterious identity was just a new fresh way to generate media buzz. The picture of his carving that ran alongside the column was too small to see every detail, but what she could see was intriguing. She plugged in her AirCard and crossed her fingers.

Yes! The Internet connection was slow, but it was there. It was also free, a nice boon to her tight budget. She hated to dip into her secret stashes of emergency cash.

A Google search on Reed Kimball yielded a list of names from across the country, but none seemed applicable to the man she'd met that afternoon. The man with the green eyes she couldn't get out of her head. The search on R. S. Morgan was a different story. The man was a mystery, but photos and reviews of his sculptures were numerous. His style was unique, the lines modern with an abstract bent. All his subjects were female and nude, but not sexual. Unlike some other critically acclaimed human sculptures Jayne had seen, these had no giant boobs, no explicitly detailed or grossly enlarged sexual organs. The figures were waiflike, more elegant than erotic. If anything, the subjects' sexuality was downplayed. The bodies were thin and delicate, the expressions sad, lonely, tortured. The blend of primitive and modern made the statues compelling. The more she looked at them, the more raw despair welled from them.

Jayne stared at the pictures as she chewed hot cheese and tangy sauce. The sculptor's work was complex and fascinating, but more than a little disturbing. She was no art critic. But R. S. Morgan, whoever he was, had some serious issues.

– – –

21

He focused on the third window, for the rest were dark. Her shadow moved across the opening. The sheer curtains weren't quite closed, and he caught a quick glimpse of her bright red curls as she passed by.

As he'd already noted, she was lovely. Long limbs. Strong back. Skin creamy as fresh milk. Hair like a fiery halo. The kind of woman who could keep home and hearth, as well as wield a sword on the battlefield. Celtic blood ran thick in her veins, of that he had no doubt.

But she'd taken his picture. Not acceptable. Not for a man with secrets such as his.

Someone might find out what he'd been doing. He wasn't prepared for that yet. He needed time to prepare, to gather his power, to collect the necessary implements for the upcoming ceremony. A true Druid ritual required preparation and study.

There was so much work still to be done, and he had no one to share his burden. The others weren't ready to accept their fate. They weren't ready for the sacrifices that had to be made. His gloved fingers pulled at the hem of his coat.

But soon they would have no choice. The gods had ordained their fate.

She moved across the window again. Tall and graceful. There was something special about her. Something that stirred his own blood. If only he could pinpoint her familiarity.

The light went out in the window of the inn. He stayed in the shadowed alley that ran alongside the building a while longer. The photos she'd taken could be quite…damaging. She couldn't be allowed to leave town.

He'd be back tomorrow. She couldn't stay in the inn forever.

When she came out, he'd be waiting.

CHAPTER FOUR

Fortified by a full country breakfast, Jayne stepped out onto the inn's porch. The cold front preceding the approaching storm slapped her full in the face. But the shock was just what she needed to knock some sense into her. Her oldest brother, Pat, was keeping tabs on her paroled assailant. No news from Pat meant the scumbag was still accounted for. The danger was in Philadelphia, eight hundred miles away.

She could breathe.

With her camera bag slung over her shoulder, she tugged her knit hat over her ears and set out for the sidewalk. She would approach her search for R. S. Morgan the only way she knew how. She'd walk around, take pictures, talk to people, and hope her Irish luck played out one more time. Jayne's fingers itched to capture the town's Norman Rockwell charm anyway.

She turned down a side street. Smoke curled from chimneys and snow coated the ground like vanilla frosting. Lopsided snowmen waved mitten-covered stick hands at passing motorists. Buildings were draped with swags of greenery and wreaths.

This was what she was supposed to do. Real photography, not skulking around like a vulture waiting for celebrities to drop their guard. Knots slid from her neck muscles as she recorded images.

Her camera beeped. The memory card was full. She tugged off her gloves and changed it, shoving the full one into her jeans pocket. Her frozen fingers and the painful numbing of her toes alerted her to the passing of time. She glanced at her cell. She'd been out there for hours. No wonder her nose was frozen. She shivered and tugged her gloves back on. Her winter gear wasn't adequate for the kind of cold that Maine served up.

She squatted down and took one last picture of the rusty sign that dangled from the front of the feed store, then turned back down the empty lane that would lead her back to the inn, just a few blocks away. She slid her equipment into its padded sheath.

Her spine prickled. Jayne spun around. No one in sight. She eyed the buildings on either side. Crumbling brick facades sat close to the cracked sidewalk. Their shadows loomed near enough to conceal a person.

Chill. There's no one following you. Pat would let her know if she had reason to be afraid.

Something scraped on concrete in a narrow alley to her right.

Jayne picked up her pace, breaking into a jog as instincts overrode rational thought. Were those footsteps behind her? Her breath snagged in her dry throat. A shadow flickered in her peripheral vision and she lengthened her stride. Her feet went out from under her. She plunged ass-first into a slush puddle. Jayne scrambled to her feet.

Almost there.

Jayne glanced over her shoulder as she rounded the corner. Her boots hit a patch of ice. She scrambled for traction, but her feet slid. She slammed into a large, hard, male body.

"Umph." He absorbed the impact with barely a stagger. Hands under her elbows supported her weight easily as she righted herself.

Heart rabbiting, Jayne flattened her hands against his chest and prepared to push away. She looked up into Reed Kimball's piercing green eyes—and froze.

"Are you all right?" His expression went from surprised to suspicious in one pulse.

Jayne looked behind her. Nothing. She felt the blood rush to her chapped cheeks. Now that she was standing in front of the inn, her earlier panic felt silly. "I thought I heard someone following me, but it was probably just the wind."

His eyes narrowed on her face, then scanned the street behind her. "Really?"

She nodded bobblehead style. Could she look like more of an idiot?

The muscles of his jaw tightened as he looked her over. His parka was open, the wool of his sweater soft under her palms. Through it, his heart thumped in the solid plane of his chest. "You're all wet."

"Slush puddle." Jayne inhaled deeply in an attempt to control her racing heart. But the adrenaline flowing through her veins simply shifted gears, and she suddenly noticed that Reed smelled really, really good. A masculine mix of soap, pine needles, and wood. Just a few inches separated their bodies. If she took one step she could press her face to his neck and get a much better whiff of that scent. Her gaze followed the movement of his throat as he swallowed. Was the flush spreading up his face from the cold wind? She sure hoped not.

"You sure you're all right?" His eyes said he doubted she was, but he released her elbows, slowly, and took a step back.

"Yeah." Jayne's arms dropped to her sides as cold air swirled between them. She pulled her gaze away from his face before she did something embarrassing like hurl herself back into his arms and sniff his neck again.

His truck was parked at the curb. He retrieved a red metal toolbox from the open cargo area, closed the hatch, and followed her up the brick walk onto the porch. He reached around her to open the door. As his arm brushed hers, the heat in the lobby burned Jayne's face. *The heat, right.*

Mae wasn't in sight. Bill was walking from the rear of the house, his arms stacked with wood, his face pink as if he'd been outside. He shrank as Jayne stepped through the door and hurriedly dumped the logs in their holder.

"Reed!" Bill's eyes lit up as he looked past her. Keeping a wary eye on Jayne—or rather on her boots—he rushed forward with the speed and size of a linebacker when Reed entered. Jayne moved out of the way.

"Hey, Bill." Reed accepted the hard hug with grace and what appeared to be genuine affection.

"Excuse me," Jayne said, "I have to change." She ducked for the hall and hurried up the steps. Both men would likely be glad she left. Bill because she somehow made him uncomfortable, and Reed because he probably thought she was nuts.

Behind her, Bill sounded as excited as a grade-schooler. "Mom wants you to fix the back door. Can I help, please?"

"Sure you can." Patience filled Reed's easy drawl, and Jayne felt a smile pull at her face, despite the incident outside. Reed Kimball wasn't just sexy, he was kind. Kind in a way that made him even sexier. As if his chiseled face and broad shoulders didn't already make her toes curl.

Her self-defense classes had taught her to trust her instincts, but they were way off base today. Reed Kimball must think she had a screw loose for her behavior outside. Hopefully he'd give her the benefit of the doubt. There was something about him that didn't quite tally up. The Southern lilt didn't match the local accent any more than his too-sharp gaze belonged on a handyman. And she couldn't ignore the fact that physical contact with the man made her crave things she'd forgotten about.

Hot, sweaty, naked things.

Their voices faded. Jayne fished in her pocket for her key, but when she caught sight of her door, she stopped. Her hand rose and splayed at the base of her throat. The dark wood was covered with dozens of small white symbols. Jayne's neck quivered as she touched one of the lines. Fine powder came away on her finger. Chalk.

Graffiti? No, the weird symbols looked primitive, like hieroglyphics. Crude Trinity Knots. Spirals. Wagon wheels. A few other more complicated emblems she couldn't make sense of. Some of the signs were repeated.

"Is something wrong?" Mae hurried down the hall, a stack of towels in one arm. She frowned at the door. "What on earth?"

Before Jayne could answer, Mae wiped the emblems from the wood with rapid-fire sweeps of a towel. "I'm sorry. Bill can be childish at times." She left Jayne standing in the empty hall staring at the now-clean door like she was in an episode of *The Twilight Zone*.

What now? Go in like nothing happened?

She checked the door and her breathing relaxed when she found it still locked. A quick sweep through the room assured her nothing had been taken. Weird. Had Bill really drawn on the door like a kid? Those marks hadn't looked like aimless scribbling, but Mae was probably right. She should know. Had Jayne really been followed today? The odds were against it.

Jayne peeled off her wet jeans and yanked a dry pair out of her bag. She had good reason to be paranoid. There'd been one warm summer night when she hadn't listened to her base instincts. When the back of her neck had itched just as it had today. When she'd felt something was wrong but convinced herself otherwise.

Being dressed, dry, and warm didn't erase the goose bumps from her arms. A hand strayed to her cheek. Her scar stung as the words mouthed across a courtroom cut across her memory, sharp as a knife point in tender skin.

You'll be sorry. Someday I'll finish what I started.

— — —

Reed watched Miss Sullivan bolt for the stairs. Yesterday she'd acted nervous, but when he'd caught her in his arms outside, she'd been terrified. She'd covered it quickly, but he'd seen it.

She is none of my business.

Something inside him disagreed, a pang of desire that needed to be squashed. Reed had enough troubles of his own. He did not need to borrow problems from others—not even from a beautiful damsel in distress.

He was no knight in shining armor.

"Let's go check out that door." Reed glanced at Bill, who was standing a few feet away, staring at Jayne Sullivan's legs as she disappeared up the stairs. "Bill?"

"I-I-I'm sorry, Reed." Bill's hands curled into bowling ball–size fists.

"Nothing to be sorry about. That's a pretty lady."

Bill's face went red as a ripe tomato and he darted for the interior door that led to the family's private wing, nearly knocking Mae over as she came through. The door slammed behind him. Mae flinched as sepia photos of historical Huntsville rattled on the wall.

"Aw, I didn't mean to upset him, Mae."

"Not your fault, Reed. It's hard to tell what's going to set him off sometimes." Mae patted him on the sleeve. "We appreciate that you're so nice to him. Some folks aren't so understanding."

Reed set his toolbox on the floor. "Let me go talk to him."

Mae shook her head. "Better to let him calm down first." She ran the dust cloth in her hand over the scarred oak desktop. "He's been acting strange since our guest arrived."

Did Bill think Jayne Sullivan was attractive? Who wouldn't? Although Bill had the emotional and intellectual maturity of a young boy, he was fully equipped with the hormones of an adult man. What had Bill been doing before he'd brought the wood in? Had he followed Jayne? If so, it would've been innocent curiosity. Bill wouldn't hurt a fly—not on purpose anyway, Reed qualified. Big Bill didn't have the best coordination.

"I'll try later. If that doesn't work, I'll bring Scott by. If Bill's still uncomfortable with your guest, he can stay with us for a couple of days."

"Bill would love to see Scott." Mae came around the desk and enveloped him in a giant hug. "You're a good man."

Reed's conscience protested. He grabbed his toolbox. "Let me get that door fixed."

Would Mae still think he was a good man if she'd read the headlines?

– – –

In his dedicated workspace, he approached his altar and donned his robe.

On the narrow table, two tall candles flanked a silver disk engraved with a pentagram. Its five points represented the five elements: fire, water, earth, air, and spirit. He lit the wicks. Fire was reflected in the mirrored surface of the silver. The other elements were placed around the disk. Water filled a tall goblet. A bowl of salt stood for the earth. Incense burned in the air. And after he'd prayed for the gods' presence, spirit would unite all.

Concrete bit into his knees as he knelt. Meditating, he called the gods forth and asked them for guidance and strength. Peace settled over him as they granted his request, the only respite in an otherwise torturous life.

His worship area was consecrated; he was ready to begin.

With the gods' blessing, he pulled a jug from the minifridge and filled a small pitcher. Pouring a fine line, he cast a circle to confine his energy. On the outside circumference, aligned with the corners of the room, four white candles marked the cardinal directions. The North candle lined up with his altar.

All was in balance.

He knelt within his sacred space and placed his materials on the floor: a small leather pouch, a piece of paper, a quill, his knife, a shallow bowl, and another candle, red to symbolize energy, life. Blood.

When the red wick was aflame, he smoothed the paper out in front of him. Then he drew the sharp blade of the knife against his palm. Blood welled from the cut.

Something from him.

He wiped the quill across his bloody pad and wrote his name on the paper in bright red letters three times, rewetting the tip of the quill as necessary. There was no rush. The more energy he infused into the ceremony, the more he would gain from it. After folding the paper in half, he opened the leather pouch and withdrew the tangle of long red curls he'd taken from her hairbrush earlier.

Something from her.

The red strands were coiled on the crease. He folded the paper twice more, visualizing their joined souls, her strength and vitality flowing over him, into him. He extended his arm. The candle reached for his offering. The paper caught fire and was quickly consumed. A small plume of smoke and the odor of burnt hair wafted from the flames. He held the packet until the flames reached his fingertips, then dropped it into the bowl.

There was something about this woman. Something familiar. But exhaustion had taken its toll on him. He had more gaps in his mind than memory these days. No matter. She would soon be his.

Earlier, he'd marked his earthly claim on her with his symbols. Now she was bound to him in spirit as well.

CHAPTER FIVE

Jayne stepped out onto the inn's porch. She glanced down the street. Walk or drive? Drive. Definitely. The diner was only a half-dozen blocks away, but after this morning's incidents, she felt safer in her vehicle with the doors locked. Irrational or not, she had no desire for a repeat panic attack. Plus, as she'd learned during her earlier walkabout, Maine was a lot colder than she'd anticipated. Numbers on a weather map just didn't do the frigid air justice.

She parked in the small lot behind the diner. Leaning against the cutting wind, she dashed across the asphalt square and around the side of the building to the glass door. The rush of heat from the lobby ceiling vent was pure bliss. She stood for a few seconds, flexing cold-reddened fingers. Utensils clattered over the murmur of voices, and the aroma of homemade soup filled her nose. A standing sign instructed patrons to Please Seat Yourself. Jayne scanned the half-empty dining room before slipping into a tattered booth. She angled her back to the wall. The position gave her a clear view of the frosted bank of windows.

"Be right with you." The gorgeous waitress hurried by with a tray of food, which she distributed with a smile to a hunter dressed completely in camouflage and trimmed in road-cone orange.

A minute later, Jayne ordered a club sandwich from the dark-haired beauty queen. Her name tag read Mandy. While Mandy the waitress hurried off, Jayne pulled out last Sunday's *NYT* Arts

& Leisure section and put it next to her place setting, folding the paper so the column about R. S. Morgan was faceup. The most important questions were the ones she had never asked. She sensed that this close-knit community would be all *talk to the hand* if she openly investigated one of their own. Subtlety was key.

Jayne mentally crossed her fingers and hoped one more time that R. S. Morgan didn't even live here. She could hang here through the weekend and still be home for Christmas. Five days of unproductive snooping would convince Jason his informant was wrong. Given her absurd anxiety attack this morning, she clearly needed a break from the situation back home. She hadn't taken a vacation in years. Four to be exact.

Jayne blinked out of her thoughts. The hunter across the aisle was looking at her scar. He dropped his eyes and flushed. Not for the first time Jayne lamented the fact that her scar was too deep for cover-up. Not that it was anything to be ashamed of. The mark was a symbol of survival—hers. Dedicated martial arts training had earned her a black belt and a new level of confidence. On the outside anyway. Inside, she still cringed when people stared.

"Hey, Nathan." Across the aisle, hunter-guy rose to greet a blond man in his midforties. Movie-star handsome with even white teeth and a light, suspiciously even tan, he had just enough of a beard shadow to keep him from looking feminine.

"Jed." Nathan nodded.

"How's your uncle? He up to having visitors?" Jed the hunter asked.

"No. Uncle Aaron's not supposed to be around any people right now." Sadness crossed the blond man's face. "His immune system's depressed from the chemo."

"Oh. Right." Jed deflated. "Damned shame. Aaron's the best tracker around. He totally missed deer *and* moose season."

"I'll let him know you were asking for him." Nathan turned to Jayne. His bright blue eyes barely touched on her cheek. "Who do we have here?"

"I'm Jayne."

"Hello, Jayne. And welcome. I'm Nathan Hall, owner of this modest establishment and mayor of Huntsville." He enveloped her hand with both of his. His palms were rougher than she'd expected, but his demeanor was smoother than Ben and Jerry's Dulce Delish. Though the mayor was polished enough to keep his gaze off her scar, it lingered on her boobs for a second too long. "What brings you to our little hamlet?"

Jayne extracted her fingers and leaned back. "I'm a photographer."

"Really?" Nathan gestured toward the seat opposite Jayne. "May I?"

The mayor was a bit of a letch, but he probably knew everyone in town. Jayne couldn't afford to pass up any possible source of information. She surveyed the dining room. A dozen other patrons were scattered among the booths and tables. Safe enough. "Sure."

"Mandy, could I get some coffee, please?" Nathan motioned to the waitress. His gaze lingered a little too long on the pretty brunette, but he wasn't leering. His eyes were filled with real warmth when he looked at Mandy. Clearly there was something going on between the diner owner and his employee. He turned the *Times* article so he could read it. "Interesting. I suppose you like art?"

"Oh, yes. Are you familiar with R. S. Morgan?"

"No. Can't say that I am." The mayor shook his head. "I'm afraid Huntsville is a very humble town. No exclusive art galleries. We do have some excellent local artisans, though, including our own excellent wood-carver." The mayor paused to sip his coffee.

Could it be that easy?

Jayne popped a French fry into her mouth and rearranged her poker face, but her pulse did a quick jig. Next to her, Jed stood in the aisle, leaning over to get a better view of the picture.

The mayor set his cup in the saucer. "Mark Stewart at the lumberyard carves the most lifelike ducks. And Martha at the Craft Depot sells handmade quilts."

"Sounds lovely." Jayne hid her disappointment by finishing off her club sandwich. Her editor wasn't going to pay for pictures of a duck carver.

"I'd be happy to give you a personal tour of our town," Mayor Hall offered. "Including introductions to all Huntsville's artists."

Jayne swallowed. Looking for an excuse to make a hasty exit, she checked the display on her phone. The mayor's interest didn't feel entirely professional, and even if it was, she did not get into cars with strange men. "I'd love to, but I have to run. Can I have a rain check?"

Nathan considered. "How about tomorrow? The snow shouldn't be an issue until midday. You're staying at the inn, right?"

"Yes." This town wasn't small; it was microscopic. She had no problem with a tiny white lie to avoid spending time alone with the mayor. "But I'll have to let you know. I have a conference call."

"I'll stop by in the morning." Ugh. The mayor had crossed into the too-pushy-for-comfort zone. She glanced at his left hand, casual-like. No wedding ring. Double ugh.

"OK." Jayne's face ached as she faked enthusiasm. "But no promises."

"I understand. Tell Mae to save me a blueberry muffin."

"You bet. I should get moving." Jayne scooted out of the booth. The hunter was still standing in the aisle, staring at the article and blocking her exit.

He glanced up at her sheepishly, like he'd been caught doing something wrong, as he stepped out of her way. "Sorry."

"No problem."

Did the hunter know R. S. Morgan?

Jayne bit back the question and made a mental note to "run into" Jed in a more private location. She stopped to pay her tab at the tinsel-trimmed counter. A minute later, zipped and gloved, she pushed through the glass door. The cold wind was an eye-watering shock. Inhaling was like swallowing razor blades.

A second gust froze her right down to her cotton bikini, and she braced against its breath-robbing bite. She'd thought Philadelphia got cold in the winter, with the damp that drifted off the Delaware River, but Maine made Philly feel like Aruba.

Jayne huddled inside her down jacket, more fashionable than functional, as she race-walked around the corner of the building. In the overcast gloom of the rear parking lot, her Jeep listed oddly toward one side. She rounded the vehicle. Both tires were completely flat. Could she have run over nails or glass? Jayne bent closer. Both sidewalls bore six-inch slits. She raised her eyes. Shock pushed her back two steps. Her windshield was covered with the same symbols that had been on her door at the inn.

– – –

Reed flattened his palms on the reception desk of the tiny police station in the basement of the town hall. Huntsville only employed two cops, Chief Hugh Bailey and his lieutenant. Hugh's office was dark. The lieutenant's office door was closed, but light glowed behind the glass.

The scrawny, goateed guy working the front desk looked up from his computer screen and gave Reed a tired sigh.

"Is Hugh around?" Reed asked. He was pretty sure the kid was the mayor's son, Evan, home from college for winter break. Nepotism was alive and well in Huntsville.

"Nope." The kid yawned and rubbed his bloodshot eyes. "And the lieutenant's on the phone. Whatcha need?"

"Don't know. Hugh called me." Reed was not going to get into it with Lieutenant Doug Lang, egomaniac extraordinaire. Three minutes in the same room as the lieutenant was enough to make Reed's molars ache.

"The chief should be back in a few. You can wait or leave him a message. Whatever." The *I don't give a shit* was implied.

The phone rang. Reed helped himself to paper and a pen, more than happy to leave the chief a note and delay the inevitable confrontation. As he pushed through the doors onto the sidewalk, the outside air felt refreshing as opposed to blistering cold.

"Reed?" The voice was female—and distressed.

Reed turned. And every thought in his head leaked out of his slack-jawed mouth. It was her, his goddess. Again.

"Hi." Relief flashed briefly in her eyes before her tone shifted to all business. "I need to talk to a policeman."

"You need Chief Bailey." Reed tore his eyes away. Sure, Lieutenant Doug Lang was inside, but goddesses should not have to consort with assholes. "But he's not in his office now."

Her pale skin was pink from the cold. The tinge emphasized the odd scar on her cheek, a shiny circular depression the size of a quarter. With better light than during yesterday's dusk encounter,

Reed could see that the wound hadn't been large, but it'd been deep. His chest went taut as he considered the various ways she could have been injured. Thanks to his former career, the list of possibilities was long, varied, and violent. His desire to press his lips against the mark, on the other hand, was totally inexplicable.

"Any idea when he'll be back?"

"Should be soon." *Don't ask. Don't get involved. Shit.* The desire to help her was a compulsion. He might as well try to stop breathing. "What's wrong?"

Something flashed in eyes the soft, pale blue of an aquamarine. Relief? Or something more?

Reed stared into their clear depths, momentarily riveted. Was she attracted to him? The mere thought sent a wave of heat through Reed. He hadn't considered dating since he'd moved up here. There were some pretty, single women in town. A few had made their interest clear, but Reed hadn't felt the tiniest spark of chemistry.

Jayne Sullivan had ignited an explosion in two ridiculously brief meetings.

Danger Will Robinson.

Reed blinked, breaking the connection. He unzipped his parka, letting a wave of cold wrap itself around his chest to lower the heat wave that was building up underneath his wool sweater. He kept his eyes and his imagination off the wave of hair that curled over one shoulder and tumbled across her breast. Which he should *not* picture naked in his head. Too late. He knew it'd be as perfect as the rest of her.

The lady needed help. *Say something, moron.* But his vocal cords refused to cooperate. And his brain was occupied with mentally stripping off each piece of her clothing. Reed's blood began to flow in a southerly direction.

She chewed a full pink lip and nervous fingers pulled a tiny tube from her pocket. Her purple gloves were knit, with little rubber dots on the insides of the palm and fingers. Reed swallowed. Watching someone apply Chapstick had never been so erotic. He shifted his weight. His jeans definitely hadn't been this tight when he'd left the house. He took a moment to admire the concrete under his Timberlands. And to get a grip on reality. This woman was here to see Hugh. She needed a cop. Not a horny handyman.

"The chief should be back in a few minutes." Reed nodded in the direction of the door behind him. In his peripheral vision, he caught Hugh's squat figure hustling toward them. "And here he is."

Reed gave Hugh's extended hand a quick shake. "Hugh. This is Jayne Sullivan. She needs to speak with you."

"Hey, Reed." Hugh's gaze passed over Reed with a flicker of acknowledgment, then settled on Jayne. Surprise and a rare smile spread across his bulldog face. "How can I help you?"

She stepped forward and extended a gloved hand toward the chief. "I need to report a crime. My tires were slashed right in the parking lot of the diner. And there's this weird graffiti all over the windshield."

"Why don't you show me?" Hugh raised his chin to look over her shoulder and catch Reed's eye. "Care to tag along, Reed?"

"Yeah. Sure, Hugh."

Hugh turned back to Jayne. "Tell me more."

She stepped into place beside the chief. Reed followed. Damned if the back view wasn't just as sexy as the front. Snug, low-rise jeans hugged her perfect body and highlighted every mouth-watering curve. While admiring her, Reed kept his ears tuned to the conversation as she succinctly outlined her situation for Hugh. Someone had written weird symbols on her door at the inn as well, but Mae had blown it off as Bill's scribble.

"Was anything stolen?" Hugh asked as they rounded the diner and strode across the back lot.

"No. There wasn't anything of value in there." As they approached her vehicle, Jayne's shoulders hunched against the wind, and she shoved her hands into her jacket pockets. Her posture stiffened as she walked to the front of the Jeep, which listed drunkenly from the two flats.

Hugh stooped to examine her tires. "Son of a b—gun."

Jayne stared. "It's gone. Five minutes ago there were weird symbols all over the windshield."

"I don't see anything there now," Hugh said evenly, but Reed could hear the hint of disbelief in his tone.

"Wait. I can prove it." Jayne reached into her purse for her digital camera.

Reed stepped up to the Jeep and leaned close. "The windshield is cleaner that the rest of the vehicle." He swiped a fingernail along the edge. Tiny white shavings came away on his nail. "What color was the writing?"

"White. Looked like soap." Jayne's camera beeped as she turned it on.

Reed extended his hand toward Hugh.

The chief fished out his reading glasses and grasped Reed's hand to adjust the distance between it and his face. "Could be soap. But if someone took the time to soap your windows, why would he wipe it off minutes later?"

Jayne pulled the picture up on the LCD display on the back of her camera. "See."

Hugh leaned in. "Looks like a bunch of scribbling to me."

Reed scanned the parking lot. If the miscreant had wiped the soap off her windshield, the miscreant was nearby. Maybe watching them right now. Daylight reflected off the back windows of the diner, the darker interior making the customers inside invisible.

There was a pause as Hugh considered. "We'll fill out a report and ask around, but unless we get lucky and someone actually saw the incident, there isn't much I can do."

"What about getting the surveillance tapes from the parking lot?"

"Nathan doesn't have cameras out there," Hugh said.

"So, there's nothing you can do?" Jayne's frustration bubbled into her voice.

"Again, I'm sorry, Miss Sullivan. This kind of thing doesn't happen too often practically next door to the police station. Did you argue with anybody?" Hugh asked.

Her resigned exhalation signaled surrender. "I've been here less than a day. I checked into the inn. I took some pictures. I ate lunch at the diner. That's it."

"I'm sorry you had such an inhospitable welcome, Miss Sullivan." Hugh sighed. "It was probably teenagers. Even small towns have their share of juvenile delinquents. We have more vandalism than you'd think. I'll do what I can, but I can't promise anything. Let's go to my office. You can give me a list of everyone you've interacted with since you arrived."

Hugh led the way back toward the station.

"There's something else." Jayne's voice lowered as she reluctantly fell into step beside the chief, but Reed could still hear her. "A man my testimony put in prison was granted parole last week. During the trial, he made threats."

"But he's in Pennsylvania?" The chief was sharper than he looked. He'd noticed her license plates.

"Last I heard he was still in Philadelphia."

"Keep in mind that a stranger stands out in Huntsville. He can't hide in plain sight here. Someone would notice him right away," the chief pointed out. "Why don't you give me his information so I can get a picture? That way I can keep an eye out for him. I'll call the auto shop for you, too. We'll take pictures of the damage and have the auto shop pick up your vehicle."

"All right. Thank you." But she didn't sound relieved by Hugh's offer.

As their feet hit the sidewalk, Reed gave the diner parking lot another quick scan. The odd crime did not sit well in his gut. If Jayne was telling the truth, someone was following her. If it was Bill, Reed doubted she was in any danger. But Bill wouldn't slash her tires. Would he?

They descended into the municipal building's basement. Hugh opened the door to the station and held it for Jayne. He escorted her into his office and filled out a report while Reed waited in the lobby. "I'll need a copy of that picture."

"Your computer's a little old. It doesn't have the right memory card slot. I'll e-mail it to you as soon as I get back to the inn." Jayne gave Hugh her personal information.

Ten minutes later, Hugh ushered her toward the exit. "Can you come back tomorrow and sign your statement?"

"Yes. Looks like I'm stuck here anyway." She bit the words off, her body rigid. "I'm sorry. I don't do the victim thing very well."

Reed's eyes flicked back to the scar on her face. Why did it bother him so much? It wasn't like he knew her or was likely to ever see her again.

But he wanted to. And wasn't that a kick in the teeth? The first woman to attract his attention in years was just passing through. Just as well. He had no place in his life for a woman, especially a woman with baggage.

"That's OK. You've every right to be mad. It's tears I can't handle." Hugh patted her arm, a fatherly gesture he pulled off without seeming condescending or sexist. "No one likes being a victim. In my book, being pissed off is a whole lot better than crying."

She gave him her personal information, then turned toward the door. Outside, Reed knew the wind was whipping down Main Street as if it were the tundra. Despite the fashionably furry boots and puffy down jacket, she wasn't dressed for a Maine winter. She'd looked cold standing in the parking lot next door; she was going to freeze her lovely ass off walking all the way back to the inn.

"Need a lift?" Reed didn't want her to leave, especially not alone. Not after today's weird events. "I'll be done here soon."

Heat flashed in her eyes for a nanosecond, but she backed away. "No, thank you. I'll be fine."

"Hugh'll vouch for me. If I had any nefarious plans, I wouldn't make the offer in the presence of the chief of police."

"Reed's OK." Hugh nodded. "Damned fine carpenter."

"Thanks anyway. I'll manage." She gripped her bag tighter under her arm and hurried out the door.

Reluctantly, Reed ripped his eyes off her retreating figure. Jayne's predicament—and her killer body—were a lot nicer to contemplate than the reason Hugh wanted to pick his brain.

The chief hadn't called him down here to talk about carpentry. No, this was about Reed's old job, the one he'd left behind. This was about homicide.

CHAPTER SIX

"Very nice." Hugh's eyes crinkled as the outer door closed behind Jayne Sullivan. "Looks like she'll be here a few days anyway. You should go for it."

Reed turned his back on the exit—and the woman beyond the door. "If the forecast is anywhere near accurate, I'll be snowed in for the weekend. Besides, I don't have the energy for a woman like that." But my God, if his past had been nice and clean and normal, he'd be doing everything possible to spend time with her.

"For Christ's sake, man, then stock some Red Bull." Hugh led the way into his office. "Hell, if I wasn't married, I could find the energy for a woman like that."

"Doris hears you say that, she'll roast you alive, slowly." Reed's gaze strayed to the chief's desk, where Miss Sullivan's police report beckoned. She was thirty. Closer to his age than he'd thought. That fact pleased him more than it should.

"No doubt." Chuckling, Hugh waved him toward a wooden chair that looked like it'd been pilfered from an old school. "Shame she's had such a rough time here in town. Odd, though, don't you think?"

"Yeah. And I'm not a big fan of weird."

"Me either." Hugh adjusted the knob on the space heater that whirred away in the corner. "We should keep an eye on her."

Reed blinked away from Hugh's comment and eased his butt onto the cracked pine seat. "Why did you ask to see me?"

Good humor bled from Hugh's craggy face. "I appreciate you coming here. I know this is hard for you. Some hunter found one of those missing hikers from Mayfield out by the quarry. You hear about that?" The chief's sharp gray eyes bore into Reed's, accurate as any polygraph.

Reed knew what was coming next. He blinked away to study a row of framed marksmanship awards that hung over the chief's head. Hugh looked and acted deceptively laid-back. It was easy to forget that under the country-bumpkin act was a cop with thirty years of experience. Unlike his weekly plug for Reed to take over the chief position, Hugh wasn't going to let this request go without a fight.

"I did." Reed forced the words out through a constricted throat. Five years ago he'd buried his career as a homicide detective along with his wife. "I don't do that anymore, Hugh."

Hugh pressed on. The cop's voice was neutral, but anger simmered just under the calm facade. "I know you've got your reasons for leaving the Atlanta PD. All I'm asking is for an hour or two of your time."

Reed weighed guilt against responsibility. On one hand he'd promised his son he was done with police work. But dead young men were a damned heavy load. For Scott's sake he should get up and walk away, yet he didn't protest when Hugh opened the file on his blotter.

"The medical examiner listed the preliminary cause of death as accidental." Hugh dealt photos out onto his desk, the grim reaper's version of solitaire. Reed considered closing his eyes against the visual onslaught. The quiet years had softened him. Full-color glossies of gory crime scenes used to be part of a day's work. For Hugh, Reed buried his disgust and scanned the gruesome images.

"Those hikers went missing in October. Remains are in bad shape. We had some unusually warm temps around Thanksgiving. Animals and insects have been at the corpse for six solid weeks." Hugh pointed a gnarled finger at a close-up of mangled, decomposing flesh. "There wasn't much to work with. Quite a few pieces were missing."

Like the guy's head. Reed's throat soured.

"Decapitation likely occurred postmortem." Hugh chose another picture. "But due to scavenger activity, the ME won't commit to how that happened."

Reed's translation: animals and insects had chewed on the stump. Six weeks in an area teeming with wildlife had taken its toll.

The chief fished for and found an X-ray report with an accompanying sketch. "But he did note, just below the decapitation, a suspicious nick on the anterior of the vertebrae."

Reed let out a deep breath, pulling his eyes off the grisly photo and concentrating on the more clinical X-ray report. The mark on the bone looked like it had been made by a knife rather than teeth. "You think his throat was cut."

The chief flipped through pictures and selected one. "This was under the body."

Reed turned the photo for optimal light. A coin of some sort. Looked old. As in ancient, something-you'd-see-in-a-museum old.

"The coin is a bronze Celtic slater, circa 50 BC," Hugh said.

"No shit?"

"No shit." Hugh leaned back. "Now if we found an arrowhead under the remains, or if this body turned up in a peat bog in Britain, I could proceed under the assumption that it might be a coincidence. But how the hell did an ancient Celtic coin end up under a corpse in Maine?"

"How hard is it to get one of these?"

"I made some calls. It's not that hard. If this were a really rare coin, we'd be in luck. Unfortunately, this is the one of the most common types. It's only worth about thirty bucks."

"Anything else?" Reed asked.

"Nope." Hugh tossed another paper on the desk, frustration deepening the lines around his mouth. "The remains are on their way to a forensic anthropologist. I won't get any definite answers for a while. If this kid was murdered, the killer's had six weeks to cover his ass. Now that the body's been discovered, I don't want to give him more time to destroy every scrap of evidence. The trail's cold enough already. "

Reed couldn't argue with that. Forensic anthropologists were always backed up. So much crime. So little time. "What about the second kid?"

"Officially, John Mallory is still missing, but we both know the chance he's still alive is razor-thin."

Authorities had assumed both guys were dead when the initial, full-out search had been called off in mid-November due to a storm that left a foot of snow in its wake. The only reason this body'd been found was a freak warm spell right after Thanksgiving. Otherwise the remains would've been buried until the spring thaw.

"Well, what do you think?" Hugh asked.

Unfortunately, Reed's cop instincts agreed with Hugh's. "I'd say it's a strong possibility. But you need the ME to declare the death a homicide to justify an investigation. The town council will not want to deal with a murder if they don't have to."

"I know, but I can't let it go." Hugh's mouth went tight. He pulled a starched white handkerchief from his pocket, removed his glasses, and rubbed the lenses harder than necessary. "I just wanted a second opinion before I stuck my head in the noose. I'm getting close to retirement. Let 'em fire my ass." Hugh slid the photos back into the file and closed the manila cover, but Reed knew damned well the case was wide open.

But he wasn't going to bite.

"I'd really appreciate some unofficial help on this, Reed. No one has to know if that's the way you want it." Hugh reached into his desk drawer and slid out a fat legal-size mailing envelope. "Copies."

Reed crossed an ankle over his knee and contemplated the zigzag pattern in his boot treads. His conscience amplified guilt like a bullhorn. His gut didn't need corroboration. It was screaming that the chief was right. This teenager had been murdered. It all added up to a no-win situation. If Reed agreed to help, he risked exposure. If he didn't, a killer could evade justice, maybe even go after someone else—like Scott.

"You know what I went through, Hugh. I can't afford any publicity."

"I give you my word. This is just between you and me," Hugh assured him. "Please. I've got some theories, but I don't have your experience or the extra manpower for this. I can't ask the state for help until the investigation is officially declared a homicide."

"What about Doug Lang?"

"My lieutenant is vying for my job. He's too busy kissing Nathan's ass to run an investigation. Besides, I'd like to keep this quiet for now. Doug can't keep his mouth shut." Hugh reached across the desk and inched the envelope closer to Reed. "Just take the file home and give it a look-through. Any ideas come to you, call me. That's all I'm asking."

Reed kept his eyes off the envelope. He'd moved his son fourteen hundred miles to get away from violence, death, and the media attention associated with both of those things. "Sorry, Hugh. I can't."

"Can't or won't?"

Reed didn't answer. His phone vibrated. Probably a text from Scott. Reed stood and turned away. He and Scott were going to cut their Christmas tree that afternoon.

Hugh's gaze leveled him. "How old's your boy?"

"Seventeen."

Hugh reopened his file and tossed another color photo onto the desk. "That's just one year younger than Zack Miller."

Reed knew it was a mistake, but his eyes sought the image anyway. The gangly kid in the senior yearbook picture didn't even look like he needed to shave. A familiar pang of anger and loss poked at Reed as the young face, full of promise and bursting with life, smiled up at him. Zack Miller wasn't going to see another Christmas. How would his parents bear the upcoming holiday?

Reed moved toward the door. His boots felt heavier than they had on the way in. But Scott had to come first. Hadn't his son already given up enough in the name of justice? Across the reception area, Doug Lang exited his office. Jealous anger gathered in his eyes as he spotted Reed coming out of Hugh's office.

If Doug didn't despise Reed for his friendship with the chief already, Reed had just skyrocketed to the top of the lieutenant's shit list. Reed had managed to piss off both cops in a matter of minutes.

It had been that kind of day. It had been that kind of decade.

A quick look over his shoulder showed the chief stuffing the yearbook photo inside the envelope. The lines in his face looked deeper, his hair grayer, as if years had passed rather than minutes. Hugh's disappointment in him was palpable in the stale air of the tiny office. "I'm sorry, Hugh. It's complicated."

Reed stepped over the threshold. The vise in his gut tightened as the chief's voice followed him. "You know what's complicated, Reed? Telling a couple of parents their son was murdered."

With those words ringing in his ears, Reed made his escape. Outside on the sidewalk, he inhaled fresh air, but it didn't help. He pulled his phone out of his pocket and read Scott's text. *Ready at 4.*

Great. He had a half hour to kill. All he wanted to do was return to his house and hibernate for the rest of the winter. If it weren't for Scott, he'd go total hermit. Scott would be going away in the fall. Socializing would no longer be necessary. So why did the thought make Reed feel worse? It was what he wanted. Wasn't it?

An ache nested behind his eyes.

His truck was parked across the street, but Reed headed for the small drugstore half a block away. Dark had descended while he'd been talking to Hugh. Streetlights glowed along the quaint sidewalk. He pushed into the shop. Aisles were narrow. Displays crowded customers and each other to maximize limited space. Ibuprofen was in the first aisle. Reed picked up the smallest bottle and turned toward the register.

The back of a tall redhead brought him up short. Jayne stood at the counter. In three steps he was behind her. He didn't remember telling his feet to move. He was the *Enterprise* stuck in her tractor beam.

A fruity smell teased his nose. He moved a step closer. Strawberries. The scent triggered a sharp pang of hunger that shocked him. It wasn't an empty-belly kind of craving. It was instinct. Pure primal instinct. The kind that drove salmon upstream and made tomcats howl in alleys.

The kind that made him want to find out what part of Jayne smelled like strawberries.

She glanced over her shoulder. Her full mouth was curved with a hint of humor. "Stalk much?"

"Honest." Reed held up the bottle of pain reliever. "Didn't know you were in here."

She nodded, but something flashed in her eyes before she turned back to her transaction. Disappointment?

"That'll be three dollars and twelve cents." The clerk shoved a pack of gum and a strawberry-flavored lip balm into a small plastic bag. Reed's gaze lingered on her lips. Would they taste as good as they smelled?

Jayne counted out three crumpled bills and exact change from a frayed leather wallet. She opened her purse and tossed the wallet in, along with the small bag. Reed's gaze fixed on a folded newspaper tucked in an exterior pocket. *New York Times*. Arts & Leisure section. His vision tunneled down to the picture, and the store went from cozy to claustrophobic in the time it took to read the caption.

R. S. Morgan's latest sculpture: Despair.

– – –

Jayne moved aside so Reed could place his item on the counter. He paid with a twenty.

"Can I buy you a cup of coffee?" Strong muscles in his throat tightened as he swallowed. There was a sharp look in his gorgeous green eyes. Discomfort and…desire? The flutter in her belly sent Jayne's eyes skittering away.

She zipped her purse as she considered his offer. If they stayed in a public place, what was the harm? She hadn't felt this much giddy anticipation since tight end Bobby Day asked her to the prom. Her day had been pretty stressful. Spending some time with a man who made her pulse skip wasn't going to make it worse. "The diner?"

Reed tilted his head toward the door. Jayne followed him out into the cold. Now that was a tight end.

He looked up and down the sidewalk, which was empty. "No. There's a bookstore a block down that serves *good* coffee and other stuff."

This afternoon's diner brew had left an acidy aftertaste in Jayne's mouth. Though coffee didn't sound appealing, Reed's company did. The thought surprised her more than the physical attraction that simmered between them. She hadn't even dated since…Well, since.

Had she imagined the gleam in his eyes? Only one way to find out. "OK."

"Walk or drive?" he asked.

"Walk."

He snorted. "Still don't trust me?"

"I don't trust anybody." Jayne's words came out more bitter than she intended.

He fell silent. Clear eyes went flat as he studied the scar on her cheek for a few seconds. "Good habit."

Without apologizing, he started down the street at a brisk walk. Jayne kept pace. They didn't speak again until they were inside the bookstore. The coffee shop on the second floor was larger and more modern than she'd expected. Jayne ordered a large hot chocolate with extra whipped cream and chocolate syrup. As she added a giant chocolate chip cookie to her order, she glanced sideways at Reed. "It's been a really shitty day."

His face softened as their eyes met. "I hear you." He turned to the barista. "Coffee, black."

They took their order to a secluded corner table. Jayne sat down, purse in her lap, and eyed the tray of sugar, sugar, and more sugar. "I'm going to be sick."

He took the seat across from her, removing his coat and draping it over the chair back. His shoulders, encased in a gray sweater, dwarfed the chair. "Probably."

She wrapped her hands around the Styrofoam mug and took a sip. Whipped cream and rich chocolate blended on her tongue. "Worth it."

For the first time, he smiled. The expression catapulted him from handsome to Wow! Tension unfurled in Jayne's belly. Warmth spread through her from the inside out. *Must be the hot cocoa.* As if. She concentrated on her cookie for a few seconds.

"Are you an art lover?" he asked.

Jayne looked up. He was nodding at the newspaper article sticking out of her purse. "Oh, yes. I'm a photographer."

"What do you photograph?"

"Most of my paid work is travel brochures." No lie. She'd actually only sold a half-dozen tabloid photos. No need to mention those. Or the obscene amount of money she'd been paid for them. Or how much she depended on that dirty, dirty money. "Someday I'd like to go back and finish my fine art degree."

He sipped his coffee and set it aside. "Why don't you?"

She crumbled a piece of cookie between her fingers and turned her face to the window. Daylight was fading, the sky darkening to a threatening, gunmetal gray. When she turned back, his gaze found her scar again. Knowledge lurked in his eyes—and realization sparked in Jayne. Duh. He'd heard her talking to the police chief. He already knew about the attack.

"His name is Ty Jennings. He was in my art history class. We'd gone out for coffee a couple of times after class. He was friendly, attractive, and seemed nice enough. One night, he offered to walk me to my car. I'd parked in a garage a half-dozen blocks away from school. He asked me if I wanted to go back to his place. When I said no, he got really angry. He grabbed me by the hair and started dragging me toward his car. I screamed, and he hit me in the face. I kept screaming, even when he was yelling at me to stop. He pulled a knife out of his pocket and dug it into my face." She closed her mouth abruptly. She couldn't believe she'd told him all that, but she'd recited the story so many times and in much greater detail, for the police, for the prosecutor, for her therapist. The words were rote. Jennings's release gave her old terror new life, and somehow, telling Reed felt more personal, like he would see things inside her the others had missed. "If this guy hadn't come out of the elevator…"

A weight on her hand stopped her from mutilating her cookie. Reed's fingers were curled around hers, warm and solid and grounding. And the connection that sparked between them ran much deeper than skin on skin. From the expression in his eyes, both the gesture and their responses were just as much of a surprise to him. "I found out later he wasn't even enrolled in that class. He was trolling. The police suspected he was responsible for two other abductions. The other girls were raped, murdered, and dumped in Fairmont Park. The prosecutor promised if I testified, he'd go away for a long time."

"How long did he get?"

Jayne focused on his hand, strong and callused from hard work. Tiny scars crisscrossed his fingers. "It turned out that the police didn't have enough evidence to charge him with the other crimes. He got six years."

"That's not a long time."

"No. It isn't. He got out last week, more than two years early. Money talks, you know. Jennings was an Ivy League frat boy." Jayne remembered the prosecutor's face as he'd told her, after she'd testified, that the other charges hadn't stuck. No guilt whatsoever. Just another day at the office—for him.

She pushed the anger and helplessness back and drank more chocolate. Calories be damned. "He has no way to find me. Chief Bailey promised to keep an eye out for him. So, no dwelling allowed." Enough about her. So far, he'd skillfully kept the conversation off himself. Time to turn things around. "What do you do, besides handyman work?"

He pulled his hand away to lift his cup. Jayne's empty hand fisted on the table. The break in contact left her uncomfortably bereft.

"Furniture repair, general carpentry, that sort of thing." His phone buzzed. He glanced at the display. His face went stern again. "I'm sorry. The time got away from me. I need to go."

"Thanks for the chocolate." Jayne covered her disappointment with a smile. Once again, all the information had flowed in the wrong direction, from her to him.

Reed looked like he was going to say something and changed his mind. "You're welcome. I'd like to walk you back to the inn, but I totally understand if you decline."

"Thank you, but I'm going to browse for a book to spend the evening with. Even if I had wheels, it's too cold to go anywhere tonight."

His tall frame unfolded. He draped his coat over a strong forearm. "OK, then. Enjoy your stay."

He tossed the remains of his coffee in the trash on the way out.

Unable to sit still, Jayne headed for the bookstore below. She brought her nearly full cocoa with her. She felt raw and exposed after telling him about the attack. Why had she? It wasn't like her to open up to strangers. Normally, she didn't talk to anyone she hadn't known since birth. Once again, he'd asked all the questions. She, who was supposed to be doing the investigating, hadn't learned one thing about him. The way he locked down his emotions and personal information told her there was something painful in his past. She was sure of it. No one was that guarded without a reason.

She still had nothing on R. S. Morgan. If anyone in town knew him, they were excellent at keeping secrets. Given the small-town dynamics she'd witnessed so far, vital secret-keeping didn't seem likely. Either the artist didn't live here or he lived under a secret identity.

Jayne selected a historical romance from the bargain table. No more reality tonight. She stepped out onto the sidewalk. In the dull yellow cast of the streetlight, flurries blew past.

Walking briskly, she turned off Main Street onto Third. The inn sat two blocks down. She hadn't expected the street to be deserted and dark this early. It wasn't even five yet. In Philadelphia, commuters would've crowded the sidewalks at his hour. She quickened her stride.

The hairs on her nape lifted in the frigid wind. She stopped. Her head swiveled. No one behind her. No sound but dry leaves blowing in the gutter and the beat of her own heart echoing in her ears.

The feeling intensified as she began walking again. Her grip on the bookstore bag tightened. She glanced behind her. The street was empty. The light from the inn's porch beckoned from halfway up the next block. Jayne picked up her pace.

She approached the inn. Relief welled in her chest as her feet hit the brick path. She checked the street behind her again to find it clear. She'd never used medication before, but if unfounded anxiety was going to plague her like this, she might consider it. She couldn't live in a state of paranoia 24/7.

High hedges lined the walkway. Steps from the porch, she passed through their shadow.

Blinding pain and a flash of brilliant white light exploded in her head. She pitched forward and was caught. She was barely cognizant of movement and the agony that ricocheted through her skull before darkness consumed her.

CHAPTER SEVEN

"Hey, Brandon." Scott crammed his books into his backpack and shut his locker. He turned down the near-empty hallway and tapped his buddy Brandon on the shoulder. "Hang on a minute, dude."

Brandon whirled, wide-eyed.

"Whoa. Relax." Scott backed away a step, hands in front of his chest, palms forward in the classic stick-'em-up position. "I just wanted to see if you were gonna be online later for a little Halo action."

"Sorry, man. No can do." Brandon ran a shaky hand through his spiked blond hair. "I got a couple hours community service to do over at the Youth Center." Brandon's eyes shifted toward the open glass-and-metal door at the end of the hall, where a dull gray sky promised snow. "Looks like the mayor'll have me shoveling sidewalks all weekend."

Both boys turned and headed for the doors.

"Shit. I forgot. How many more hours did you get?" Scott yanked his hood out from under the back of his jacket and flipped it over his head.

Brandon huffed. "Fucking Judge Hard-Ass gave me two hundred."

"That sucks." Stiff penalty for getting caught with a couple of beers, Scott thought.

"You know how it is. People hear the name Griffin and automatically think I'm the *bad seed*." Brandon's mouth thinned down to a razor's edge. With a deadbeat dad and a brother in prison, everyone assumed Brandon was a troublemaker. The judge had handed down the harshest sentence possible for what Scott thought was a minor infraction.

"That sucks."

"Yeah." Brandon nodded.

"You working at the auto shop tonight, too?"

Brandon shook his head. "Gotta be home by eight to watch my little brothers. Mom's tending bar tonight."

"You've been putting service time in every day. Is Hall a total prick to work for?"

"No." Brandon's face flushed with emotion. Anger? Frustration? He stiffened and faced Scott, his jaw set for a fight. "Mayor Hall's cool. If he hadn't stepped in, I might've gone to jail. My mom ain't exactly rolling in cash for a fancy lawyer."

"Hey, I'm sorry, man," Scott said. Mrs. Griffin worked two jobs, but she didn't make much money.

"No. My bad. I'm kinda jumpy. We're cool." Brandon blinked hard. His gaze dropped to the backpack clenched in his hands. "But really, Hall's OK. He lets Mom waitress at the diner a couple of shifts a week."

"That's great 'cause I'm supposed to help out with the winter coat drive on Monday." Not that Scott was thrilled with spending six hours at the Youth Center sorting used clothing, but this was senior year and his college applications were sorely lacking in community service. Mayor Hall *had* been cool about letting him jump into the Teen Community Service program midyear. Maybe he wasn't all that bad. "You gonna do the clothing drive?" Scott asked.

"Yeah. I'll be there. The storm should be over, and it sure as hell beats some of the other stuff I've had to do." Brandon drifted a few feet away, heading toward the sidewalk that led to the town's center a few blocks away. "I gotta go."

"You want a ride?" Scott nodded toward his dad's truck as it pulled up to the curb.

"No, thanks." Brandon waved over his shoulder.

"See ya." Scott opened the door of the Yukon and tossed his backpack over the seat. The mayor might have done him a favor, but he still didn't envy his friend and all the hours Brandon had to spend with the guy.

– – –

Reed dished steaming lasagna onto two plates. At his feet, Sheba wagged her tail hopefully. "Scott, dinner's ready."

Reed scooped a cup of kibble into the dog's bowl. Sheba pointedly ignored her food. "That's all you're getting."

Her blue eyes said, "We'll see."

His son ambled in and slid onto a stool at the counter. Sheba planted herself under his chair, having identified Scott as the weak link five minutes after they rescued her from the animal shelter years ago.

"Are those college applications done?"

"Mostly." Scott shoveled lasagna with speed and precision. Reed did not miss the noodle his son slipped to the dog.

"Mostly?"

Scott downed half a glass of milk. "Dad, I'll get them done on time. Relax."

Reed kept his nod silent. There was no changing his son's basic personality. Scott would never feel any urgency or stress over schoolwork. So, moving on: "I have a question to ask you."

His son looked up, a forkful of pasta hovering in front of his mouth. "'Kay."

Reed let the statement out like he'd been holding his breath. "I stopped to see the chief today."

Cheeks bulging with food, Scott nodded.

Reed searched his son's eyes for any sign of distress. Mild curiosity blinked back at him. "He asked me to help with one of his cases."

Scott swallowed. "Is it about the guy they found at the quarry?"

Surprised, Reed answered, "Yes, but please don't tell anyone. Hugh wants to keep the whole thing quiet for now."

"OK, but everybody at school knows they found him." Scott put his fork down. "You're gonna help him, right?"

"It'd be OK with you?"

"Sure. The chief wouldn't ask if it weren't important." Scott pointed to the foil pan on the stove. "Is there more?"

"Uhm. Yes," Reed answered in a confused fog. Scott was acting very nonchalant about the whole police-work issue.

"Cool." Scott took his plate to the stove and filled it again. The discussion hadn't affected his appetite.

Reed had expected his son to be upset at the thought of Reed helping Hugh, especially with a murder case. But Scott was no longer a grieving twelve-year-old. His son was a young man. How much did Scott even remember about the aftermath of his mother's death? The media coverage had been vicious, but Reed had shielded him as much as possible.

On impulse, Reed blurted out, "I had coffee with that lady tourist this afternoon."

"The same one that was here yesterday? The lost one?" Scott mumbled around a mouthful of lasagna.

"Yeah."

"Cool." Scott finished his second plateful, rose, and rinsed his dish at the sink. "Back to work." He poured a second glass of milk and took it with him, along with an entire box of graham crackers. The dog followed him, casting a disdainful glance at her bowl on the way.

It hadn't been easy, but Scott had learned to deal with his mother's death. At least one of them had. Reed had been so busy helping Scott handle the grief, he hadn't dealt with his own.

Reed stared at his dinner with no appetite. He covered his untouched plate with tinfoil and stowed it in the refrigerator. Maybe later. After more than five years in an emotional standstill, his life had received a jump start, all because a beautiful redhead had supposedly missed a turn.

Or had she?

Wait. He had no reason to doubt her. He'd been a cop too long. Not everyone had ulterior motives. If he was going to let go of the past, he was going to have to learn to trust people again. The article on R. S. Morgan she'd been reading didn't mean a thing. It *was* last week's issue of *The New York Times*. Plenty of people read it. The fact that she'd saved that section of the paper didn't mean anything other than that she liked art.

He'd still Google her and check with Hugh to see if anything turned up in the background check the chief was sure to run.

As he cleaned up the kitchen, Reed's thoughts locked on Jayne, and the trauma she'd endured. She wasn't hiding. She hadn't even let the parole of her assailant keep her down. He pictured her chin, lifted in rebellion as she'd told him about the prosecutor's betrayal, and the unyielding set of her shoulders. The posture of a warrior. Fear was her constant companion, but there was no trace of cowardice in her, just raw courage.

If Jayne could recover from a vicious assault and get on with her life, Reed could deal with his wife's death—without hiding. He couldn't attract any unnecessary attention. Subjecting Scott to another media feeding frenzy wouldn't be fair, even for a young man. But Hugh had promised to keep Reed's involvement in the case quiet. Reed trusted the chief to keep his word, and Hugh had his own reasons for maintaining radio silence on the investigation.

He wasn't up to discussing the case tonight, but tomorrow he'd go see Hugh, tell the chief he'd changed his mind. The decision lifted some of the weight from his chest. But not all.

Now that he'd resolved the issue with Hugh, his parting from Jayne stood out like a flashing neon sign: EPIC FAIL. Reed reached for the phone. She'd bared her soul. She'd confided in him about her life's most traumatic moment, and he'd told her to *enjoy her stay*?

Idiot. Or as Scott would say, *lame.*

He should apologize and ask her to lunch tomorrow. So she lived far away? Buying her a meal didn't equal a lifelong commitment. It would just be a meal. Granted, it would be the first date he'd had in twenty years, but he had to start somewhere. Even if the idea made his palms sweat.

The storm was forecast to crank up in the afternoon, but he should be able to get into town for lunchtime. He'd have to drive in to pick up Scott at school anyway. The thought of talking to Jayne again sent his pulse into a jog. Warmth bloomed in his chest. Ridiculous. He felt like he was back in high school as he dialed the inn's number.

Mae answered, "Hey, handsome. How was the date?"

Damn caller ID and small-town gossip.

"It was just coffee, Mae." Reed tapped the phone on his forehead as Mae's *yeah, right* chuckle came through the line. "Can you put me through to Jayne's room, please?"

"I would love to, but she's not here. You want to leave her a message?"

Ice filled Reed's empty belly. Across the kitchen, snowflakes blew across the window. "She's not there?"

"No," Mae said. "Never came back this afternoon. My, is it eight already? I didn't realize it was that late. I hope she's OK."

"Could she have come in while you were in the back?"

"It's possible, I guess." But doubt colored Mae's voice. "But I've been catching up on the books for the past couple of hours. Haven't left the desk."

"Could you check her room?" Reed reminded himself to breathe. Jayne was probably in her room, reading.

"Yeah. Good idea. I'll call you back." Mae clicked off.

Reed watched the phone for the next five minutes, jumping when it finally rang.

"She's not in there, Reed. Doesn't look like she's been back at all."

"I'm heading over. Call Hugh." Reed hung up. His cop instincts emerged, telling him something was very wrong with the situation. Jayne was in danger.

"Scott," he shouted up the hall. His son popped his head out of his doorway. "That lady tourist is missing. I'm headed into town to help look for her."

"I'm coming, too." Scott hustled out of his room, joining Reed at the coatrack. They donned hats, parkas, gloves, and boots in silence. For once, Scott didn't ask a thousand questions.

Twenty minutes later, Reed pulled up to the curb in front of the inn. Hugh was sweeping the beam of a flashlight over the inn's front lawn.

Reed jumped down from the cab, Maglite in hand, dread roiling in his gut. "Any luck?"

Hugh shook his head. "Not yet. I checked her room. All her stuff is there, but no bookstore bag."

Scott joined them on the sidewalk, turning his back to the bone-rattling wind. "She doesn't have a car. Where could she have gone?"

Hugh consulted his pocket-sized notebook. "On my way over, I stopped at the stores on Main Street. No one's seen her since she left the bookstore. She was the last customer. According to the register, she checked out at four forty-five."

"I left a little after four." Guilt hammered Reed's conscience. He should have walked her to the inn. Scott was seventeen. He could've waited, but Reed had once again used his son as a social shield. Somehow Jayne had slid past his defenses. And he'd bolted. Like a coward. He'd had something wonderful within reach, and he'd run from it. "She said she was going to buy a book and go right back to the inn."

Hugh didn't hesitate. "OK, then. Let's start looking."

"Scott and I will walk from here to the bookstore. See if we can find any sign of her."

The chief turned toward his car. "I'll get Doug and a few other people to start driving around town, checking anywhere she could have stopped. There aren't that many places open."

Reed led the way, walking slowly and scanning the ground in front of him. He hadn't gone fifty feet when he saw it. Tucked behind the hedge at the beginning of the path, a Styrofoam cup lay on its side in a puddle of frozen chocolate. His throat constricted as he moved closer and bent down. The beam of his flashlight illuminated a bookstore bag farther under the shrubs.

Everything that had been whirling inside him collided in a dizzying sense of déjà vu. Loss lodged deep in his chest and spread in an empty ache. It took three long breaths of frigid air before his head cleared.

"Hugh, over here."

The chief squatted down and peered under the shrub. "Shit."

Reed shoved his clenched hands into his coat pockets. The cold he hadn't felt earlier now burrowed into his bones. "Jayne didn't get lost. Someone took her."

Hugh straightened. "Shit. Shit. Shit."

"Did you have a chance to check out the scumbag in Philadelphia?"

"Yeah. Far as anybody knows, he's still in town. Not due to check in again until Monday next. His parole officer promised he'd try to hunt him down, though, but I'm not holding my breath. I know how many cases these guys juggle." The sharpness had bled from the chief's gray eyes, leaving them clouded with sadness and disappointment. Disappointment in the town, his job, maybe the whole human race. Reed knew exactly what was going through Hugh's head. "I'm not ruling him out, but what are the chances this guy followed her without anyone in town noticing him? If you don't scoop your dog's poop, somebody reports it."

"If it's unlikely she was grabbed by someone from her past, it's probably someone from Huntsville's present."

"Yup." Hugh said. "And the mayor can deny it all he wants, but if my gut's right, she's the third person to disappear."

Reed's gaze swept over the quiet street. He'd come to this town to escape violence. Now one teenager was dead and another missing. Jayne had vanished. Someone in this perfect little town had a deep dark side.

The well-kept houses, the Christmas lights, the wreaths, the picket fences, it all felt like a lie. Under the quaint small-town facade lurked something evil.

CHAPTER EIGHT

The Druid kicked open the door and carried his burden down the wooden staircase. His Celtic blood hummed incessantly through his veins.

The only thing that could free him was a return to the old ways. Not the weakened, watered-down religion popular today. Wine for blood. Bread for flesh. Bah. There was no substitute for either. People just didn't want to get their hands dirty anymore.

Not a problem now that he understood. He needed to return to his roots, to the practices handed down by generations in the Old Country and cast aside in the New World. As he'd learned at his grandfather's knee, blood, fire, and water were the only real sources of energy. The only ways to restore the natural balance. The fire ceremony on Samhain had been compromised by the boys' intrusion, especially the one who'd crossed into the sacred circle.

That boy had paid the ultimate price for his transgression. Necessity had fueled the killing. The gods required the boy die for ruining the ritual. But his trespass had been a blessing in disguise. It was when blood had been spilled onto consecrated ground that the gods' message was revealed.

There was no such thing as coincidence. It was another omen. The gods had intended the boy to wander there. They wanted to show the true path to salvation. Blood was the stuff of life, from man's first nourishment in the womb until it ceased to circulate upon his death. Only a blood offering could save him. He knew that now.

Blood was his only hope.

He shifted her body in his arms.

Her blood.

He had no time to waste. He could feel his health slipping away, like water through cupped hands. The winter solstice was his last chance. This holiest of Druid celebrations, the rebirth of the earth from its darkest day, the dawning of new life.

He lowered the woman to the floor, grimacing at the filth she'd have to endure. Not for long, though. He only had to keep her confined for a few days.

He removed her jacket, hat, and gloves. Her limp body slid in the dirt as he adjusted her position and clamped the handcuffs around her slender wrists. She was a marvel. Fine-boned and feminine, yet simultaneously long-limbed and strong. His palms stroked up her biceps, squeezed the firm muscle of her shoulder, then moved upward to cup her jaw. And now he knew exactly why she'd seemed so familiar the first time he'd seen her.

His gaze moved to the tapestry he'd brought down and hung on the cinder-block wall. One of the prizes of his collection, it depicted the story of another tall, graceful redhead with creamy skin and a warrior's bearing: the goddess, the healer, the Druidess, Brigid.

Jayne was Brigid in the flesh. And, like the goddess, she'd been sent here to heal him.

He turned back to his captive. Long eyelashes rested against skin the color of fresh cream. She was lovely. Absolutely lovely. And pure as the clean snow falling outside. His fingertip traced the scar on her cheek. A crude spiral. The symbol for ethereal power. Exactly what he needed to end his torment. The woman had been marked by the gods.

He pulled her camera from her jacket pocket and turned it over in his hands. He scrolled through the digital images. His photo was not among them. She must have another. Perhaps she'd left it in her room at the inn. No matter. He'd get it. The picture wasn't that important anymore. Not after the revelation had come to him.

The winter solstice loomed just a few days away. Until then he'd pass the night hours awake and lonely. On the solstice, she'd be bound to him forever. Her life would flow from her body to his. Life and death would be mingled in the strongest earthly connection.

Until then—

He pulled his *boline* from his pocket. The white handle of the ritual knife fit comfortably in his palm; its curved, sickle-like blade sharp as a razor. He knelt by her side, the concrete floor unyielding under his knees. He turned her palm upward, drew the knife across her soft skin, and dipped a forefinger in the blood that welled from the shallow cut. Raising his hand to his forehead, he drew the lines of Brigid's off-kilter cross on his flesh.

Perhaps some of her power could sustain him until the solstice. Then, her sacrifice would be his salvation.

– – –

John lifted his head from the mattress and listened. Thumping and the barely discernable murmur of voices echoed through the ductwork.

The man was back. Terror coiled around John's heart like a python and squeezed. His gaze darted to the open cardboard box next to the door. The usual bottles of water and meal replacement bars were still piled inside from this morning's visit. Unless it was tomorrow.

Had he blanked out an entire day? Or was this a new, unexpected visit? A steady dose of some sort of tranquilizer made days difficult to track, but a change in the daily routine could mean his time was up. Despite the man's promises, John knew in his soul that death was on the agenda.

A shiver passed over him, but this third-story room wasn't as cold as the basement prison he'd occupied those first few weeks. His heavy wool sweater and jeans were filthy but warm. The heat register gave an occasional puff of warmth. They'd taken his boots, though, so his feet were always cold.

With a groan, he rolled to his side, then slid off the mattress onto his hands and knees. The chain that attached his ankle to the iron bed frame clanked to the floor. Limbs stiff with disuse trembled. The impact with bare wood amplified the aches in his dehydrated joints. Unnaturally loose muscles protested and threatened to let his face flop onto the hardwood. Again.

Mustering energy from fear, he crawled toward the window. The tether played out before he was quite to the wall. Stretching, his fingers grasped the sash and he heaved to his knees. He closed one eye to peer through the half-inch gap between the trim and the plywood sheet screwed into the frame.

Lazy white flakes swirled across his field of vision. The overcast sky gave no clues as to the time of day.

The rough grate of wood on swollen wood paralyzed him. He knew that sound well, the scrape of the door to the basement. He couldn't prevent the tremors that seized his limbs any more than Pavlov's dogs could've stopped salivating.

Panic pulled at his remaining sanity. The strange symbols drawn in the cellar flashed through his mind in a terrifying montage.

The door rasped again. John's bowels pinched. Memories of gut-searing hunger and debilitating blows received in those first days flooded his brain. Days when he'd hung on to life with both hands. Now he almost wished he hadn't. A quick death would sure beat this slo-mo dying routine he had going on now. But he hadn't known that then. And even if he had, he wasn't sure he could've made a different decision.

Survival dominated all other instincts, hijacked the body and brain when necessary. He'd learned that the hard way. Imminent death brought forth the animal in him.

John held his breath and strained his ears for more sounds. Footsteps on the bare wood treads of the basement steps rang through the heat duct. More thumps. More footsteps. A vehicle passed beneath his window. Then silence.

He wasn't coming upstairs.

John's bones shook as relief swept through him. Then he stiffened.

Those noises meant one thing. Someone else had been imprisoned in that cold and dank cellar. Someone else was chained like an animal, ready to be beaten and starved into submission. Someone else was going to be left with no options but to obey or die.

Bile surged into his throat. Helplessness drained his soul like a parasite. But what could he do? Escape attempts were futile and resulted in more pain. He couldn't withstand any more pain.

A yearning was fanned inside him. He should shout down the register to the new prisoner. Just thinking about contact with another person other than his kidnapper sent a wave of giddiness through him. But terror muted any sound that vibrated in his throat.

Bad things happened when he disobeyed.

He turned and looked across the few feet of space to his mattress. So far. Too far. His body curled into itself, wrapped in the fear of an unknown fate. As his eyelids drifted shut, he felt his humanity slip further away.

– – –

In the back office of the diner, Nathan looked up from his invoices at three sharp raps on his door. "Come in."

Chief Hugh Bailey stood in the doorway "We have a serious problem."

"What's up, Hugh?" Nathan set aside his paperwork and straightened his spine. Unease whispered along the back of his neck.

Hugh swept his red knit hat from his head. A few snowflakes drifted to the commercial tile. "Just got back from the Black Bear Inn. Mae had a tourist check in earlier today. Went out this afternoon. Never came back."

Grease from the hamburger Nathan had eaten for dinner rose into the back of his throat. "Was she tall, with long red hair?"

"Yeah."

"She was in the diner today," Nathan volunteered. No doubt Hugh already knew the girl had eaten here.

Hugh whipped out a pocket-sized notebook and clicked open his pen. "What time?"

Hugh probably knew that too.

"I'm not sure exactly. Toward the end of lunchtime."

"Anything seem odd about her?" Hugh asked.

"Not really. City girl. Pretty. Looked out of place. Other than that, nothing."

"You talk to her?"

"Sure. Introduced myself." Nathan fiddled with a paper clip. "We talked for a few minutes. She expressed some interest in local artists. I offered to take her to see Mark's ducks and Martha's quilts in the morning, weather permitting of course."

Hugh flattened his mouth and gave his head a curt shake. "While you were chatting her up, someone slashed two of her tires in your parking lot."

"Really?" Indignation laced Nathan's voice. "No one told me about that."

Hugh looked down at his notebook. "The tow truck picked up the car around three."

"Oh, I had some errands to run. Did you check inside the vehicle?"

Hugh's nod was far too casual. "Nothing unusual in it."

"This is a small town. Where could she have gone?" Nathan followed Hugh's gaze as it shifted to the window. Outside, snowflakes danced in the glow of the rear parking lot light. A spare inch coated the asphalt.

"It's damned cold out," Hugh said. "She had hot chocolate with Reed Kimball at the bookstore. She bought a book and left the store at four forty-five. Hasn't been seen since. We found a Styrofoam cup and her purchase in the hedge outside the inn."

"Not good."

"No. Definitely not. Doug and I did a drive around. No sign of her. With this storm gearing up for tomorrow, I want to dispense with the usual wait and start looking for this girl in a major way. I need volunteers. Appreciate it if you could handle organizing them. Doug's already started making calls."

"Sure thing." Nathan rose. "I'll see how many people I can scrape up. Maybe she fell or something. Hit her head. I can't think of any other possibilities."

"If she fell outside the inn, she'd still be outside the inn." Hugh tugged on his cap and rose. "I don't like this one bit, not after that body turned up last week."

Nathan rose to his feet and splayed his palms on the desk. "Hugh, we talked about that. Do not go starting any rumors unless the medical examiner officially rules that death a homicide. Chances are that kid died of exposure."

"Don't you think it's odd, having two strange events in such a short period of time?" Hugh cocked his head.

"No. Pure coincidence. There's nothing unusual about someone getting lost and freezing to death. Happens every year."

"But now we have a missing kid and a missing tourist."

"Christ, Hugh. That kid disappeared over six weeks ago. You can't possibly connect the two events. This town can't afford bad publicity. This was the slowest hunting season on record. One more like that and this town'll shrivel up and die."

A rap on the door frame cut Nathan off before he could threaten Hugh with town council intervention. A uniformed Lieutenant Doug Lang stood in the hall, a black knit hat clenched in both hands.

"The Rotary Club is going to help." Doug's gaze passed over Hugh and settled on Nathan. "Do you want to use the diner as a base?"

"Good idea, Doug," Nathan answered.

Doug flushed.

"I'll get on the phone to the state and county boys, but I doubt we'll get any help yet." Hugh grunted and stepped into the hall. "We need to find her. Before we have another body on our hands."

Doug's eyes followed Hugh's exit.

"So how many volunteers do we have in the Rotary?" Nathan pulled paper and a pencil from his desk drawer.

Doug pulled a small notebook from his pocket. "A dozen. We're calling the volunteer firemen, too."

"Good."

Doug scratched his head with the tip of his finger. He glanced at the door and lowered his voice. "Just so you know, Hugh's been talking to Reed Kimball about that dead kid."

Nathan snapped the pencil in two. "Has he?"

"Yeah. Hugh isn't telling you everything about this Jayne Sullivan. I think it's a huge coincidence that one of the last people to see her alive was Reed Kimball, considering."

"Considering what?" Other than that Hugh wanted Reed to take over as chief. Really, Hugh wanted anyone but Doug to take over as chief. Nathan couldn't blame Hugh. Doug was an idiot, but his daddy owned the local bank. Nathan found the lieutenant easily manipulated and therefore useful on occasion.

Doug expression went smug and mean. "You didn't know?"

CHAPTER NINE

Jayne raised her eyelids and immediately squeezed them shut again. Her head felt like a bowling ball mounted on a Popsicle stick, with her neck not nearly strong enough to support its bloated burden. Pain and nausea competed for top billing as she clawed her way out of a drugged stupor. A weak shiver coursed through her limbs.

Had she been at a party? Had someone slipped her something? Her memory was a deep dark hole. The fact that she couldn't remember the previous night washed over her consciousness like an ice-cold shower.

She tried to raise a hand to her head. A tug on her other wrist and a metallic jingle made her eyelids snap open. Pain shot through her left hand. Her vision blurred in the dim light. She blinked hard and focused as the images in front of her sharpened.

Handcuffs linked her wrists. A thick chain fastened her bound hands to the stone wall four feet away. She stared at them as if they were figments of her imagination. She turned over her left hand. A fresh cut was just beginning to scab over. Adrenaline pushed the first twinge of terror through the drug-induced haze.

This can't be happening.

Ignoring the pressure behind her eyeballs, she scanned her surroundings. Four walls of irregular stone. Dirt floor. Low ceiling. A bare lightbulb was attached directly to a rough-hewn beam. A steep wooden staircase rose in the center of the space. High on the opposite wall, faint gray light filtered in through two narrow, rectangular windows. An ancient furnace hunkered in the far corner.

OK. She was in a basement. But where? And how long had she been down here? She glanced toward the closest small window. With the heavy cloud cover, it could be dawn, dusk, or anywhere in between.

She forced herself to a sitting position. The room spun briefly, and she closed her eyes for three slow breaths. A gentle probe with her fingertips found the egg-size lump behind her ear. When she pressed on it, pain bounced through her head like a pinball.

Jayne blinked hard to sharpen her focus. The walls were covered with hundreds of those strange symbols. As her head cleared, Jayne connected the dots. She sucked a shaky breath into her lungs, controlled the exhalation.

She'd been knocked unconscious, drugged, and kidnapped by whoever was following her around town. This sort of thing happened to other people. She heard it on the news, read about it in the newspaper. She watched *CSI* with the same morbid fascination as everyone else.

But this sort of violence didn't actually strike the average person. Twice. And how had he grabbed her without making a sound? She was always vigilant.

Fear swept the remaining fuzz from her brain. Her situation crystallized. If she couldn't find a way to escape, she would die here. She refused to contemplate that option. There was always a way out, a counter to every attack. She just had to find it.

She would escape.

But how?

Both windows were barred. No bulkhead doors. The only way out was at the top of the staircase. It was also the only way in, and the way that her captor would enter when he came back.

Because whoever he was, he *would* come back. The faces of the men she'd met in Huntsville flashed through her mind: Nathan, Jed, Chief Bailey, Bill. She forced herself to add Reed to the list. Her attraction to him didn't alter the fact that he was essentially a stranger.

What if Reed wasn't R. S. Morgan? Could one of the other men be the sculptor? Could the sculptor be mentally ill? How desperate was he to keep his identity a secret? She hadn't heard from Chief Bailey, so she didn't know for sure that Ty Jennings was still in Philadelphia.

Jayne drew in more stale air and refocused with a quick, painful shake of her head. Next to her, directly under the place where the chain was fastened to the stone, three bottles of water tempted her. It looked like her captor wouldn't be back right away, and that he wanted her alive—for now.

Jayne licked her chapped lips as she picked up a bottle and examined it. The seals were broken; the water was probably laced with a sedative. She set it back on the floor. Like she'd drink anything supplied to her by a kidnapper who'd already drugged her once.

A faint moan sounded from above.

Jayne held her breath and strained her ears for sounds. Only silence greeted her ears. No footsteps echoed from overhead. No squeaking of floorboards. No hum of appliances. Nothing.

Must have been the old house above her settling or the wind through the trees outside.

Scooting back to lean against the rough wall, she squinted at the tiny window across the room. Through it, she could see the edge of the forest. Fat snowflakes fell against a colorless sky. From the lack of other visible roofs and the silence, she doubted she was still in town. The vastness of the wilderness surrounding Huntsville flashed through her mind. Didn't matter. She'd take her chances out there over what was in store for her in this basement.

She didn't want to die, but she *really* didn't want to be tortured, then die.

Jayne pounded a fist on her knee. Death wasn't an option. Not only did she have plenty of living to do, she couldn't do that to her brothers. They'd never be able to cope with losing her, especially Danny. He'd already sacrificed enough. His mental state was far too fragile to cope with another loss.

Time to get off her butt and out of this prison.

The room was cold but not as freezing as outside. Jayne felt the dampness seep into her bones. She was dressed exactly as she'd been when she left the bookstore: wool sweater, jeans, and boots. Her jacket, hat, and gloves were missing. No doubt to discourage an escape attempt.

Jayne examined the handcuffs. Too tight to slip out. There was a tiny keyhole in each, and Jayne wasted a few minutes searching her pockets and the surrounding dirt for anything that would fit into the hole. She was no angel. She'd picked a few locks in her day.

Finding nothing useful, she tucked her feet under her body and rose to a kneeling position. Whatever drug she'd been administered was wearing off rapidly, because she only wavered for a brief moment before getting to her feet. Her legs felt steadier than she'd expected.

She tested the length of chain with a yank. It didn't give, but a few minuscule granules of gray dust trickled down to the floor to accumulate in a hopeful pile. Jayne pulled harder. The metal cuffs bit into her flesh. Blood seeped from the thin skin over her wrist bones.

She ignored the pain and stepped to the wall to inspect the fastening, a giant eyehook set directly into the mortar. Jayne grasped the eye with her fingers. In the next few minutes, she managed a painstaking eighth of a turn, watching optimistically as more dried mortar dust emerged from the hole and trickled slowly down to the dirt floor.

Freeing the hook was going to be a slow process.

But how much time did she have before her captor returned?

Jayne said a silent prayer and wiggled the hook again.

– – –

"I'll be in the truck, Scott!" Reed shrugged back into his coat and snagged his keys from the hook by the door.

"Coming," his son called from his bedroom at the other end of the one-story house.

Juggling two travel mugs of coffee, Reed opened the door and stepped out into the predawn gray. He was raw and numb from the night's lack of success in finding Jayne. How could she be gone?

Snow fell, the density of the dancing white curtain thickening by the hour. Three inches had accumulated since midnight. Sheba brushed past his legs to chase a squirrel up a nearby tree. Reed leaned in and started the red Yukon. A blistering gust burned his unshaven jaw, sending a fresh ache of cold through his bones. The tall pines overhead bowed to the wind. Jayne's Caribbean-blue eyes filled his mind while emptiness crushed his chest.

Where was she? Was she warm? Was she injured? He refused to think about the possibility of her being dead, even though his inner cop told him the chances increased with each hour that passed.

Never mind the fact that 90 percent of women taken to a secondary location didn't survive.

Pushing the sick feeling back, he opened the back door of the truck. "Come here, girl."

Sheba leaped into the vehicle. Reed closed the rear door and climbed behind the wheel, grateful for the dog's silent company. Scott burst from the house and loped down the short walk. Slinging a backpack to the floor, he hopped into the truck. He removed the Pop-Tart that protruded from his front teeth, rooted through the bag, and pulled out a blue box. He handed Reed a cold toaster pastry. "Here."

"Thanks." Reed took it. His stomach protested the first bite, but he forced it down. The sugar would have to serve as a stand-in for sleep. It took a few seconds for the artificial flavor to come to life on his tongue.

Strawberry.

He closed his eyes, the scent conjuring images of Jayne in his mind. Her wide smile, the vivid turquoise of her eyes, the stubborn set of her jaw.

The small shake of her head as she refused his escort to the inn.

The pastry went back into the package. Food would not fill the void inside him. Just like wallowing in guilt and loss wouldn't find Jayne.

He shifted into gear and the truck rolled down the drive.

"You OK?" Scott asked.

Reed glanced at his son. Scott's eyes were underscored. The night's search had been long and cold, but the teen had held up. Like a man. Even if Reed had fucked up every other aspect of his life, Scott had turned out OK.

"Yeah. You?"

"I'm fine." Scott's slip into a slush puddle had prompted their brief trip home for a hot shower and dry clothes. "Where to?"

"I don't know. We'll check in with the chief." What could they do? A dozen volunteers and two hunting dogs had failed to find Jayne overnight. Huntsville was a small town. Reed's gut said Jayne wasn't in it, unless someone had hidden her somewhere.

But who? And why?

Had her paroled assailant followed her or was a resident of Huntsville not what he seemed? The fact that two teens had disappeared in the woods wasn't necessarily an indication of foul play. A few people died in the wilderness every year. Even seasoned woodsmen could suffer an accident or get lost. But when Reed factored in the possibility that the boy's throat could've been cut, then threw Jayne's sudden disappearance into the mix, his instincts went ballistic.

Malevolence in the snapping cold of the air clung to the town like static electricity.

He scraped a hand through his hair, as if the pressure of his fingertips on his scalp could contain the grisly images pulsing through his head. Visions of dead bodies from former cases scrambled inside his skull. Jayne's face was superimposed on old corpses. Fear for her fate throbbed in his chest with every beat of his heart.

What had happened to her?

Scott reached behind the seat and ruffled Sheba's fur. "She's coming with us?"

"Yeah. That way we don't have to worry about coming back to feed her or let her out. Besides, she might be useful." Sheba's eyes and ears were sharper than any man's. She'd proven to be an excellent judge of character over the years. She didn't like Doug Lang. "Keep your eyes open."

"'Kay." Scott turned his head toward the passenger window.

On the main road that led back into Huntsville, Reed spotted the chief's cruiser parked on the shoulder, right behind Jed Garrett's beat-up black F-150. Reed pulled off the road. The chief must have expanded the search beyond the town limits.

Spying Jed's orange hunting cap through a stand of pine trees, Reed stepped out of the cab. Sheba jumped into the driver's seat, wagging her tail expectantly.

"You stay here." He pointed his finger at the dog. Her tail froze and drooped midwag. Reed shifted his eyes to Scott, who was reaching for the door latch. "You, too."

Scott opened his mouth to protest but closed it after meeting Reed's gaze, which was surely filled with dread at what the chief and Jed might have found. Reed closed the heavy vehicle door. His feet dragged and his muscles cramped with trepidation as he strode through the trees. Hardpack crunched under his boots, the snap of ice echoing ominously in the still-quiet woods. "Hugh?" His voice was gritty over the incessant pounding of his heart.

Hugh's head lifted. Snow dotted his red knit cap. His face was ruddy, windburned, and exhausted but held no trace of horror. "It's not her, Reed. Jed found a dead moose."

Reed exhaled, relief nearly making him dizzy. A fresh lungful of cold air settled his stomach. He stepped into the small clearing. The two men stared down at the frozen, partially mauled remains of a bull moose. The carcass was largely intact, indicating it hadn't been there long. A dead moose was the wilderness equivalent of a free lunch.

Frustration stirred in Reed's chest. Who the hell cared about a dead moose? They should be out looking for Jayne.

Jed pointed to a neat hole in the animal's chest and jerked a thumb at the beast's thick neck. "This is the third animal we found like this since summer."

Reed flinched as Jed kicked a mangled hind leg with the callousness of a toddler angry at a broken tricycle. The frozen limb bobbed stiffly.

The hunter spat. "A thousand pounds of good meat, wasted."

Reed started to turn away. This was a fucking waste of time.

"Let's stay focused. We're looking for a missing woman, remember?" Hugh's tone sharpened. "But this is real strange."

Reed swiveled back at the odd pitch of Hugh's voice.

"They bled him." Jed pointed to a slit in the animal's jugular. The carcass was positioned head-down on enough of an incline that blood would have run out of the vein even after the beast's heart stopped pumping.

"Somebody killed three half-ton animals just for their blood?" Reed leaned closer. The hair on the back of his neck rose. Blood collecting was not a good sign. Not a good sign at all.

"Jed, what do you think?" Hugh asked. If you needed something tracked, Jed was your man. He and Nathan's uncle Aaron were the best guides around.

Jed scanned the area around the moose. "Can't see tracks with the new snow. But there's no reason to leave the meat. Can't see this spot that good from the road. If I wasn't looking for something, even I wouldn't have found the carcass."

Placing two hands on his thighs for support, the chief straightened his lean but aging frame with a huff. "OK. This is weird, but let's get back to the search."

The three men were silent as they made their way back to their vehicles. Reed followed the chief to his cruiser.

"About the case." Reed glanced behind him. Jed's pickup was pulling onto the road. "I'll do it."

Hugh nodded and tossed his hat onto the passenger seat. His face was somber, but his eyes were pleased. "Thanks. I knew you wouldn't let me down."

Reed's face heated. "There're too many odd things happening around here."

"That's the way I see it, too." Hugh fired up the engine and reached for the door handle. His wipers brushed fresh snow off the windshield with a squeak. "Normally, this is a pretty boring town."

"All these recent weird events can't be coincidental," Reed said. He and Hugh exchanged a look. Cops weren't big believers in coincidence. Bloody visions from a cult murder case he'd investigated years before swam in Reed's head. The thought of Jayne mixed up with something like that made his stomach roil.

"I agree. But I'd appreciate it if you'd keep my request quiet. As far as anyone else needs to know, you're just helping with the search for the missing lady. No need to upset anybody until I have more information. Nathan doesn't want to believe any of these things are connected." Hugh didn't need to spell it out. Many of the businesses in town depended on campers, hikers, and hunters. Murder was hell on tourism.

"I'm heading back to the diner. Nathan's called in more volunteers." Hugh cast a worried eye toward the sky. "According to the forecast, we have maybe six more hours before we have to call off the search until the storm passes. Though, frankly, I don't know where else to look. Maybe we'll get lucky."

Reed swallowed. Lady Luck had never liked him very much.

"I could use some help organizing volunteers," Hugh said.

"Right behind you." Reed's stomach churned. As he climbed into his truck, his eyes drifted back to the moose carcass.

Someone in Huntsville was literally out for blood.

– – –

Jayne continued to work, keeping her ears open for any sound that'd indicate her kidnapper had returned. A shiver moved up her spine as she thought of her abductor. A strange psycho serial killer had been watching her. Following her. He'd slashed her tires. But why?

The answer stood out like a marquee.

To keep you from leaving town. Duh.

Jayne's numb fingers slipped on the curved metal, and she snapped off her thumbnail below the quick. The spark of pain that shot into her hand was blunted by the cold. She flexed her fingers to force blood through the digits before returning to her task.

As she wiggled and turned the hook, an unfocused memory edged into her mind. Hands lifted her body. A voice murmured. The picture faded as suddenly as it formed. Jayne tried to yank the impression back into her head, but the harder she concentrated, the more her brain refused to cooperate.

Jayne shook herself and bent down to inspect her progress. The hook felt just a little bit looser and turned with less resistance.

She supposed it could be worse. Whoever had abducted her could have stripped her naked. He could have raped, tortured, and murdered her by now. Instead, she was still looking forward to those upcoming festivities. Occult-type visions of black candles and chicken blood swam through her head.

Why else would he keep her alive?

She stifled a hysterical sob and applied more pressure to the hook in the wall as she turned it. The cut on her palm reopened.

The falling snow thickened, blowing and drifting against the small windows. As daylight gradually abandoned her, Jayne's eyesight adjusted. She worked methodically on turning and circling the metal pin long after her cramped fingers began to bleed. Until she heard a sound that brought fresh panic bubbling into her throat. A hot rush of adrenaline wiped out any thoughts of exhaustion.

Upstairs, a door had opened.

CHAPTER TEN

Footsteps tracked across the ceiling above Jayne's head and echoed in the empty space.

Despite the cold, despite dehydration, fear pushed sweat from her body. She grasped the chain in both hands and pulled frantically. Fresh blood oozed from her wrists and fingertips. Jayne felt the hook slip, just a bit, and pulled harder, throwing all her weight backward with each heave. She choked up on the chain and braced one foot up on the wall. Her shoulders and back strained. The mortar gave suddenly with a way-too-loud jangle of metal. Jayne fell backward onto her butt in shock and froze.

Had he heard that?

She'd planned on running, but there was only one way out of this basement. And her captor was up there.

She could try to sneak out. Was the basement door even locked? She'd been chained. Her kidnapper *might* have assumed a lock wasn't necessary. No. If he caught her on the steps, he'd have the advantage of higher ground, and possibly knock her down the steps. She'd wait. See what he did. He had no idea she was trained in martial arts. She had surprise on her side. What could she do to look even more helpless?

She quickly reached for a bottle of water, opened it and poured it out behind the steps, out of sight, bringing the empty bottle back and leaving it on its side in the dirt. If he'd doctored the water, let him think she'd drunk it. The old house had a low basement ceiling. Jayne stood on her toes and loosened the light-bulb in its fixture. Her eyes had adjusted to the gloom. Maybe his hadn't.

Footsteps neared the basement door. Jayne's heart thumped at the base of her throat. All her training boiled down to the next few minutes.

But would it work?

She turned to the wall, stuck the hook back in its hole and brushed away the pile of fresh dust on the floor. Squatting down onto her butt, she eased down onto the floor, curling on her side and keeping her feet between her and her captor. Her legs were her strongest weapons. She left some space to maneuver between her body and the wall.

Panic stiffened her neck. She fought the tension and allowed her head to loll onto the dirt floor. Feeling the heavy chain sag on her wrists, she grasped the links between her hands a few inches above the cuffs. She tilted her face down and let her long hair fall across her eyes.

The footsteps came closer. The basement door opened with a rough scrape. Jayne peered through the curtain of hair. Light illuminated the stairs as a silhouetted figure stepped down onto the first tread. Against the bright light of the open doorway, her captor was a shadow. A hulking, black silhouette.

He flipped a switch on the wall and grunted when the bulb didn't illuminate.

Inside its ribbed cage, her heart pumped frantically. Adrenaline screamed through her veins. Her body protested the stillness, pleading with her to move. She fought her flight instinct and the ragged breaths that hitched from her lungs.

She'd trained for this. She could do it.

But panic still skittered through her head like a desperate rodent bolting for its hole.

The man switched on a flashlight and yanked the door shut behind him. The beam swept the dark recesses. Jayne closed her eyes as it passed over her. His boots rang as loud as gunshots on the wooden treads as he descended.

He stopped at the bottom of the stairs with a rustle of nylon. Jayne's heart stuttered when he trained the bright beam directly in her face. Unsure how much her hair covered, Jayne forced her facial muscles to relax.

Through her lids, the light flickered and dimmed.

Her captor hesitated, as if deciding if he should approach her. Jayne peered through her lashes and forced lungs that wanted to pant in terror to maintain a slow, even rhythm. She grew light-headed from the effort and perceived oxygen deprivation.

He took a few steps forward—close enough that she could smell the mix of evergreen and sweat his body emitted. His foot stopped next to her hip. He nudged her with the toe of his boot. Jayne let her body go lax; her head lolled.

He shifted his weight as if still uncertain. He pulled his leg back and kicked her sharply in the thigh. Pain shot up Jayne's leg. She couldn't hold back a soft moan as she rolled to her back, drawing her knees up to her chest as if in agony.

The beam from the flashlight flickered again, then went out. He tapped it in his palm.

Taking advantage of the momentary diversion, Jayne grabbed the ankle next to her hip. She simultaneously shot both feet into his pelvis and yanked his leg out from under him. He fell backward onto his ass. Before he could recover, she dropped a heel onto his groin.

A wet gasp emanated from her captor. The flashlight dropped to the floor as he cupped his genitals with both hands and curled to the side.

She leaped to her feet and swung the chain in her hands in a wide arc. He levered his shoulders off the ground, raised one hand and blocked most of the blow with a beefy forearm, but the tail whipped around and slapped him on the back of the head. His body sagged onto the dirt floor. One hand still clutched his groin as Jayne backed away.

The flashlight on the ground flickered. In its beam, something small and silver lay in the dirt next to his prone body. She scooped up both the light and the object, shoving them into her pocket before sprinting for the steps. Her boots slipped on bare wood as she scrambled up the stairs. Her fingers were stiff from cold and slippery with her own blood. She fumbled with the knob.

She wiped her palms on her jeans, twisted the knob, and pushed. The door, swollen from dampness, stuck fast.

A scrape sounded at the foot of the steps. She risked a look back. Her captor was pushing to his feet. Jayne turned back to the door as his boot rang on a wood tread.

Fresh terror gave her strength, and she threw her shoulder against the door. Behind her, her captor scrambled on the steps. She slammed into the solid frame again. Bloated wood gave with a scrape. Jayne's momentum carried her forward. She fell to her knees. Her palms slapped worn linoleum.

A hand grabbed her left ankle, dragging her back onto the steps. She snagged the door frame with her bound hands and glanced over her shoulder. Light poured onto the upper portion of the stairwell, illuminating her ski-masked captor four steps below her. He jerked on her foot. Jayne's fingers dug in.

Instinct developed during long hours of intense training took over. She rolled to her left hip, drew her right knee to her chest and fired a sidekick. The sole of her boot plowed straight into his chest. The breath whooshed out of him. He fell backward and crashed down the stairs.

Jayne jumped to her feet and shot through the door with a burst of frantic energy. She yanked the chain clear, slammed the door behind her and braced her back on it. Her gaze raced around the room looking for a way to secure the door. If he got out, that was the end of her. She'd never be able to take him by surprise a second time, nor could she outrun him in her weakened condition. She'd only get so far on fear and its associated rush of adrenaline.

The basement door had opened into a run-down kitchen. A heavy table and several chairs stood in the center. She seized a chair and jammed it under the doorknob. Then she dragged the heavy table over and shoved it against the chair.

Only then did she take a few seconds to pull the tiny key from her pocket, and with shaking fingers, free her hands. The chain and cuffs clattered to the floor.

The door reverberated as her abductor rammed into the other side, but the solid old wood held. Muffled, infuriated swearing faded as Jayne ran along the main corridor. Despite her panic and disorientation, she found the front exit. She bolted through it into the snowstorm with no hesitation, greeting the killing cold with enthusiasm.

— — —

A door slammed downstairs. Despite the startling noise, John's body sank farther into the mattress as the fresh tranquilizer, courtesy of his captor's daily visit just a short while ago, chugged through his bloodstream.

Furious banging erupted from below. The house trembled. Profanity echoed in the heat duct. Shock at the unexpected event—never good in John's predicament—sent a minute charge of adrenaline through his sedated system.

His captor was pissed.

John belly-crawled to his window. Kneeling, he dragged his reluctant body into an upright position and peered through the slit. A blurry figure sprinted away from the house. John blinked hard. The image cleared. He caught a flash of long red hair against a backdrop of snowy white. The runner moved with feminine grace.

A woman. And she'd gotten away.

John slid to the cold floor. It was ridiculous to feel abandoned by someone who didn't even know he was here. If he'd had the courage to shout out to her last night she might have rescued him. Or at the very least, let someone know he was here. But his courage had condemned him. He'd failed the ultimate test. Now he'd pay the ultimate price.

He hugged his knees to his chest. Pressure built behind his eyes, but his body didn't contain enough moisture for tears.

When the man came back, John would pay for the prisoner's escape.

CHAPTER ELEVEN

Jayne leaped from the peeling porch. A sharp wind full of icy crystals pelted her face. She hunched against it and plowed through calf-deep powder to what she assumed was the driveway, a ribbon of white that neatly cleaved the thick forest. A glance backward at boarded-up windows and a sagging roofline told her she'd been kept in a run-down farmhouse. Three stories of neglect loomed over her, and she turned away from its menacing shadow.

Could she steal her captor's vehicle? It would be ironic if the skill that had nearly put her into juvenile hall in high school saved her life.

A skinny set of strange tracks marked the path of her captor's vehicle around the side of the building. Snowmobile? She followed, peering around the corner into the rear yard. The trail led to a ramshackle detached garage. Behind it, the carcass of a collapsed barn rested on the snow like the bleached bones of a beached whale. Jayne jogged across the open yard. A heavy-duty padlock and chain secured the overhead door. No windows. No luck.

She backed into the shadow of an evergreen, which cut the driving wind in half. A shiver raced from her feet to her nape and lodged in her bones. She needed to keep moving. Snow clung to her hair and clothes, and then melted from diffusing body heat. Water invaded her crewneck and slid down her spine. Her body temperature had already dropped during her long day in the cellar. Wet clothing wasn't going to help. She needed to find help or shelter—soon. Both would be even better.

Had Mae noticed Jayne never returned to the inn? Was anyone looking for her? Like Reed Kimball? Wishful thinking. He'd bolted from their impromptu "date" like a man with something else on his mind. But she'd had an appointment to meet with the mayor this morning. Maybe he'd get concerned when she missed it. Regardless, at the moment she was on her own.

How far from town was she?

She scanned the wilderness around her. Nothing but trees and white stuff as far as she could see. White obscured everything, including the air. She'd get lost out there in a heartbeat. On the drive up, her GPS had shown a lot of large green blotches all around Huntsville. Even with the risk her assailant would break free and follow her, it would be better to keep to the road than wander aimlessly into thousands of acres of frozen nothing. If she possessed one ounce of luck, the falling snow would fill in her footprints before he broke out of the cellar.

Jayne listened. No sound to indicate her captor had escaped. Yet.

She skirted the house and followed the vehicle tracks down the long driveway. Her boots swished through the fluffy layer of dry powder with little effort. Still, how long could she keep going? Four karate classes a week kept her strong. She'd gotten through a grueling black belt test last fall. Every Sunday she and her brother Conor ran an eight-mile loop along the Schuylkill River. But she'd never run without a jacket in the middle of a winter storm with zero food or water for at least twenty-four hours, maybe longer.

Eating snow would hydrate her, but would also lower her body temperature even more. At the moment, hypothermia was a bigger threat than dehydration.

She pulled the sleeves of her sweater down over her aching hands. Her feet, encased in fashionable but not waterproof boots, turned to blocks of painful ice in minutes. Her toes felt as if they'd break off with each step.

Jayne assessed her surroundings. The road did not appear to have been plowed recently. There were no mounds of snow on the roadsides. Jayne stopped and dug underneath the fresh powder with her boot, but all she found was more packed snow. Nope. This road hadn't been plowed since the last storm two weeks ago. That would make it a secondary road or private drive with little or no traffic. Not good.

She faltered when the lane ended in a T with another, wider road, wide enough to be an actual public road. Jayne could see the partially filled depressions where multiple sets of tires had traveled not too long ago. Snow banks lined each side of the road. Hope squeezed her chest. She dug through the fresh snow. *Pavement!* This road must be on the plow route.

Her excitement at finding a more frequently traveled street was dimmed by the next question. Should she go left or right? Which way would take her toward civilization? The road looked completely identical in either direction: long, white, and empty. Tree limbs bowed overhead, forming a tunnel of white-coated lattice.

A gust of wind rocked her. She had to keep moving. Jayne flipped a mental coin and turned right. Her feet stumbled for the first few steps until she fell into an awkward rhythm. Soaked wool and denim weighted her limbs. Her steps felt slower than before, as if she were wading through mud instead of light, fresh powder.

How far did she have to go?

She pushed the question from her head and focused on each individual step.

Swish, swish, swish. Jayne's legs crumbled under her. Her knees sank into the snow. She wasn't going to make it. Her chances of surviving this situation were minuscule. She had no idea how to survive in the forest. A groan from the trees startled her. Her head whipped around. Was that the wind moving ice-encased branches or could that have been an animal? Bears hibernated, didn't they?

She pushed to her feet. A plow or salt truck was bound to come through eventually. If she didn't get up, it would run right over her collapsed and frozen body. They wouldn't find her until the spring thaw.

A faint, high-pitched sound drifted through the trees, and Jayne swallowed a whimper. *Wind or snowmobile?* Fear drove her forward.

Strangely enough, once she progressed beyond numb, the cold faded. Her body actually began to feel warmer. Hypothermia might not be such a bad way to go after all. Definitely preferable to whatever her kidnapper had in store for her.

Jayne thought of her three brothers and took another step. They needed her. She couldn't abandon them.

The low purr of an engine cut through the storm's furious howl. It came from in front of her, the opposite direction that her kidnapper would use if he were following her trail.

But was the sound real or an illusion conjured up by her desperate imagination like an oasis mirage to a desert wanderer?

She moved toward the sound and lost her footing. Unable to catch herself with sluggish reflexes, she fell face-first into the foot-deep powder, directly in the path of the oncoming vehicle. White flakes bombarded her face like tiny needles as she lifted her head and squinted at the vision. A set of lights approached. She tried to belly-crawl off the road, but her arms gave out.

The headlights drew closer. From the woods, a buzzing sound, much too high-pitched to be an automobile, sent a fresh wave of panic into her frozen brain. She ordered her body to rise and run but it refused to respond.

– – –

Reed kept the Yukon to a crawl. His head throbbed from squinting at the road through the storm, and he was filled with a sense of failure.

They hadn't found Jayne. Hugh had called off the search until the storm passed. The chief wouldn't risk any more lives to find a woman who was probably dead. Jayne's long odds were in the eyes of every volunteer.

The intensity of the sadness that welled up inside Reed stunned him. He'd barely known her, yet her death rocked him with a wave of crippling grief. He was drowning in sorrow and couldn't draw a deep breath.

The wipers slapped back and forth, swiping melted flakes from the windshield. Packed slush accumulated on the blade, leaving a blurry arc in its wake. Equipped with chains and a plow mounted on the front, the big four-wheel drive chugged steadily.

Scott stirred in the passenger seat. He'd been silent since the chief had sent them home for the duration. "How long is this supposed to last?"

Reed cleared his throat. His voice felt scratchy, his throat raw. "Don't know. Depends if the storm goes straight or veers out toward the coast." He flipped the defrosters to high. The sound of rushing air competed with the grinding of tires on snow.

Scott leaned his head on the window. "Think she's still alive?"

Reed couldn't answer. Scott didn't repeat the question.

The Yukon slipped sideways. Millions of tiny flakes danced lightly across the windshield, obscuring visibility to the headlights' reach. The truck shifted, and Reed tugged it back into line. Crystals were hitting the windshield faster than the wipers could clear it. And the little pinging noises on the glass sounded more like ice than flakes. "See if you can get the weather report on the radio."

Anything was better than contemplating Jayne's fate.

Scott reached for the knob and fine-tuned into a news report. The on-air meteorologist didn't mention sleet or freezing rain, but he officially upgraded the storm to a blizzard.

Scott snorted. "Duh."

Exactly, thought Reed as he switched the wipers to their highest speed. Didn't help much. The blurry arcs just moved faster.

A gust of wind pushed against the truck. Reed shifted into low gear to maximize traction. At this rate, it would take them another half hour to travel the last few miles. Hugh had wanted them to stay in town, but the thought of sharing his grief was more than Reed could handle.

Through the swirl of white, Reed caught a glimpse of blue in the middle of the road.

What was that?

He blinked to clear his dry eyes. A figure turned toward them and then slid to the ground in a boneless heap. Reed pressed his foot hard on the brakes, praying his antilock technology was enough to stop the heavy vehicle. He turned the wheel to the side, but the truck continued its forward slide. The brake vibrated under his foot. Tires slid, gripped, and slid again. With a shuddering groan, the truck ground to a halt less than ten feet in front of the blue lump in the road.

Reed exhaled the breath he'd been holding. Relief and hope sent his heart into a sloppy jog.

Could it be?

"That was close." Scott leaned forward, then reached for his door handle. "Holy cow. It's a person." Excitement tinted his voice. "Think it's her?"

Reed was already climbing out of the SUV, the possibility racing through his mind. "Stay here and lock the doors." He tugged his hood up and ignored Scott's scowl. A dozen years in homicide put suspicion front and center of Reed's mind in any unusual situation.

The force of the storm struck him before his boots touched the ground. Wind-driven ice pellets scratched and clawed their way across his exposed face and deep into his lungs.

He hesitated, almost afraid to look.

Ten feet in front of the yellow plow attachment on Reed's Yukon, a tall woman sprawled facedown in the snow. There was no mistaking the long hair that trailed through the snow in a matted rope. Even wet, he could tell it was red.

Jayne.

His initial excitement passed in one heartbeat as he approached her. What condition was she in?

She was still dressed in the jeans, boots, and bulky sweater she'd worn at the bookstore, but no coat, hat, or gloves. He dropped to one knee. A prickling on the back of his neck warned his internal cop of danger. "Jayne? Can you hear me?"

Reed grasped her shoulders and turned her over slowly, then felt at the base of her exposed throat for her pulse. Her milky white skin was cold and wet. Her pulse fluttered against his fingers.

"Jayne?"

Her eyes, pale blue as a clear winter sky and glazed with terror, opened wide.

"It's OK." Reed held his hands out, palms forward. "I'm going to help you."

She didn't meet his gaze. Her head swiveled, her eyes darting over his shoulder.

"Oh, God! *Oh, God*! We don't have time for this." She grabbed his forearm. Reed gasped. Her wrists were bloody all the way around.

Ligature wounds? A lump of tension balled up in his gut.

"Please. We have to get away! Before he catches us." She scooted on her backside toward the truck.

Reed jolted into action. Whoever had hurt her might be close by. He scooped her off the ground. Jayne slipped in his arms. Her hands clutched the front of his parka. Blood smeared on the nylon.

"Take it easy. I've got you." Reed hiked her up. His thighs burned as he straightened, but he welcomed the weight of her. He scanned the trees for any sign of a pursuer, but he could neither see nor hear anything in the forest. Between gusts of angry wind, the naked woods were as silent as they can only be during a heavy snowfall. All the sensible creatures had taken shelter.

Scott stared over the back of the seat as Reed pulled open the rear door and climbed into the back with Jayne on his lap.

"Drive, Scott. Keep it in low gear. Lock the doors and keep a sharp eye out."

Scott nodded, slid over the bench seat, and turned his attention to the road. At the click of the door locks, Jayne went limp.

Reed's heart lurched. *She trusted him to keep her safe.* He pulled her closer. The solid weight of her against his body reassured him that she was really there. It wasn't a cruel dream.

She was alive.

But whoever had kidnapped her couldn't be far away.

– – –

The Druid stood at the edge of the road. A set of taillights faded into the whiteout. He blinked snowflakes from his eyelashes.

She's gone.

Someone had picked her up in the road.

Anger warred with relief. She was alive and safe. His goddess had fought well. He was the one who had failed. He should have expected her to fight. The fault was entirely his own.

No doubt the gods were disappointed in him.

He'd find her, though. The minute the storm passed. There weren't that many places for her to hide out here.

He retuned to his snowmobile, parked behind a stand of evergreens, and marked his location on his handheld GPS. Even an experienced woodsman benefited from technology. When he returned home, he'd pinpoint all the homes in the area.

She was his last hope. He'd find her if he had to search each and every one.

CHAPTER TWELVE

Reed twisted and reached over the backseat into the cargo area for a blanket. After unzipping his coat, he pulled her against his chest, then covered them both. Water from her clothing seeped into his sweater.

Sheba jumped over the back of the front seat and sat next to them, giving the stranger a few sniffs and a halfhearted wag.

"Here, girl. Down." Reed patted his thigh. Instinct kicked in and the dog settled across Jayne's legs. The Husky's thick coat would help warm Jayne.

"Should I turn around? Head for the hospital?" Scott's gaze caught Reed's in the rearview mirror.

Good question. How badly was she hurt?

His gut quivered as he made the decision. Her life depended on it. "No. We're only a few miles from home. She needs to get warm now. It would take us hours to get to the hospital in this mess—if we got there at all." With the emergency supplies he kept in the truck, he and Scott would be able to survive being stranded overnight. Jayne might not.

Reed glanced down at the face resting against his chest. Her skin was so pale it had taken on a bluish hue. Her cheeks were chapped pink from windburn and cold, but he didn't see any of the telltale blotches that would indicate frostbite. Her scar stood out crimson against her skin, reminding him that she'd been hurt before. One of her hands, bloody and raw-looking, slipped out from under his coat. He tucked it back inside, resting it over his heart.

"She gonna be OK?" Scott asked in a low voice.

A shiver seized Jayne, indicating her body was still trying to generate heat. Reed hugged her tighter. "I don't think she's been out here for very long. She was still on her feet a few minutes ago."

"Where do you think she came from? She's not even wearing a coat, and we haven't passed any abandoned vehicles."

Reed hesitated, tempted to shield his son from the unpleasant details, but Scott needed to know the truth. He wasn't a child anymore. He'd be leaving for college next fall. "Her wrists have ligature wounds. She must have been tied up somewhere around here."

"What?" Reed caught Scott's surprise in the rearview mirror. "Someone kidnapped—"

The Yukon lurched and Reed cut him off. "Keep your eyes on the road, please. Just get us home for now. We're not going to get any answers until she wakes up."

It took them thirty minutes to navigate the remaining few miles to their house. Jayne remained unconscious, her body slack except for short periods of intense shivering that wracked her lean frame. Reed could only hope she didn't have any serious injuries as he carried her inside the chilled living room.

Scott flicked a light switch. Nothing. "I'll get the fire going."

He stoked glowing embers in the woodstove and added logs. Flames leaped in the iron box as the fire licked dry wood. Preferring the cold, Sheba headed for her bed in the opposite corner.

Reed set Jayne down on the floor in front of the burning stove and began to remove her boots. "Scott, get me some towels and a sleeping bag, please." He remembered the wounds that circled her wrists and her bloody hands. "I'll need the first aid kit too."

Scott moved off toward the kitchen. Reed switched on a camp lantern, then tossed Jayne's boots aside and tugged on her sodden jeans. He peeled the soggy material over her hips, which were covered in fitted, moisture-wicking long johns. She'd been more prepared for the weather than he'd thought. The sopping wool sweater came off next, then a T-shirt, leaving Jayne in a tank made from the same synthetic fabric as the long johns. He tugged off her wool socks. No sign of frostbite on her feet or toes. Both a miracle and affirmation that she hadn't been outside for long.

Reed examined her hands. No frostbite there either, but broken, bloody blisters tipped her fingers. Her nails were jagged and torn. A shallow cut crossed her palm. Respect swelled Reed's chest. These hands had fought for their freedom and won.

Scott returned with the supplies, draping the open sleeping bag over Jayne. He clasped her cold hands between his own to warm them while Reed cleaned the ligature wounds and other cuts, then applied a thick coating of antibacterial ointment and bandages.

Reed felt a warm rush of pride at the gentleness in Scott's touch. Scott's chronic procrastination didn't seem as important as it had this morning.

Scott poked the fire in the woodstove and added another log. "I'll go outside and start the generator." He bent to pick up Jayne's clothes.

"Wait. The chief'll want them for evidence. Lay her clothes out on a clean sheet in the washroom. When they're dry, we'll put them and the sheet in a paper grocery bag. Try to touch them as little as possible."

Scott followed instructions, lifting her jeans with one finger under a belt loop.

"Guess the phone's out?" Reed asked.

"Yep. No satellite reception either."

"Of course." The landline was unreliable, but satellite TV and Internet would return as soon as the sky cleared. As far as cell service was concerned, the area north of town was a giant dead zone. They had no way to call for help until the storm passed.

Scott grabbed his coat on his way to the door. After he'd left, Reed slipped his hand under the sleeping bag to feel the skin on her chest. It rose and fell with steady breaths, but she was still ice-cold. Damn. Apprehension gnawed at his gut. She wasn't warming up fast enough.

He stripped off his sweater and T-shirt, then lifted the quilted flap of the sleeping bag. Stretching out next to the unconscious woman, he pulled her body against his bare chest and pulled the covers over them both. His skin protested with a wave of goose bumps. It was like hugging a refrigerated side of beef.

But he prayed Jayne didn't freak out when she woke up.

Someone had actually tied this woman up. Someone nearby. Someone he possibly knew. The faces of his neighbors began to flip through his head in a mental lineup of potential suspects, and for once he wished he were more social. There were more than a dozen small places around here; at least two or three were vacation homes, unoccupied most of the year. Who knew how many hunting cabins lurked out there in the surrounding forest?

Could be a transient, holing up in someone else's empty house.

Or the culprit could be one of them.

Any one of Huntsville's normal-looking residents could harbor a dark side.

Reed shifted Jayne's frozen body in his arms to a fresh patch of his chest that hadn't yet been chilled by the contact. Her hair trailed across his skin and curled into ringlets as it dried to a bright shade of copper. He brushed a damp curl off her cheek. She stirred. Reed's heart kicked.

How would she react to being squashed up against him?

She stiffened in his arms.

"It's all right. You're safe. I'm just trying to get you warm."

Reed fought to remain still and detached as she squirmed against him. Long legs brushed against his jeans. Through the thin tank, her breasts rubbed against his chest. One popped into view as she wiggled around, and he jerked his eyes away to study a small water spot on the ceiling.

No denying it, though. That was a nipple in his peripheral vision.

He reached across her body to pull the sleeping bag over her shoulders, covering her torso. She squirmed, smashing her hips against his groin. Pain and pleasure rocketed up Reed's spine. He shifted her body off his hips and started to slide out of the sleeping bag.

She raised her head an inch or so from his shoulder and blinked hard. Her body lifted.

She rocked him with an elbow to the jaw, and colors burst through Reed's head.

— — —

Jayne pushed hard against a warm, muscular—and *bare*—chest as her vision cleared. There was no mistaking that square jaw and those intense green eyes. Lying on his back beneath her, Reed Kimball blinked and rubbed his chin. He held his other hand in front of his face, ready to block another strike, but Jayne could still feel the hot imprint where his palm had splayed across her lower back, holding her snugly against his body.

Memories flooded her head. He'd found her in the road. He'd *rescued* her. And she'd repaid him with an elbow in the face. Luckily their close proximity kept the strike light. Heat rushed into her cheeks.

"Oh my God. Reed. I'm so sorry." The words scratched her dry throat. "Are you OK?"

He grunted and closed his eyes for a second. When he reopened them, their gazes locked, and a sense of security slid over her. She was safe with this man. She felt certain down to her bones with every solid thud of his heart against hers. Though she was usually slow to warm up to a guy, he *had* saved her life.

"I'm fine. How are you?" Deep and soft, his Southern lilt caressed her battered nerves.

Jayne took stock. She'd been cold, so cold she'd thought she'd freeze to death. But thanks to Reed, she was warm and dry, cocooned in a thick sleeping bag chest-to-chest with him. He threw off heat like a furnace, and her body had wrapped itself around his muscled body, soaking up his warmth like a cat basking in a patch of sun. Considering everything she'd been through, just being alive felt freaking peachy. "I'm OK."

Apparently, the heated bliss of togetherness only went one way. Barely two seconds after she woke up, Reed wormed his way out of the sleeping bag. The empty space went cold in his absence. Jayne instantly missed the contact with his warm body—and the perception of security that went with it. Feeling her fingers on her scarred cheek, she lowered her hand, noting thick bandages around her wrists and left hand. She'd have more scars, more reminders of the violence she'd suffered. Every inch of her body began to ache.

"Do you know how you got here?"

Memories of her imprisonment and flight assaulted her, a fast-forward barrage of terrifying sensations and images. Fear closed her throat, and she could only nod in response.

Reed scooped a shirt off the floor and tugged it over his head, but not before Jayne got a brief glimpse of a rock-hard six-pack. Accepting a drink of water with two trembling hands, she raised it to her chapped lips. The lukewarm fluid felt like liquid silk in her throat as she swallowed. She drained the glass and turned to the fleece pullover and sweatpants Reed set on the floor next to her.

"These are Scott's. They should fit well enough. Why don't you get dressed? Then we'll see what you remember." He started to turn his back.

Memories she had no interest in dredging up swamped her, intertwining with flashbacks from her past. Jayne's forefinger traced her scar twice before she jerked her hand down and clasped it tightly with her other one. Enough of that bad habit. Time to get a grip. She'd survived a horrific attack—again. There was no reason for self-pity.

"Are you OK?" Reed caught the movement and squatted in front of her.

"Yeah. Fine." But Jayne sat up too quickly and wavered. Her sore muscles were stiff and clumsy, her limbs rag-dollish with weakness.

"Easy does it. Here, I'll help you." He dropped one knee to the floor and supported her shoulders, then helped her draw the soft fabric over her head and torso. She reached for a pair of white crew socks and fumbled. Her injured fingers refused to cooperate. A fresh wave of chilling memories washed over her. Without Reed's body to keep the cold at bay, she shivered. The dampness of the basement was imprinted in her bones. She wouldn't feel warm right now if she were on a tropical beach. She might never be warm again.

"Let me get that."

The touch of Reed's warm hands on her skin brought Jayne back into the present as he stretched a thick sock over her toes. His fingers brushed her bare arch. In one fluid motion, Reed scooped her from the floor and set her gently on the couch. His lean physique was deceptively strong. Jayne's hand lingered on a heavily muscled shoulder as if she could soak up his strength as well as his warmth. He ducked away to whisk the sleeping bag from the floor and tuck it around her like a blanket.

A door banged, and Jayne jumped. A minute later, a tall, gangly teen walked into the room. "Got the generator going."

"Great. We'll have food, heat, and hot water." Reed gestured toward the youth. "Jayne, this is my son, Scott. Scott, this is Jayne."

"Nice to meet you," he said. The green eyes and dark mop of hair matched his father's, but his smile was easy and outgoing, compared to Reed's more reserved expressions. The teen's face was ruddy and his hair damp as he spread his hands to the woodstove. "Feel OK?"

"Yeah. I'm good, thanks."

"Scott, please make Jayne a bowl of soup and a cup of tea, extra sugar. She needs calories and heat."

"OK." Scott disappeared through a doorway.

After the teen exited, Reed drew a yellow legal pad from the end table. "Do you remember what happened?"

"Some." A clock on the wall to Jayne's left read six o'clock. Darkness pressed on the windows. If it was evening, she'd been held for over twenty-four hours. Unless she'd been unconscious for more than one night. "What day is it?"

"Friday." Reed followed her gaze to the window, then crossed the room to open the wooden blinds. The yard was dark but not pitch-black. The view was obstructed by a thick, shifting curtain of snowflakes. Trees across the yard waved in a sudden gust of wind. White dust blew from their limbs. Tiny ice pellets tapped a faint tattoo on the glass, as if the storm were trying to get in.

Definitely evening. She'd only been held one day. Just over twenty-four hours. Seemed like much longer. Jayne crossed her arms and rubbed her biceps.

"It's OK. You're safe. I doubt anyone's moving around out there."

He was right. The chances that her captor could've tracked her here in this storm were slim. With that revelation, the brutal weather morphed from enemy to dear friend.

Reed left the blinds open as if he knew she needed a reminder of the insulation afforded her by the blizzard. He sat down on an ottoman next to her and clicked open a pen. "What did you do after you left the bookstore?"

Jayne took a deep breath. "I headed back to the inn. I got as far as the walkway out front. Then…Nothing. I don't remember anything until I woke up this morning. The whole night's a blank. I'm pretty sure he drugged me."

Jayne gave him a brief rundown of her imprisonment and escape.

He set aside the tablet and perched on the edge of the sofa next to her, sliding his fingertips through the still-damp hair over her scalp. The effect was hypnotizing until he pressed behind her ear. She flinched as pain bounced through her head. He parted her hair and held the lantern closer for a better look. Jayne's nose picked up the scent of a musky aftershave layered over wood smoke.

"You've got a nice goose egg back here, but the skin's not broken. Does it hurt?"

"A little, but not as much as when I first woke up this morning."

"Considering how cold you are, I think we'll skip an ice pack. Tell me more. Do you have any idea how far you ran before we picked you up?"

She spread her hands toward the woodstove. Heat infused the sensitive skin of her sore fingers. "No. But I can't imagine it was too far."

"No. Not in this weather. Can you describe your attacker?"

"Not really. He was wearing a ski mask." Jayne tried to detach herself from the scene, but fear crawled over her skin like a swarm of insects. She hugged her shoulders and huddled farther under the covers.

"Was he taller than you?"

"I think so." A memory flashed. *Her body bounced. The world was inverted. Pressure built as blood rushed to her head. A thick shoulder dug into her stomach.* Goose bumps rippled across Jayne's flesh. "He carried me. Over his shoulder. Fireman-style."

Reed nodded. "So, he was strong. Do you remember what was he wearing?"

She closed her eyes and refocused, but the mental image of her captor remained a dark blur. "I don't know."

"That's OK." Reed's pen hovered over the tablet. "What about the house? Can you describe it?"

The basement she had down cold, but the rest? "Not really. Looked like an old farmhouse."

"One story or two?"

Once she'd escaped, her mind had focused on getting away, not analyzing where she'd been held. She'd only glanced over her shoulder, but the house had felt taller than normal. "Three, I think."

With Reed's pointed questions, Jayne remembered more details than she'd thought. There'd been lights, so the house had electricity. The furnace in the corner of the basement must have been working because the temperature in the basement hadn't been nearly as low as outside. Not an abandoned house, just neglected. Reed gleaned more facts from her reluctant memory until Jayne pressed a forefinger to her temple, which had begun a slow bass-drum throb.

Reed clicked the pen closed. "That's enough for now. I'm not sure how many houses are along that stretch of road, but the police chief'll know. Hugh knows everybody. I'll put the tablet on the table over here in case you remember anything else. I assume you no longer have the camera you used to take those pictures of the symbols on your Jeep."

"It was in my purse. He must have it."

"Do you think you can draw some of those symbols?"

"I'll try." Jayne thought his interview skills were awfully well developed. "Are you sure you're not a cop?"

"I'm sure." Reed stiffened. For a few seconds he watched the storm rage on the other side of the glass. "But I used to be." His mouth closed abruptly, and Jayne was sure he hadn't meant to divulge that bit of information.

"I'll check on your dinner." He ducked into the kitchen as if he couldn't get away from her and her questions fast enough.

So, what was Reed hiding?

– – –

He stowed the vehicle in the small shed far in the back of the property, removing his thick waterproof gloves to fasten the door.

Pushing his goggles onto his forehead, he faced the woods. No one was more at home in the forest. People fought nature instead of communing with it, allowing it inside them, to strengthen, to soothe, to heal. He embraced the blizzard. The trees called to him; the storm was a gift from the gods to help him with his quest.

Ice stuck to the exposed skin around his eyes. He ripped off the knitted balaclava and welcomed the bitter wind on his face. The cold was no matter. Huntsville's isolation and climate had been part of its appeal all those years ago, when he'd moved here, needing a fresh start.

A bit of guilt wormed its way into his belly. He shook it off. Everything he'd done had been for his family's benefit. Even the things he could never tell them. Especially what he was about to do.

It was a huge request, and the gods rightly demanded a great sacrifice. The woman would be a perfect addition to the ceremony. The gods had sent her to him. He could feel their power in the icy wind. As if answering his prayers, snow thunder rumbled across the empty yard.

Once he recovered her, one more offering needed to be chosen.

Three was the magic number.

If his own life were asked, he'd give it willingly and with honor. The gods assured him that the next life was far superior to this one.

He wondered who had rescued his Brigid tonight. Would he take good care of her? Treat her with the respect she deserved? How difficult would it be to reacquire her? He would do anything to get her back. A battle against a worthy foe would increase his power and give him the edge he needed.

Warriors craved—no, needed—battle.

Perhaps the sickness inside him was a result of an easy life. With no wars to wage, his body fought with itself. Didn't matter. In two days, it would all be over. One way or the other.

Bitter wind stung his face as he turned toward the house. But first he needed to make a sacrifice to atone for his failure in letting her escape. He pushed up his sleeve, then slipped a knife from his pocket and opened the blade. A quick slash across his forearm. Blood dripped onto the snow.

Just like that boy on Samhain.

The first blood sacrifice. The one that had started it all.

A tree limb creaked.

The gods were satisfied.

CHAPTER THIRTEEN

Reed's gaze flickered across the room to the couch, where Jayne murmured in her sleep, then back to the file in his lap. Outside the wind howled. Ice pelted the windows. He rolled his head on his neck to stretch muscles that had stiffened during the few hours of rest he'd managed.

He adjusted the lantern next to his reading chair in the far corner of the room, as far away from the stove as he could get while still keeping Jayne in sight. The temperature of the room hovered at sweat lodge, perfect for someone recovering from hypothermia, sweltering for anyone else. Usually insomnia drove him to his workshop until dawn broke, which explained the depressing nature of his work.

But tonight, Reed couldn't leave the room.

The urge to watch over Jayne was too powerful to ignore. It thrummed through his veins, like the low-level hum of an electrical transformer. His brain insisted she was safe from her captor, insulated by the powerful storm that raged outside, but primal instinct overruled common sense.

That beautiful woman had been abducted and held prisoner and had nearly died yesterday. Like a warrior, she'd trained and valiantly fought her opponent. She'd rest safely if he had to guard her all night long. She'd earned it.

His instincts were also telling him there was a strong possibility Jayne's abduction was related to the murder case that he was about to dive into. Cops didn't believe in coincidence. The chance of two violent crimes of this nature occurring in this rural spot in such a short period of time was practically nil. Huntsville wasn't a stranger to crime, but its violent troubles tended to be of the more personal variety: domestic disturbances, barroom brawls, and the like.

Reed turned to the page in his lap, but the words on the medical examiner's report blurred, and the thick file felt heavier on his thighs. He could feel his carefully maintained low profile slipping away.

He could look at grisly crime scene photos. He could read autopsy reports. But the one thing he couldn't handle was media exposure. Unfortunately nothing drew the press like kidnapping and murder. And if there was a juicy scandal attached, reporters would home in on Huntsville like buzzards on roadkill.

Reed was a walking, talking scandal. He needed to keep his name out of the reports and pass Jayne off to Hugh ASAP. Ironically, it was Jayne who had awakened something in him that wanted to do more than simply exist. Something that wanted to start living like the future was more than an endless stretch of sleepless nights.

Jayne snored softly and snuggled deeper into the sleeping bag. The window of the woodstove threw a flicker of light across her pale face, highlighting her scar. Reed watched, mesmerized. A dull ache spread through the center of his chest when he thought of her lucky escape—and what would have happened if she hadn't managed to get away from her abductor this afternoon.

She'd be dead, just like that college kid from Mayfield.

The ache swelled, amplifying in the vast emptiness of Reed's heart. Jayne's courage, strength, and beauty called to him. They threatened to take hold, to root themselves in that place deep within that he'd closed off to everyone except Scott.

He couldn't get attached to her. After his wife had died, he had vowed to never open his heart again. He couldn't take another loss.

Jayne turned on her side with a soft sigh. A tendril of hair fell across her cheek. Reed suppressed the urge to sweep it from her face.

Barely.

His gaze dropped to her lips. Her mouth would be hot and soft. He already knew what her body felt like against his. All that was left to imagine was the way she'd taste. Every inch of her. The biggest decision would be whether he started at her slender feet and kissed his way to her core, or worked down from her mouth and across her breasts to get to her center. Blood rushed to his groin as he imagined licking inside her heat.

The strength of his desire shocked him, and his vulnerability pierced him to the soul.

Oh, yeah. The sooner he passed Jayne off to Hugh the better. He'd start clearing the driveway and paths at daybreak. If the storm weakened through the night, as the meteorologist on Reed's radio predicted, he could get her to town by late afternoon. Then she'd be Hugh's responsibility. Reed would be in the clear.

She'd be out of his life before the spark in his chest ignited.

But Reed knew the damage was done. He knew what he was missing, why one-night stands weren't his thing. Closeness. Intimacy. The emotional bond that gave sex its zing.

The very thing he'd purposefully avoided since his life had imploded.

When Jayne left, how would he continue to ignore the giant, gaping hole in his existence?

Scott would leave next fall. Reed would be left with a dog and a hundred acres of lonely wilderness. That was what he wanted, wasn't it? He'd purposefully bought a house in the middle of nowhere. After five years in it, he only knew a handful of people in town well. So why did time stretch out in front of him like an open road in the desert? No reason to move forward except that the future was unavoidable.

Shit. He was getting morose. Midnight was a very bad time for in-depth life analyses.

Death was the ultimate distraction, so Reed turned back to the preliminary autopsy report on Zack Miller. Hugh was right. The kid's throat could've been slashed. But why? And by whom?

Reed's brain flipped through the available scenarios. The college kids got lost. Weather conditions had changed rapidly that weekend, with an unexpected light snowfall. Zack was an Eagle Scout, and his father had insisted the boy had packed extra provisions. His son knew how to survive in the woods. But even experienced woodsmen weren't immune to the dangers of the wilderness.

One or both of the teens could have been hurt. But being lost or hurt wouldn't have taken them so far from their intended campsite that rescue crews couldn't find them in the extensive search that had followed their disappearance.

Had someone followed the boys with the intention of killing them? A personal grudge? Didn't seem likely according to the boys' school records and backgrounds, but Reed tucked the possibility in the back of his head.

What had happened to Zack's roommate, John Mallory? Had he been killed and dumped in a different location? Had animals dragged his remains away? Would his body turn up next spring?

Then there was the coin. How did a two-thousand-year-old Celtic slater end up under a corpse in Maine?

A sudden gust rattled the windows. A muffled creak pulled Reed from his chair. He held his breath while a series of cracks split the air.

Tree.

The thud that followed shook the house. Scott's middle-school graduation picture slid to the floor with a clatter. Glass shattered. Reed exhaled. It hadn't sounded like the tree hit the house.

Jayne rolled off the sofa, landing on the floor in a tangle of long limbs. Her wide-open eyes sought his. Fear lingered in their clear depths. Reed's stomach knotted.

He extended one hand, palm out. "It's all right."

Relief crossed her face, and the rope in Reed's gut tightened. Her trust rattled him nearly as much as the downed tree. He turned toward the kitchen, away from Jayne and her needs.

"What was that?" A bleary-eyed and barefoot Scott stumbled from the hall, hip bones and sinewy abs in stark relief above low-riding sweatpants.

"Tree, I think. Stay with Jayne." Reed moved through the kitchen, stepped into his boots, and shrugged into his parka on the way out the door. He scanned the yard. Nothing. Reed rounded the house and stopped cold.

Shit.

A mature oak, with a trunk too thick for Reed's arms to encircle, lay directly across the drive, right behind the rear wheels of the Yukon.

So much for his plans. Jayne wasn't going anywhere today.

– – –

The first thing Jayne noticed upon waking was the gray morning light filtering through the wooden blinds. The second thing she realized was that she wasn't at home or in a motel. Pain, dark memories, and panic flooded through her, and the foggy remnants of sleep evaporated from her head.

She bolted upright, sending a zing through the stiff muscles of her back. Cold fear shoved the pain away.

Where was she?

Her gaze ping-ponged around the room and landed on the chair in the corner, now empty. A memory of Reed, alternatively sleeping and reading through the night, popped into her head. A wave of relief followed in its wake. He'd saved her; then he'd watched over her so she could rest.

She sucked in air and blew it out, but her heart was locked in a full-out sprint that threatened to steal the oxygen from her lungs. Jayne concentrated, inhaled, and held the breath deep in her chest. She focused inward, expelling a breath from her core and focusing as she'd been trained. Karate had taught her to control her breathing and function in a high-stress situation. Both skills had come in damned handy yesterday. The light-headed feeling ebbed away as her heart rate slowed.

Hyperventilation averted.

She pushed the heavy sleeping bag down to her waist. Her body was coated with a thin layer of sweat. Her frame ached from head to toe. But all of this paled against the alternative of being dead.

As she stretched her arms to the ceiling, her muscles resisted. A hot bath would be just the thing to loosen her up. Besides, she couldn't possibly smell like a rose after all she'd been through. Thankfully that was a quick fix as soon as she found Reed.

His house was simple and manly in decor, something she hadn't even noticed the night before. An overstuffed sofa and chair in chocolate brown, bookshelves, and clean-lined furniture gave it a Pottery Barn feel, which continued down to the wide-planked wood floor and flat, Berber-type area rugs.

The house was comfortable and neat but lacked personal touches. No artwork, no magazines, no clutter. Reed's halfhearted Christmas decorations were comprised of one poinsettia and a cinnamon-scented jar candle on the coffee table. The only other evidence of habitation was a few of Scott's electronic gadgets left lying around: an iPod, a cell phone. Wait! A cell phone? Did he have service out here? Didn't matter, she supposed. Her phone was in her purse, wherever that was.

She knew she was lucky to be alive. Things were just things. But she didn't have the money to replace her equipment. Because of the weather, she'd been carrying her compact camera when she'd been abducted. Hopefully her large single-lens reflex model was still in her room at the inn. Getting photos of R. S. Morgan wasn't looking likely, but the loss of her main camera meant no more travel brochure business either. Thin as those checks were, it was honest pay, which was more than she could say for her tabloid income.

The smell of coffee and bacon drew her from the sofa. She eased to her feet and shuffled into the kitchen. Her first impression was *wow*. The utilitarian space was a shiny acre of slate, granite, and stainless steel, a professional chef's dream. Sleek and gorgeous but impersonal. Jayne preferred a bit of clutter. Or maybe she was just used to a mess since her three brothers were complete slobs. Either way, Reed's sterile kitchen felt as warm and homey as an operating room.

She made use of the empty mug that sat next to the coffee-maker and helped herself to a piece of bacon from a plate on the center island. Both seemed to have been left out for her. Without thinking, she polished off the remaining bacon. Her stomach rumbled for more food.

So where was Reed? And how rude would it be to rummage through his kitchen or go looking for the shower without permission? Too rude, she decided with a regretful sigh.

Coffee in hand, she wandered to the breakfast nook. The bay window overlooked the backyard. Everything in sight was shrouded in a shiny white glaze. Squinting, she caught a flash of movement by an outbuilding on the corner of the property. Standing in a trench they'd obviously just dug, Reed and Scott leaned shovels on the side of the shed and wrestled the double doors open.

How long would they be out there? Her stomach groaned and her scalp itched. All she needed to do was ask him if she could use the shower and help herself to more food. It looked cold, but she'd only be outside for a minute or two.

While she watched, Reed wheeled a snowblower into the open. They weren't coming in anytime soon.

Jayne headed for the nearest interior door. A mudroom opened onto a small side porch. A freshly cut evergreen leaned into the corner, its stem submerged in a bucket of water. Next to the door, coats and hats hung on wooden pegs over a long rubber tray of boots. She helped herself to a parka and boots.

Jayne stepped outside. On the porch, she pulled the zipper to her chin and sniffed. Pine and wood smoke. The wind, though cold, felt fresh on her cheeks after she'd been held prisoner in that dank basement.

At that thought, Jayne cast a worried glance around the perimeter of the yard. The storm had slowed. Reed and Scott would dig out today.

So would her captor. The fresh air turned bitter as it blasted her face.

A bark drifted across the woods, and Jayne caught a glimpse of gray fur tearing through the trees toward Reed. Sheba. He whistled and winged a snowball at her. The dog leaped, snatched it from the air, and pranced away. Reed grinned. The rare smile on his handsome face pulled Jayne toward him.

She raised a hand to smooth her tangled hair. Her fingertip brushed across the recessed scar before she yanked it back down. This attack had brought all her buried insecurities to the surface.

A narrow path cut through the thigh-high accumulation. Not having any desire to be wet again, she stuck to it. The oversized boots flopped on her feet. A fierce wind slapped against Jayne's back, and a shiver coursed through her bones. After her experience the previous day, she wasn't going to last more than a few minutes out here. The boots swished though the layer of powder that had blown and fallen on the path since they'd shoveled it.

Scott disappeared into the shed.

Reed must've heard her approach because he whirled and squinted hard at her. "You should've stayed inside. It's too cold out here for you."

Not much of a greeting. "Good morning."

He pulled off his knit cap, stepped closer, and tugged it over Jayne's head. His short hair stood up in damp tufts, and his big body was close enough to shelter her from the wind. He scanned the yard before allowing his gaze to meet hers again for a heartbeat. Regret crossed his face, and his eyes softened. "I'm sorry, but hypothermia's serious. You need to keep warm. How do you feel?"

She raised her eyes to his lean and chiseled face. Emotions warred in his expression for a few seconds. Then his poker face slid back into place, rock-solid, as he stepped back to put a few feet of snow between them. Something was up with him. Jayne remembered their initial meeting, when he'd barely spoken to her and purposefully kept her off his property. Did he feel like she was intruding on his privacy? He'd acted friendlier when they'd talked at the bookstore, although he hadn't been forthcoming with any personal tidbits then either. Once again she thought maybe Reed had something to hide.

Jayne swallowed hard as she tried to mimic his self-control. Not likely, but she could fake it. "I'm OK. I'm no hot-house orchid."

He glanced at her. Surprise flared in his eyes, then a quick flash of humor. "No. That you aren't." His mouth opened again, but instead of speaking he clamped it shut. His eyes looked wounded for a second before his features smoothed out into his usual blank mask.

"Is everything all right?" Jayne asked, taking a step toward him unconsciously.

Reed backed away, turning to the machine he'd been setting up when she'd interrupted him. He opened the snowblower's fuel tank. "The storm hasn't lived up to its expectations. So far, the heaviest precipitation stayed south and east of us. The coast is getting hammered all the way down to DC."

Jayne lowered the hand that had reached for his forearm to comfort him, sticking it in the pocket of the borrowed parka. "I wish I could call my brothers and check on them. If Washington's being hit hard, Philly probably is too."

Scott emerged from the shed, gas can in hand. He flashed Jayne a wide smile. "Hey. Good to see you up."

Reed cast a glance at the steel-gray sky. "This is clearing out fast. We have satellite Internet. You should be able to able to contact your family tomorrow."

"OK. Good." Wind swirled powder around Jayne's feet and she shivered.

"You'd better get inside." Reed straightened and brushed snow from his gloves. "You must be hungry. I'll get you some breakfast."

Jayne's stomach rumbled audibly at the cue. "I'm starving. But I really came out here to ask if I could use the shower."

Reed paused and his shoulders tensed. "I'm sorry. I should've thought of that."

"No biggie. I don't expect you to think of everything, and I'm perfectly capable of taking care of myself."

"That you are." Reed nodded, his posture relaxed, and his eyes settled solidly on hers. Heat flared in their green depths as he frowned. There was the same attraction she'd seen in the bookstore, but now he wasn't thrilled with the idea. Why? Did he resent her presence in his home? Was there some reason he didn't want her here?

Jayne hugged her arms, the warmth and security she'd felt at seeing him a few minutes earlier abandoning her. Maybe she was just being overly sensitive. He hadn't mentioned Scott's mother once. Maybe a bad divorce had thrown him off women.

"Come on, Jayne." Scott handed the gas can to his dad. "I could use breakfast too."

Jayne followed Scott. The prospects of food and a shower lightened her step. On the porch, she glanced over her shoulder. Reed was still standing in the same place, staring at the red fuel can in his hand as if he didn't know what it was.

It was a good thing her stay with the Kimballs would be short. Reed had saved her, but he obviously couldn't deal with her presence. Something traumatic in his past had left its mark, stunted his ability to connect with other people.

Reed was far more adept at hiding his feelings, but the man clearly had plenty of his own scars. Just because his were on the inside didn't make him any less damaged.

CHAPTER FOURTEEN

Reed parked the fueled snowblower on the porch and faced the house. Through the window, he watched Jayne move around the kitchen. She'd pulled her hair back into a ponytail, the mass of curly hair hanging down her back. Scott's sweats hung low on her hips. She handled the kitchen equipment deftly, with an efficiency that suggested she was no stranger to household chores.

Jayne was definitely not a hothouse orchid. If she were a flower, she'd be a tiger lily, tall, resilient, and bright. The fact that he'd almost said those words made his palms clammy under his insulated work gloves.

She'd been abducted and held prisoner, and still had the ability to smile, to give. *She'd* been about to comfort *him* for Christ's sake. Had he ever met anyone so strong? So kind? So generous?

No. No. And *no*.

But along with jolting his sleeping soul back to life, Jayne had stirred up his carefully orchestrated life, a life in which he didn't dare allow anyone to get close. Men with secrets couldn't afford scrutiny or complete honesty. Tough to have a relationship without those and the trust that went along with them. So far, he hadn't been tempted to try, but Jayne was different. He'd been alone for years, but he'd never felt lonely until she showed up. Honest, courageous, valiant. All the things he wasn't.

He'd contemplated backing out of his promise to Hugh just a few hours ago.

What would she do if she knew everything? Would she feel as safe with him? Or would she sleep behind a locked door with one eye open? She deserved better, someone without all his baggage. Face it, he had a wagon full, far too heavy a load for a twice-assaulted woman to share.

He stepped into the mudroom and shook the flakes from his parka before hanging it to dry. His gloves had their own pegs. Boots went on the rubber tray. Reed turned toward the kitchen and hesitated at the threshold.

A redheaded tornado had blown through his kitchen. Food containers littered the counters. Frying pans sizzled on the stove. Jayne held a bowl in one Band-Aid-tipped hand and a whisk in the other. Her hair was a warm copper against a backdrop of sleek gray and black, a shock of color in his monochromatic kitchen. She gestured to Scott, who lounged at the center island. A yellow glob flew off the whisk and landed on the formerly pristine ebony granite. Through the doorway beyond, the bare Christmas tree stood crookedly in its stand. Boxes of decorations littered the floor.

"Oh, hi." Jayne whirled as he padded into the room in damp socks. "I started breakfast. I hope you don't mind."

"Um. No. That's fine."

Scott beamed. "Jayne's gonna help with the tree, too."

A tiny kernel of resentment lodged in Reed's chest. The tree was the one Christmas tradition he shared with his son. Father-son bonding experiences were few and far between these days. Next year, Scott would be leaving for college.

"It's the least I can do." Jayne slipped a piece of bread from a plate, dunked it into the beaten eggs, and slid it into a sizzling pan. She stopped to turn the bacon frying on the next burner before repeating the process with three more slices.

"You don't have to do anything," Reed said.

"It's OK. I'd rather keep busy." She shot him a brittle smile. Ridiculously, Reed was relieved that her sunny disposition was a brave front. The woman had been through hell. He felt like a total shit for resenting her participation in their Christmas ritual, even if it had only been for a split second. Jayne needed activity to keep her imagination off her abductor and where he might be right now, not to mention the horrors she'd already suffered. "Scott wanted French toast."

"Did he?" Reed pulled a paper towel off the roll and wiped the dots of egg off the floor.

His son grinned and rested his chin on his fists. "Dad doesn't cook much."

"I saw the pile of Hungry-Mans in the freezer." Jayne traded the whisk for a spatula and slid food onto plates with the competence of a short-order cook. More bacon and French toast went on the stove. Grease splattered. "That's a shame. You have restaurant-quality appliances here."

"That's what the realtor said." Reed took the stool seat next to his son and watched Jayne's nervous bustle. He liked the kitchen clean and free of clutter, like his workshop—and his life.

"We eat a lot of sandwiches," Scott said.

Jayne set loaded plates in front of them both.

"I cook sometimes. I make eggs and bacon every weekend." Reed cringed at the whiny edge in his voice as he cut off a corner of French toast and stuffed it into his mouth. More eating, less talking. There was no reason for him to get to know Jayne any better. She'd be gone tomorrow. Jayne was meant to live in the spotlight, while he was destined to live in the dark.

"Fried eggs on Saturday. Pancakes on Sunday. The frozen kind. Precooked microwave bacon." Scott shot Reed a smug look.

"There's nothing wrong with keeping to a schedule." A routine kept life from disintegrating into chaos and kept Reed sane. "Nothing seems to stop you from eating vast quantities of everything."

Scott had too much food in his mouth to respond, but he gave Reed an eye roll that adequately communicated his opinion of their meal routine.

Jayne reloaded Scott's plate before he'd cleared it. Without lifting his head, Scott grunted his thanks.

"Hey." Reed lightly slapped his son's shoulder, then turned to Jayne. "Please excuse his manners."

"It's fine. Eating is serious business for teenage boys. I have brothers. Two older and one younger. They used to eat every meal like they were never gonna see another one. I learned how to stretch a stew early."

Scott swallowed. "Stew. Yum."

Jayne filled her own plate. Reed covered a wince with a cough as frying pans were dumped in the sink and topped with a few squirts of dish soap. Water followed with a hiss and corresponding billow of steam. Jayne left the pans to soak and took the seat next to Reed. Her silverware clattered and she pushed the food around on her plate. Very few forkfuls made it into her mouth. "Do you cook a lot?" Scott asked between shovelfuls of food.

"Didn't have much of a choice. My parents died when I was twelve. The four of us were on our own. My oldest brother, Pat, was twenty-two. He took over the bar. The rest of us were stuck with house duty until we were old enough to help him." Pride and affection edged her chatter as she cut her French toast over and over into absurdly small pieces. "Pat did whatever he had to do to keep us all together. And to thank him, we gave him a lot of gray hair."

A sense of inadequacy slid over Reed. Jayne's brother had barely been an adult when he raised his siblings and took over the family business. Jayne was keeping house at twelve. Reed struggled to raise one child, and he'd failed miserably as a husband. Since his wife's death, he'd avoided personal relationships and all the vulnerability and complications that went with them. Caring about people twisted him up inside, like now, when he watched a beautiful woman bravely struggling to be normal after a terrible trauma. And look how his one semifriendship, with Hugh, had turned around to bite him on the ass. Friends expected to be able to ask for favors occasionally.

Reed used his napkin to wipe an egg splatter from the sleek granite counter. "That's young to take on three kids and a business."

Jayne shrugged. "Well, Conor was twenty. He was pretty much raised. But Pat should still be sainted. Danny was only eleven, and the two of us were a huge pain in his butt."

Reed's heart clenched. Scott had lost his mother at the same age as Jayne. The first couple of years had been rough. Both Scott and Jayne had learned to live again, though. Unlike Reed.

Scott swallowed half a glass of orange juice and came up for air. "What're your brothers like?"

"Pat's married. I live with him, his wife, and their three kids. He's big and patient and he works all the time. Worries about the rest of us nonstop. He's a great dad." Jayne's face was animated; her eyes went liquid and she seemed to calm as she talked about her brothers. "We all work the bar, but Pat's definitely the boss. Conor's the quiet one. He's also the practical joker. Danny's the rebel. He went into the army after high school. He was injured in Iraq and went through a severe bout of depression. But we got him the help he needed—and the rest of us are on his case enough that he's snapping out of it."

"I wish I had brothers or sisters," Scott said. "Mom couldn't have any more kids."

Unpleasant memories turned the French toast in Reed's mouth to paste. The truth was, Madeline had had enough trouble dealing with one child and a cop husband. She hadn't wanted any more kids. Something Scott did not need to know.

He cleared his throat. Time to put an end to this morning's show-and-tell session. "So, the plan is for me and Scott to clear the drive today. The weather's improving. I should be able to get you to town tomorrow. Either the phone or Internet should be up by then, too."

Jayne looked down. She pushed her plate away mostly full. "You guys go ahead. I'll take care of the kitchen. Then I'll use the shower if it's OK."

"Of course it's OK. There a Jacuzzi if you want to use it." Reed stood. His arms ached with the need to comfort her. The desire to pull her close was as disconcerting as her turmoil. But after tomorrow, it would be Hugh's job to ensure her safety. Reed would be off the hook. Better to keep his distance. Jayne's presence threatened the invisible life he'd worked so hard to attain.

Reed backed away. "Scott, please restock the wood on the porch and load the stove before you come out."

His son patted Jayne on the arm on his way to the mudroom. Jayne gave him a sad smile.

"Don't worry, Jayne. Dad'll make sure you're OK."

Scott's promise hit Reed like an uppercut to the belly.

Keeping Jayne safe was Hugh's job. Reed hadn't asked for the responsibility. If he turned her over to Hugh, Reed's duty would be done. He could restore his life to its former order. No more complications. No more risk.

Jayne would take her bright smile back to Philadelphia, and Reed would crawl back into the shadows.

— — —

Jayne glanced out the window as she set the last plate in the dishwasher. Nothing was coming out of the sky. Tomorrow Reed would take her into town.

Then what?

She'd report the crime, collect her Jeep, and head back to Philadelphia as soon as the roads were clear? Now that her courage had petered out, the thought of driving eight hundred miles alone made her knees weak and her eyes swell with tears. She couldn't do it. She'd call Pat. One of her brothers would fly up and drive her home.

The only problem was that home didn't feel safe either. Getting away from Philly hadn't made a difference. Once she left Reed's isolated house in the woods, she might never feel secure again. Of course, given what had happened, she wasn't safe here either.

Would she ever feel safe again?

She reached under the sink for steel wool, tripping over the dog sleeping at her feet. After patting Sheba's fluffy head, Jayne straightened and plunged her hand into the soapy water in search of the cast-iron pan.

When it was clean and dried, she stared out the window, watching Scott cross the yard. He was headed for the tarp-covered woodpile next to the shed. He'd need someone to hold the porch door open for him. She stopped in the mudroom to borrow boots and a jacket, but a movement through the panes in the door pulled her to the threshold before she had a chance to don them. Sheba butted her knees. The dog's hackles lifted.

A feeling of unease passed over her as she pushed the storm door open and sidled through the opening, pushing Sheba firmly back into the house. "Stay."

Scott grabbed another piece of wood and added to the pile in his arms. Jayne scanned the area. The hair on her neck tickled. Something was out there. On the other side of the door, Sheba let out a furious bark. Jayne's gaze swept the trees.

And she saw it.

A small wolf stood about thirty feet away from Scott, teeth bared in a vicious snarl. Thin, scraggly gray fur stood up on the back of its neck. It stepped forward. A low growl emanated from its throat.

Scott.

Ice crawled down Jayne's spine and liquefied in her belly. Driven by instinct, she stepped out into the yard. She barely felt the moisture soak through her socks. Her heart protested, banging furiously on the inside of her breastbone.

Scott eased back. He dropped all but one of the logs, holding the remaining piece in front of him as a weapon.

Jayne ran on numb feet, passing a fat tree stump, yanking free the ax buried in its scarred surface without stopping. It was heavier than she'd imagined. She tested the weight of the metal head. If the animal attacked, there'd be little time for a big, slow swing. Her best option was a straightforward thrust of the honed edge. She choked up on the handle and prayed it was sharp.

Jayne drew even with Scott. "Get in the house!"

Scott shook his head. He didn't take his eyes off the wolf.

"Now." Jayne planted herself between Scott and the wolf. She waved the ax. Her legs shook from cold and terror. "Shoo."

The wolf snapped its jaws. Saliva dripped from its muzzle as it focused yellow eyes on Jayne.

CHAPTER FIFTEEN

The snowblower hitched in Reed's hands as he rounded the house. He shut off the engine and bent to examine the blades for stick or rocks. He wasn't even close to the fallen tree yet.

"Scram. Get out of here!"

The panic in Jayne's voice cut through the brittle air. Reed whirled and sprinted toward the house. Her yell had come from around back. He raced around the corner and came to an awkward, sliding stop.

Jayne stood in the center of the yard, brandishing an ax at a damned big coyote. Coyotes didn't generally attack adults, but this one looked hungry. The coat was a dull, dirty gray; its ribs visible through the sparse fur.

Scott reached out to touch Jayne's shoulder. "It's OK. It's just a coyote."

Jayne held her position. She waved the ax at the coyote like a mother bear defending her cub.

Reed ran forward. Inside the house, Sheba hurled her body at the closed door. Scratching and angry barking accompanied the rattling of the frame. With a nervous glance at Reed's approach, the coyote turned and slunk into the woods.

Jayne didn't move. Reed kept jogging until he stood in front of her. Her eyes were wide open, her features frozen with shock. He pried the ax out of her trembling hands.

"Thank you."

Scott stepped up. "It was just a coyote. He probably wouldn't have hurt me, but thanks anyway."

But Jayne hadn't known that. Reed would never forget the image of her wielding an ax to protect his son.

Jayne didn't respond for a few seconds, just stood staring out into the woods, shivering. "That was a coyote?" Her voice quivered.

Reed's eyes traveled the length of her. No hat. No coat. No boots. Pants wet to midthigh. Snowflakes in her hair. No thought to her own comfort or safety.

"You're going to get pneumonia." He scooped her off her feet. "We'd better get you dried and thawed—again."

"I thought coyotes were small." Her body shrank and curled into his. "I could've sworn that was a wolf."

Reed tried not to like the way she felt in his arms—and failed. This was not the distance he'd sworn to keep. "No wolves in Maine, but the coyotes can be pretty darned big."

On the porch, Scott opened the door for them. Reed carried Jayne right through to the master bathroom. He set her on the tiled lip of the tub.

"Shower or bath?"

"Uhm. Bath."

Reed turned the water on in the Jacuzzi.

"Can you manage?"

She nodded but just sat there, trembling and staring at the tile. Lost. Overwhelmed by the surge and ebb of adrenaline no doubt. Reed stacked clean towels and prepared to make his escape.

Eighteen hours. That's how long he had to keep his distance. Deep in his soul he knew if he let Jayne into his heart, he'd never get her out again.

At the door, Reed glanced back. Jayne hadn't moved. Her face was as white as his fiberglass tub.

Shit.

He returned to the tub and adjusted the water temperature before approaching Jayne. Kneeling at her feet, he grasped her ankle and peeled off her sopping socks. A clump of slush fell to the tile floor. Jayne started as he wrapped both his palms around one slender foot and gently rubbed the ice-cold skin.

He lifted his eyes to hers, an infinite turquoise, clear as the Caribbean. Drowning in their depths would be heaven. His gaze dropped to her mouth. Her tongue slid out to moisten lips. Reed's body leaned forward until he could feel her breath on his face, light as a whisper.

Jayne blinked up at him. Her head tilted slightly. Her pupils widened, her eyes darkening from tropical sea to stormy ocean.

"Dad?" Scott's voice came from the hall.

Reed jolted and sat back.

Jayne didn't move.

"Tub's almost ready." He scrambled to his feet before bolting from the room. A glance back showed her face was flushed—with surprise and something else.

Reed sincerely hoped he'd imagined the return desire in her eyes. Attraction not returned was far easier to resist than mutual passion.

– – –

Jayne stared at the closed door. Several seconds passed before she realized the water in the tub was inches from overflow. She lunged over and turned off the tap. Steam rose in a thick cloud over the tub.

What on earth had just happened? Had Reed been about to kiss her? She didn't even know what she thought of that, except that she'd been wrong about him. He wasn't emotionally stunted. He was a pressure cooker. There'd been enough heat in his eyes to ignite them both.

A lank tendril of hair fell over her shoulder. She'd contemplate Reed and his emotional roller coaster later, after she was clean. On the bright side, she wasn't cold any longer. The warmth of Reed's gaze had flushed her with heat.

But would she have kissed him back?

Her gaze dropped to the bandages on her wrists, and a chill streaked through her belly. Had she finally met a man who could pierce through the wall of fear she'd erected after the first attack? Or was she suffering from some sort of white knight syndrome? Only time would tell, along with a fresh round of therapy.

Anger flared at the memory of Reed's hot stare. Damn! It wasn't fair. Even if he was the right man, she was not in the right frame of mind to take that step.

With a resigned sigh, she searched the bathroom for amenities. Reed had dashed out before she could even ask him for shampoo. Calling him back to request soap reeked of desperation. She couldn't stand to be helpless again. For the entire year following Ty Jennings's attack she'd been totally dependent on her brothers.

The hell with manners. The man obviously needed some alone time. At this point, she'd help herself.

Under the vanity sat a basket of hotel-size soaps and shampoos. Jayne sniffed out two bottles that smelled like spring. She dipped a hand in the water before stripping off her clothes, then unwinding the bandages on her hands. The shallow cut across her palm and thin scabs around her wrists stiffened her spine.

Was her captor looking for her right now? She didn't think it had been Jennings again. This man had seemed thicker, more mature. Of course she hadn't seen Jennings since his stint in prison. He could've bulked up. But her instincts said it wasn't him. Someone else had attacked her.

A shiver coursed through her and she slid into the hot water to scrub away the filth of the last two days. Her lathered fingers lingered over the scar on her cheek. One thing was clear. Reed definitely found her attractive, even in her unkempt state. When his eyes had blazed into hers, she'd felt beautiful for the first time in years. She'd felt like a normal, desirable woman.

Tomorrow she would return to the harsh reality of police reports, phone calls to her brothers, and the possibility that her kidnapper from Maine would follow her home. As if having one madman on parole, waiting for her in Philadelphia, wasn't bad enough.

Now she'd have a second, faceless shadow to fear.

– – –

"They haven't found that woman yet?

Standing in front of the desk in his office, Nathan took Mandy's hand between his. "No."

He was pathetic. Mandy was not only his employee, she was nearly half his age. He shouldn't have started this affair, but she'd been the one bright spot in his life for the last three months. Being with Mandy made him feel alive, instead of halfway to the grave. Half of his life was over. The best half. It was all downhill from here.

"That's so scary. One minute she's going about her business. The next, she's gone." Mandy shivered but she didn't move closer.

Nathan rubbed a hand down her arm. "Keep in mind we don't know anything about her. She could have a drug or drinking problem. She could be mentally unstable."

"I guess." Mandy didn't sound convinced. "It makes you think, though, about life and the future. It can all end in the blink of an eye. We have to make the most of every second."

Nathan pressed his mouth to Mandy's and gathered her close. She was going to end it. He could feel it. Her lips were warm as usual, but stiff, and her body was far too rigid. On the other side of the closed office door, the commercial dishwasher hissed in the empty diner. Nathan's gut clenched. He rested his temple against the long, soft fall of her shining dark hair and closed his eyes.

Here it comes. Wait for it.

His hand reflexively squeezed her hip.

Mandy's hand splayed in the center of his chest. "Stop. We need to talk."

He froze at her sharp whisper. Regret gripped his heart. *I love you.* "What is it, baby?"

"It's us, Nathan. It's not working." Huge blue eyes glistened as she looked away. "If you really cared about me, you wouldn't insist we keep our relationship a secret." Stepping back, she turned away and paced the few feet between his desk and the wall. She stopped at the window and hugged her arms. Her gaze pieced him with equal parts misery and anger. "I don't understand. You're not married. There's no reason we can't be together."

If she only knew. "People will talk. You're twenty years younger than me." And oh, so beautiful. So perfect. So clean and fresh. The blackness in Nathan's soul expanded and threatened to swallow them both. He had no right to corrupt something so pure. But that fact didn't stop him from wanting her. "Besides, I have Uncle

Aaron to take care of right now. His cancer isn't responding to treatment. I can't deal with any more stress. Like your mom. Mae would kill me if she ever found out about us."

His attempt at humor failed. Mandy wasn't buying any of his lame-ass excuses.

"Mom'd be OK with it. *She* wants me to be happy." A tempest of emotions filled her eyes as she left the rest unsaid: that he didn't.

He cared, more than she knew, which was the reason he had to let her go. The only thing Nathan could give her was more misery.

"And you can't wait to get out of this town," he said.

"I'd stay for you." Her eyes welled up, sparkling pools of baby blue in a porcelain face. How short, sturdy Mae Brown had given birth to such a perfect creature was beyond comprehension.

"And likely regret it for the rest of your life. There's a big world out there, and you should see it. I'm holding you back."

Only Mandy could make a shrug simultaneously innocent and sexy. "I'm not sure I can leave anyway. Mom needs me at the inn. She's getting older. She can't run it all by herself. That old place barely generates enough income to cover expenses. If you didn't let me work here, I wouldn't be able to cover my tuition. There's Bill to think of, too. My brother is a perpetual seven-year-old. He'll never be independent."

Nathan knew all about sacrifices made for family, but the thought of Mandy giving up her life for her mother and brother compounded the ache in his chest. "You shouldn't give up your dreams for another person. You're young and smart. You're meant for bigger things, Mandy. What about your degree?"

"I can finish that here."

He shook his head. "Honey, we're in different phases of our lives. The road in front of you is wide open. For me, it's all in the rearview mirror."

Mandy's breath hitched but she didn't disagree. She could have a long, full life. She was beautiful, kind, and intelligent.

Mandy gave her cheek a quick forefinger swipe. "I just don't want to sneak around anymore." Her eyes turned toward the door before her face followed. She'd already decided, he thought, before she'd even come in here. Good. If the breakup was her idea, she'd move on faster. "I want a real relationship."

"I know. But I can't give you what you need." Except for his son, Evan, she was the only thing that kept hopelessness from dragging him under. What would Evan think of his affair with Mandy? She was closer to Evan's age than Nathan's. One more reason to end it now. "I'll miss you, though."

What else did he have to live for?

His uncle's death wouldn't be easy or quick. Nathan would care for him until the gruesome end. What kind of life could he offer Mandy?

Mandy sniffed and shook her frame straight, bringing Nathan back to the issue. She was through with him. "You know I don't care what people say."

"I know you don't." Nathan's arm itched to pull her back, to hold her close, to beg her not to abandon him in the dark. But he didn't. Even though her exit from his life was like the final seal on his coffin, he needed to let her go. It was better this way. Really.

So why did he feel like cannonballing off the bridge? His responsibilities would weight him down better than concrete blocks.

"Can I give you a ride home?"

The Black Bear Inn was only a few blocks away, but Nathan would feel better if he saw her inside just the same. Just because she was through with his sorry old ass didn't mean he wouldn't continue to love her.

"No. Jed's waiting outside."

"You shouldn't string him along like that, Mandy." Nathan felt the fatherlike frown pull at his mouth. It wasn't the first time he'd felt paternal toward her, and that dynamic to their relationship disturbed him. Mandy's dad had died when she was young. Had Nathan taken advantage of her yearning for a father? If so, he was a poor excuse for a human being.

Again, the river called.

Mandy shook her head. Denial tinged her voice with irritation. "Jed and I are just friends. I've known him since grade school."

"Honey, that man is in love with you. Probably been that way since grade school."

"No way. Yeah, he cares, but like a brother."

Nathan held back the retort. Mandy was clueless about Jed. The hunting guide looked at her with big soulful eyes like one of his faithful Labrador retrievers. Jed wasn't very smart, but he'd figured out that he wouldn't have a future with Mandy. Still, the hunter would do anything for her. Nathan saw the pain in Jed's eyes every time he was in the same room as Mandy. Nathan could empathize. He felt like a million gallons of water were pressing on his chest as she turned and walked out of his office—and his life.

The jingle of the bell on the glass door and the *vroom* of Jed's truck punctuated her exit. An empty silence, hollow as Nathan's heart, filled the diner as he grabbed his coat and headed out the back door, the confines of his small office suddenly intolerable.

His official office in the municipal building next door was more spacious but lacked privacy.

White flakes danced in the beam of the streetlight. Slush packed under his feet. He sniffed, looking for that crisp dampness to refresh him, but the winter night just felt dark, cold, and endless.

His SUV huddled alone in the back lot. He'd plowed the rectangle several times, although a few inches had accumulated since the last once-over. South of Maine, the East Coast had gotten slammed. Three feet of snow was a state of emergency in the lower states, but in this neck of the woods it wasn't a big deal.

Plows had cleared Main Street and moved on to the secondary roads with practiced efficiency. The two-mile-long trip home took all of ten minutes. Evan had run the blower. Neatly cleaved banks of snow flanked the driveway. Nathan parked in the attached garage and depressed the automatic door button.

With the engine still running, he sat for a few long minutes. Wouldn't be a bad way to go. Easier than a swan dive off the bridge. Peaceful. Quiet. Painless. Sure as hell beat a slow decaying of the brain. How long would it take? A garden hose hung on the far wall. *That* would speed things up. All his problems would just fade away.

Evan's inside.

If his son heard the door close and the engine still running, he'd be out here in a minute. Besides, Nathan couldn't abandon his boy. Evan was far too young to be saddled with their uncle's long, drawn-out illness and death.

Uncle Aaron wouldn't go gently into that good night.

Nathan turned the key and shut off the engine. He held his breath as he pushed open the door and stepped into the kitchen.

Evan was pouring boiling water from the kettle into a cracked old teapot on the granite island. Nathan exhaled. Nothing terrible had happened. Maybe they could have an almost normal, quiet evening.

He turned and hung his coat on the rack in the corner, then toed off his boots.

Evan turned. The blond goatee didn't make him look as old as he hoped. At twenty-two, Evan could pass for sixteen. "Hey, Dad."

"Hey. Uncle Aaron's tea?"

"Yeah." Evan set the steaming kettle on the unlit stove. The aromatic concoction of his uncle's special tea wafted toward him. Uncle Aaron was grasping at the straws of alternative medicine. Nathan could hardly blame him. Once his uncle had been a professor. To watch the former scholar in him slide into madness broke Nathan's heart. "Think this stuff is OK for him to drink? I thought mistletoe was poisonous."

"The berries, yes. But with the leaves it depends on the variety." Nathan shrugged. His uncle's disease was progressing, defying all medical treatment. "Doubt it matters much."

Uncle Aaron was dying. But the end wouldn't come before he'd endured a year of suffering, just like Nathan's mother, Aaron's sister. Nathan almost wished he had the balls to end it for his uncle now, but there was always that grain of hope germinating in the back of his mind.

Uncle Aaron's voice carried from the basement stairwell, the place where they'd stored his collection. "The crow. The crow is here again."

Evan sighed hard. "He keeps talking about a crow following him around down there. Been at it for hours."

Hallucinations were new. The relief Nathan felt at arriving home and finding relative peace evaporated in one beat of his pulse.

Crows portended death.

CHAPTER SIXTEEN

Jayne awoke to darkness, and for a brief second she was back in that dim, frigid basement. Sweat-dampened sheets clung to her limbs. Despite the warm blankets that covered her, a chill burrowed into her body and lodged itself in her bones.

Her body tumbled onto concrete. She rolled, helpless and limp. A distorted and blurry shadow loomed. Callused hands grasped her wrists. Metal bit into her flesh as her wrists were bound. Fingers stroked her face, lovingly circled the scar on her cheek. A knife sliced her palm. Her stomach heaved.

The scene was extinguished as quickly as a struck match in the rain, leaving behind a lingering scent of evil as distinct as burnt sulfur.

Reality returned with the feel of flannel sheets against her cheek, the softness of the pillow under her head. Jayne turned her head toward the nightstand. Large orange digits on the clock read three fifty. She shuddered under the pile of thick covers. The room felt cold and empty, and she was alone in Reed's guest room.

She was safe.

For the moment.

But tomorrow—no, today—she'd leave Reed's house and the security it represented. Helplessness clawed at her throat. There'd be no more sleep for her tonight.

She flipped back the comforter and rose into the chill of the bedroom fully dressed. The woodstove's warmth didn't penetrate the back of the house as efficiently as the front rooms, but the guest bed was more comfortable than the couch. Jayne drew a second pair of socks onto her feet and sought the warmth of the living room. The fire burned brightly, and Jayne held her hands out to absorb its dry heat. She peered in the stove's small glass window. Someone had added fresh logs recently.

She paced to the bookcase, stuffed with dog-eared bestsellers. None of the many titles appealed. She was too tense to read. She perched on the edge of a chair, closed her eyes, and attempted a few deep breaths. The nightmare had imprinted images and sensations on her mind. Even after she opened her lids to the reassuring sight of Reed's living room, her chest constricted and her heart pounded relentlessly.

Rubbing the knot beneath her sternum, Jayne crossed to the wide window and looked over the yard. Light glowed in the windows of Reed's workshop. The electricity must have been restored during the night. But why was he working at three o'clock in the morning?

Maybe he couldn't sleep either.

The possibility of companionship pulled at her. There were several hours still until dawn, hours that would drag if she passed them alone. She stepped into a pair of boots and donned Scott's parka. A shoveled path led to the old converted barn that housed Reed's workshop.

Jayne stepped out into the cold.

– – –

Reed turned off the carving saw. The whirring ceased and silence descended on the small back room of his workshop. He circled his project. She was long and lean, the birch trunk straighter than his typical sculpture. The last piece had been thin as well, but huddling inward, sinking, in the process of collapsing in despair, a typical emotion for his carvings.

But not this time.

He set down the saw and reached for a leather-covered photo album on the shelf behind him. Opening it, he flipped through pictures of his previous pieces. All the sculptures had names like *Misery*, *Anguish*, or *Despair*. As their names suggested, the figures stared back at him with desolation—and accusation.

He returned his attention to the new piece. One hand swept out to caress the rough wood. He'd seen strength and resilience in the pale birch from the very first time he'd touched it. Raw power emanated from the wood, yet he was not tempted to make the subject masculine. The lines remained wholly feminine, with fertile curves despite her ample musculature.

This project would be different, the beginning of something new.

Closing the book, he picked up a marker and began to map details. He fine-tuned the length of her hair and the angle of her chin. This woman would stand tall, with her face turned to the sky in challenge. Her cheekbones would be sharper, more angular than the almost childish figure of *Despair*.

The scrape of a branch on the skylight broke his concentration, and his gaze swept to the clock. Only a couple of hours remained until dawn. As usual, he'd lost track of time while absorbed in his work. He'd intended to spend an hour or so out here once he was sure Jayne was asleep. He couldn't work on his sculpture while she was awake. She didn't miss a trick, and he couldn't risk anyone seeing his work in process, especially a woman who'd been read-ing an article on R. S. Morgan.

One look at this roughed-out piece and Jayne might well real-ize he was the famous sculptor. His cover would be blown. As long as she was in his house, he'd limit his carving to the hours when she slept.

He scrubbed a hand over his face. Was it worth going to bed at this point or should he work another hour or two?

The long section of bare wood begged for him to give it life.

— — —

Jayne knocked lightly on the door. The latch must not have caught completely because the door swung open, revealing a neat work-shop. Reed was emerging from a back room. He started and quickly pulled the door closed behind him. His face registered surprise and a trace of alarm before he neutralized his features.

Storage room? Or was something hidden behind that closed door?

"I'm sorry. Am I interrupting you?"

"No," he answered. "It's OK. Come on in."

Jayne walked toward a table in the center of the small space. A small antique chest sat in the center, its top sanded smooth. Scott's boots, loose on Jayne's narrow feet, scuffed across the floor as she moved toward the piece. "This is nice."

Reed avoided her gaze by focusing on the furniture. "It's Mae's. Some guest's kid gouged the top."

Sheba rose from a dog bed in the corner farthest from the kerosene heater. After a full-body stretch, the dog trotted over to Jayne, sat, and presented her with a large paw. Jayne scratched the dog's chest.

"Is anything wrong?" he asked.

"No." Jayne shook her head and straightened. The heater was doing its job in the small space. She slipped off her coat and draped it over one arm. "I just couldn't sleep."

Reed turned to the sink and washed his hands. He glanced over his shoulder at her. "Nightmare?"

The vision edged into her consciousness. *Angry eyes, glittering with the reflection of her fear, glared at her through a black mask.* Jayne's chest tightened, and she shoved the images away. *Too soon.* "I don't want to talk about it right now. Maybe later."

"OK." He dried his hands on a clean towel.

Jayne sneezed. The air carried the clean scent of sawdust, with an oily undercurrent. "What's that smell?"

"Linseed oil. It's a wood finish."

"Is that what you'll use on Mae's chest?"

"No. I'll try to match the existing finish. Is there anything I can do for you?" Reed tucked his thumbs into the front pockets of his jeans and waited for her response.

Erasing her memory would be great.

Blood. Pain. Panic. Her bare legs scraping on asphalt. Agony shooting through her head as he dragged her by the ponytail. Dry terror choking off her screams as her feet kicked and scrambled uselessly for traction.

Time blurred. Wrong attack.

Her eyes squeezed shut as the images raced through her head and collided with one another. Assaults blended together in a terrifying barrage of sensation. The sound of rushing water, loud as Niagara Falls, blocked out her hearing.

– – –

Reed reached for her shoulders. "Jayne."

She opened her eyes. The agony in their turquoise depths cleaved a rift in the center of his chest. And when she straightened, lifting her chin bravely with a shaky sigh, his shield of objectivity shattered. He was open. Raw. As vulnerable as the woman before him.

There was no use pretending her turmoil didn't touch him.

She mattered. Beyond Hugh's case. Beyond keeping her physically safe. Beyond any sense of duty. What happened to Jayne mattered to *him*. He couldn't abandon her emotional need any more than he could have left her collapsed in the blizzard.

"I'm sorry." She shifted her weight as if to step back, but her eyes were still liquid pools of pain. Her pulse throbbed visibly in the curve of her neck and she trembled in a valiant attempt to slow her respiration.

"Nothing to be sorry about." Reed pulled her close, ignoring the screaming of his brain. *This is a bad idea. She's a storm ripping through your soul, and she will leave a hole as great as Sherman's march to Savannah in her wake.* He told his brain to shut up and rested his forehead against her temple. He was taking this minute and storing every sensation for the long, cold season ahead. "Nobody should have to face what you did alone."

She stiffened for a second, then settled against his chest. Just a few inches shorter than he was, she turned her head so her face nestled in the hollow of his shoulder. A perfect fit. He stroked her spine, the muscles long and firm under his hand, as he inhaled the floral scent of her hair. Her back relaxed under the gentle sweep of his palm.

Her breaths slowed. The pounding of her heart against his lessened. A surge of satisfaction flowed through Reed, along with the sense that he'd just willingly stepped into the path of disaster.

Her hips settled against his, and Reed's next breath locked in his chest for a few seconds as passion awakened inside him from its half-decade nap. He shifted his weight to avoid transmitting his libido's sudden rise and shine.

Jayne lifted her head. Something flickered through her eyes. Regret? Embarrassment? For what? A momentary weakness? There was nothing weak about the embrace. If anything, Reed could feel strength flowing between them. Mingling. Growing. Making him wonder which one of them needed the contact more. The surge of desire through his veins was primitive, powerful, and raw.

He couldn't speak. His throat was clogged with things he couldn't explain, emotions he hadn't experienced in so long they felt like strangers. He'd thought he'd gone permanently numb, but he'd been wrong. Emotions still chugged through him, like water flowing under a frozen river.

She'd either given him an awesome gift…or pushed him out onto thin ice.

The question remained: What would happen after she left? Would he continue to feel or refreeze?

And would he be able to deal with either outcome?

"Thank you." She stepped back, moving out of his arms, leaving a chill behind that forecasted a brutal, lonely winter ahead.

– – –

Jayne rubbed her arms. Reed's woodsy scent clung to her nostrils as she fought the urge to step back into his arms, rest her head against his broad chest, and inhale deeply once again. The gentle slide of his fingertips along her backbone mesmerized, soothed—and warmed her from the inside out.

It had been years since she'd allowed a man to touch her. Desire wasn't the only thing she felt. Reed made her feel strong and capable. Something she hadn't thought she'd experience again. Her cheeks flamed.

Did he notice her flush? Of course he did. Her skin was so fair, a blush stood out like a signal flare. She tried to look away, but her eyes were locked on Reed's, where she saw her own confusion reflected right back at her. His detached mask had slipped away, leaving behind equal amounts of shock and sadness.

And heat.

A tingle passed through her belly, and she savored it for a moment. Her body was ready to answer even if she knew her head wasn't in the right place. She hadn't felt any amount of attraction for a man in so many years. Just the knowledge that the sexual being inside her wasn't dead was a relief.

She blinked. The door behind him came into focus and she latched onto a new train of thought. What was he hiding back there?

Following her gaze, he cleared his throat. "We should go back to the house. Check the Internet and phone service."

She tugged on her coat and moved toward the exit. He grabbed his own jacket, then reached around her and opened the exterior door. As he ushered her over the threshold, his palm settled on the small of her back, hot as a brand. His hand remained on her hip as he walked closely behind her down the path to the house. Did he feel the electricity that flowed between them? She glanced over her shoulder, but Reed's eyes were busy scanning the surrounding woods.

Oh.

He wasn't getting familiar with her. He was looking for danger and shielding her with his body. The realization was a much-needed jolt of reality. Lack of sleep must be making her wonky.

Thank God one of them had some common sense. Someone had kidnapped her and held her prisoner. If she hadn't escaped, she'd be dead. Psychos didn't abduct women and set them free unharmed.

They left their coats in the mudroom. Reed left the kitchen dark until he'd closed all the blinds. Another reminder of the danger that lurked outside. Who knew where her captor was right now?

"Do you want something to eat or drink? Tea? Coffee?" Reed opened a laptop on the kitchen table. "Feel free to browse the fridge and cabinets."

Jayne glanced at the clock on the microwave. Four thirty. Too late to return to bed. A dull lack-of-sleep headache thudded through her head. "I'll make coffee."

While the computer booted up, Reed picked up the cordless phone. Holding it to his ear, he shook his head. "Nothing yet."

Jayne measured grounds, filled the pot, and pressed the On switch.

Reed clicked at the keyboard. "Aha. Internet. I'll send the police chief an e-mail."

Jayne rummaged for food, coming up with apples and cheese.

"We're in luck. Hugh's online. He'll meet us at his office at eight."

Jayne set the plate of food next to Reed's elbow and turned toward the coffeepot, her appetite fading. In three hours, she'd be leaving this house.

And Reed.

CHAPTER SEVENTEEN

The heavy vehicle lurched and slid to a stop. Unfortunately, John kept moving. His face slid on the carpeted cargo mat. He tilted his head and drew in a quivering breath. At the edge of the blindfold, a slice of black night appeared through the vehicle's tinted window.

"Don't move. I'll be back." The whispered command came from the front of the SUV.

Like he could go anywhere. John lay still as possible. The black hood he was required to wear whenever his captor was present blocked all available light. His wrists and ankles were bound and connected to a rope looped round his neck. Any struggling simply tightened the noose. He should pull it tight and suffocate himself. But he couldn't. He didn't want to die, even though he knew his demise was inevitable.

After all, his captor had already killed Zack and beat John without mercy. The man's moods were hard to predict. Fits of anger warred with equally terrifying cold-blooded calculation. Oh, yeah. John was going to die eventually if he stayed in this man's control.

A door opened. Someone rummaged in the backseat. That door closed with a bang, and John was left alone. He could hear movement outside the vehicle. Footsteps. Scraping. An occasional grunt.

An indefinite period of time passed. John waited. Nothing horrible was happening at the moment. He'd learned to live with that. And the drug that chugged through his system kept him unnaturally calm.

The rear of the vehicle opened. Rough hands hauled John to a sitting position. His feet dropped off the tailgate. The rope bit into his neck, cutting off his air. The quick swish of a knife removed the pressure. John gulped cool air. His heart stuttered. Terror overrode the sedative.

Another slice and his feet were freed.

"Walk."

As he stood, the drape of the hood allowed him to see his feet on the snowy ground. Icy crystals underfoot soaked through his socks in two steps. The hand stayed on his arm as he swayed on a narrow shoveled path. The trek from the car was short, and John was shoved through a doorway. Beneath the hood, he could see weathered wooden boards under his feet.

"I started the stove."

John concentrated to hear the whispered instructions. Disobeying even a single one always turned out badly for him.

"Wood's on the porch. There's nothing around for miles. Scream away. Nobody will hear you. Burn the place down, you'll burn with it."

The handcuffs were removed. He rubbed at his wrists as a thick metal shackle was fastened around his ankle, the same one he'd been restrained with at the old house. John heard the clinking of chain links being dragged across the floor.

"Count to one hundred before you take the hood off, or I'll slit your throat."

The door slammed shut. The engine rumbled to life, then faded.

But John did exactly as he was told. One hundred seconds later, he lifted the blindfold.

He was standing in a one-room cabin. Heat poured from a cast-iron potbellied stove in the corner. The chain attached to his ankle was fastened around its feet, which were bolted to the floor. John did a quick sweep of the cabin. The chain was just long enough for him to reach the front porch to retrieve wood and take two steps out the rear door. The single cabinet was empty save for a metal bowl and a plastic cup. No knives. No can opener. There wasn't even a cot, just a sleeping bag on the floor. Logs were piled waist-high by the door. His captor had left the usual supply of protein bars and bottled water.

A tiny seed of hope formed in John's chest. He could melt snow to drink. Without the tainted water, he'd be able to think. Unless the protein bars were drugged. He'd go without for a while and see if he felt clearheaded.

He pulled the sleeping bag closer to the stove and extended his wet feet toward its warmth. His brain was still mush. Tomorrow, though, he had to figure a way out of here. Moving him to this even more remote location wasn't a good sign. It meant something was going to happen.

And John knew it wasn't going to be something good.

– – –

He glanced at the small rectangular window high on the cellar wall. Dawn brightened the sky. Tomorrow at midnight he would usher in the winter solstice with three deaths. By the time the sun rose on the darkest day, three men would be reborn.

He pulled a box from the rows of shelves and set it on the workbench. An English associate had sent him the package after a very special request. He carefully lifted the boughs from the white paper wrapping. A white berry fell from the greenery and rolled to the floor.

Fresh mistletoe. Cut from a great oak by a Druid priest with a golden sickle on the sixth day of the new moon.

He began to lay out his ceremonial supplies on the workbench next to the mistletoe.

The burnt stub of last year's Yule log, along with the thick section of oak he'd selected for the coming ceremony. He wrapped his hand around the amulet that hung from his neck. The tiny vial contained ashes from the previous year's fire—and therefore a bit of power from the sun's rebirth.

Two gallons of moose blood in plastic milk jugs went on dry ice in an igloo cooler. The circle must be consecrated.

Sturdy rope.

Three thin leather garrotes.

His *boline,* its sickle-like blade freshly sharpened.

Three hand-carved oak vessels to catch the lifeblood that would be their salvation.

Only three things were missing: the boy he'd already collected and moved during the night to the cabin near the clearing, the woman who'd escaped, and the final, yet unnamed, sacrifice.

Whom should he choose? Someone who wouldn't be missed right away. Someone whose disappearance could be easily excused.

The answer came in a sudden rush of divine epiphany.

One of the troubled teens at the Youth Center would be perfect. A few had run away in the past.

Perfect.

Everything was lining up perfectly.

A sign from the gods that he was on the true path to redemption.

CHAPTER EIGHTEEN

"I'll call you later." Reed watched Scott gather the bag of fresh bagels and the gallon of orange juice from the backseat. The roads in town had been plowed and salted with Yankee efficiency.

"You'll be here all morning, right?"

"Yeah. Brandon's mom is working the breakfast shift at the diner. He has to stay with his little brothers." Scott's breath clouded in the morning chill.

"Let me know if you guys go anywhere else," Reed said.

"'Kay." Scott jumped down from the cab. He paused at the passenger window. Jayne lowered the glass. "It was nice to meet you, Jayne. Good luck."

"Thanks, Scott. You too." Jayne leaned out and gave him a quick hug.

With a final wave Scott walked up the shoveled walk to the front door of the tiny Cape Cod. Across the street, the sun rose over the trees behind the cemetery. Only the tallest headstones poked out of the thick drifts.

With a crunch of tires on ice, Reed pulled back out onto the street. Next to him, Jayne rested her head on the passenger window.

Reed took a gulp of scalding coffee from his travel mug and pushed back the guilt. He'd deliver Jayne safely into Hugh's custody and make sure that all was well before leaving her there.

He'd miss her, but she'd go on with her life. She had a family that loved her. Her three brothers would make sure the scumbag in Philadelphia didn't bother her.

The very idea of her assailant walking the streets burned in Reed's gut. He'd seen countless violent predators evade the system. The fact that Reed was well versed in reality didn't help him deal with the truth. A woman like Jayne didn't deserve to have the jerk who'd attacked her on the loose. For that matter, no woman did. But Jayne was special.

To him.

Shit. How had that happened?

Jayne didn't need to be bogged down with him. So why did he feel like someone was carving a chunk from his heart with a spoon? And why had he spent the rest of last night thinking about running away with her to a tropical island, somewhere far away from Huntsville or Philadelphia? In this fantasy land, Reed wouldn't have to worry about the media. Jayne wouldn't be in danger. They could get to know each other without the stress of either of their pasts.

He could kiss her without worrying about taking advantage of her vulnerability. He'd barely resisted last night, despite her fragile state.

The spoon's dull edge dug deeper.

Damn it. He was doing the right thing. She couldn't stay here. It wasn't safe.

"It'll be OK." He glanced at Jayne, but her face was still turned away from him. She nodded and picked at the edge of a bandage poking from her sleeve.

The ache in Reed's chest deepened. "Hugh'll take care of you. He's one of the good guys."

Hugh wouldn't shirk responsibility. Ever.

Reed's conscience nagged as he made the turn onto Main Street and parked in front of the municipal building. Hugh's truck wasn't there yet. Reed glanced at the dashboard clock, his fingers clenched on the steering wheel. Hugh had specified he wanted to interview Jayne early, before the nine o'clock church service swarmed the town with well-intentioned busybodies. Except for the police, the township building would be empty on a Sunday morning.

Hugh pulled in next to him and got out of his car. Instead of his uniform, he wore a navy-blue parka, jeans, and work boots. He walked up to the passenger window of the Yukon and opened Jayne's door. "My goodness, am I glad to see you safe and sound."

Reed loosened his fingers as he resisted the urge to drive away with her.

Jayne slid out of his truck. A Lincoln Town Car pulled in at the diner next door. The old man at the wheel pointed at Jayne and said something to his wife. Reed jumped out of the Yukon, rounded the front of the vehicle, and planted his body between Jayne and the gapers.

Everyone in town knew by now that she'd been abducted. The press would be here any minute. If Jayne didn't leave town soon, she'd suffer an onslaught of media exposure. Reed would spare her that horror no matter what her departure did to his heart.

"Let's get her inside. It's cold out here." Hugh frowned and drew a ring of keys from his pocket as they trooped up the rock salt–dusted steps to the porch. He blew on his gloveless free hand as he inserted his key into the lock and shoved the door open. "What the hell?"

Smoke wafted down the hallway. Reed pulled Jayne back.

"Get her to a safe place, Reed." Hugh rushed ahead. "I'll make sure there's no one inside. I forget what time I told Evan to come in."

"Don't go in there, Hugh." Reed turned and propelled Jayne away from the building, keeping his body between her and the smoke. He yelled at the old folks in the Lincoln, "Call the fire department!"

Reed shoved Jayne into the Yukon and handed her the keys. His heart kicked as he turned to look back at the building. The smoke was still thin, but the building was old and mostly wood. "Park down the street and wait for me. Lock the doors. Drive away if anything seems suspicious."

"What's going on?" Nathan rushed out of the diner, sliding into his coat as he jogged toward Reed.

"Fire. Hugh went in. He wanted to make sure there wasn't anyone inside." Reed ran toward the municipal building.

"Why would there be anyone in there? It's Sunday."

"He was worried about Evan."

Nathan kept pace. "Evan's at home. He's not due in until ten."

"Good." Reed pointed at the mayor's chest. "Stay here and show the firemen where to go." The last thing Reed needed was a civilian getting in the way.

Nathan backed away from the doorway with a nod. He was a little too easily convinced, Reed thought as he pushed through the door. He pulled his collar over his mouth and nose as he navigated the stairs. Downstairs, yellow smoke filled the top half of the hall. "Hugh?"

Reed coughed at the invasion of smoke in his lungs and crouched to get under the worst of it.

"Hugh!"

The chief stood in front of the police station door, handkerchief-wrapped hand on the knob. Another hand splayed on the door, probably testing for heat. At the bottom crack, yellow smoke puffed and was sucked back under the door.

Backdraft.

"Don't open that, Hugh!"

The sound of approaching sirens drowned out Reed's warning. Hugh looked over his shoulder as he yanked the door open. "What?" he mouthed.

The door blew out with a gigantic ball of fire as oxygen rushed into the starved blaze. Reed's world muted as the force of the explosion knocked him backward. He hit the floor flat on his spine. Pain slammed through his head as it bounced off the commercial tile. The little air he had in his lungs whooshed out. His chest locked down like someone had dropped an anvil on him, and he sucked at the smoky air in vain.

Reed rolled onto his hands and knees. His heartbeat echoed inside his head as he squinted into the haze. A blurry shape lay unmoving at the end of the hall. Reed crawled toward it. Heat seared the side of his face. Embers hit his exposed skin as burning pinpricks.

Huge black boots ran past his head.

"Easy, buddy." A hollow voice sounded in his ear. Gloved hands hooked under his armpits and dragged him up the stairs. Pain zinged through his legs as his shins bounced on the treads.

"The chief." Reed coughed and pointed into the smoke. Flames leaped from the doorway below.

Hugh's office was an inferno.

- - -

167

A full block down on Main Street, Jayne turned the truck around and parked so she had a clear view of the municipal building. A fire engine roared past, sirens wailing. Down the street, people gathered across from the burning building. Firemen leaped from two engines and got to work with practiced efficiency amid the chaos.

Jayne gnawed on her lip. Several volunteer vehicles flew down Main. Single blue lights flashed from their car roofs. Emergency personnel milled about.

Jayne searched the crowd but couldn't see Reed's tall form anywhere.

Emergency workers sped up with a flurry of renewed urgency. Something was happening. Her heart stuttered. She locked her gaze on the front of the municipal building. No Reed. The firemen were pushing people away from the building, their movements insistent. Jayne cracked the window and strained to hear.

A muffled explosion split the air and rattled the windows of the Yukon. Glass shattered somewhere. The scent of smoke drifted to her nostrils on the frigid air. Up the street smoke poured from the front of the old building.

Jayne's chest tightened as she jumped from the truck. She moved toward the fire, eyes trained on the disaster scene.

Her upper body jerked backward. She gasped as an arm hooked around her neck and dragged her back into the narrow alley between two stores.

Her brain shut down in disbelief for a few seconds before her training overrode the panic.

Jayne tucked her chin to protect her airway. The soles of her boots dragged on the sidewalk as she dropped her weight, making her body heavier, harder to pull. She slammed her head backward. Her assailant grunted as Jayne's skull connected with his jaw.

But the arm around her neck tightened.

"Do what I say or I'll hurt you." The whisper was deep, male, and angry, with an edge of desperation.

Jayne grasped his wrist and elbow, pinning his forearm to her chest. She turned her chin to the crook of his elbow for breathing room. Releasing her left grip, she drilled her elbow straight back into his solar plexus and dropped a hammer fist into his groin.

He doubled over and coughed. "Bitch."

In her peripheral vision, Jayne caught a flash of blue eyes through the opening of a ski mask. Then she shot her elbow up under his chin.

The pressure around her neck disappeared. Jayne fell forward onto all fours and clutched her throat. Her knees burned on the concrete. Footsteps retreated. She crawled forward out of the alley and gulped cool air in greedy swallows. A glance over her shoulder confirmed that her assailant had taken off. The alley behind her was empty.

Jayne's heart sprinted as she climbed to her feet. The alley had been shoveled. No footprints. She hesitated. Should she try to follow him?

External noise gradually replaced the sound of her own labored breathing. Sirens. People yelling.

"Call for medevac!"

Jayne whirled.

Reed. Fire.

Her belly clenched as she stumbled up the block. Smoke poured from the municipal building. Firemen doused the buildings on both sides. The double doors were propped open. Hoses snaked inside the smoky hole of a doorway.

Jayne searched for Reed among the milling professionals. He was tall. She should be able to see him. If he was standing.

A great shudder passed over the old clapboard building. Jayne turned. Smoke billowed from the roof, windows, and doors.

Through the thick, black cloud, a fireman jogged from the door. He carried a body draped over his shoulder. The legs were denim-clad. The jacket was dark. Jayne's heart stopped.

Reed!

CHAPTER NINETEEN

Jayne stumbled forward.

"Give Doc room." The crowd parted. A tall, lanky man pushed through, black bag in hand. A white lab coat flapped around his legs under the hem of an unbuttoned wool jacket. Kneeling men blocked Jayne's view of the body in the street. She stood on her toes but still couldn't see the victim. Trying to get closer, she pushed ineffectually at a row of broad shoulders.

Adrenaline and fear skittered through her veins and a sick feeling gathered in her stomach.

"What's the ETA on that medevac helicopter?" a soot-streaked fireman shouted back from the inner circle.

A short, stocky man in a tan uniform and dark brown police-issue jacket put a hand on his shoulder and shook his head. "He's gone, Lou. Sorry."

Silence spread through the men in a devastated wave. Heads hung. Bodies deflated.

"You a doctor, Doug?" The doctor shot the uniform a nasty look.

The uniform shrugged. "It's obvious."

Jayne's chest contracted, squeezing every ounce of air from her lungs. Her throat closed on a choking moan. Smoke burned her eyes. Her knees nearly gave out as she turned away, stumbling.

"Jayne!" Her name cut off on a hacking cough.

Her head swiveled, and her heart stopped.

Reed sat on the back of a fire truck, his green eyes blood-shot over the oxygen mask. Soot coated his face and clothes. Like the dead man, he also wore jeans, boots, and a dark coat. But as Jayne glanced around, she realized that so did three-quarters of the male population not in firefighting gear.

Reed was alive.

It took a few seconds for that fact to sink into her stunned brain.

She rushed forward. Relief bubbled from her throat with a sob. He dropped the oxygen mask to his lap and caught her in his arms. His shoulders were solid and real under her grip as she lifted her face. All thoughts of protecting her heart and Reed's inhibitions fled as their mouths met. His lips tasted of smoke and sweat and sadness. The kiss was fierce, raw with need. His tongue swept in, hot and demanding, as he claimed her mouth.

She welcomed his invasion, tilting her head back in surrender as his control broke.

He lifted his head. His eyes searched hers, bewilderment and passion both naked in his gaze, before the moment was broken by a cough.

Still numb with disbelief at Reed's survival, Jayne pressed her face into his throat. His broad chest spasmed. She breathed him in and mumbled into his skin, "I thought you were dead."

He shook his head and swallowed. A shudder passed through him, then a sigh as he lowered his head. He breathed in her ear, "Hugh."

Guilt cut into Jayne's relief. "Oh. I'm sorry." The police chief had seemed like a nice man, but she couldn't shake her joy that Reed was alive.

Jayne pulled back and studied his face. His red-rimmed eyes looked moist. He blinked hard.

She dropped her head to his chest to revel in the beat of his heart against her face. When she lifted her head, his sooty shirt was wet. She swiped a hand across her cheeks. Her fingers came away streaked with black.

Reed's gaze dropped to her legs. His jaw clenched. "What happened?"

Jayne looked down. Scott's borrowed jeans were torn and her knees bloody through the rips in the denim. "Someone grabbed me."

The vein on Reed's temple jumped, matching the intensity in his eyes.

"Reed." The doctor approached, gray hair disheveled, glasses askew, grief etched in the deep lines of a weathered and ruddy face. He scanned Reed from head to foot. "My office. Now."

They stood, and Reed swayed.

The doctor grabbed his arm and draped it over his shoulders. "Can you make it down the block?"

"I could get the truck." Jayne backed away.

"I can make it." Reed grabbed her hand and wheezed, "I'm not letting you out of my sight."

– – –

Jayne huddled in an uncomfortable chair against the wall, watching the doctor examine Reed. From her position she could see the waiting room and the curtained-off triage area.

The exterior door opened and a uniformed man strutted through the waiting room. A shiver rippled up Jayne's spine as the cold outside air invaded the clinic. From the examination table, a shirtless Reed squinted at the cop over his oxygen mask. Reed's eyes went flat.

Jayne ripped her gaze off Reed's lean, hard torso and focused on the cop. It was the same officer who'd announced the chief's death so abruptly in the street. Black hair, blue eyes, average height, thick-bodied, overflowing with attitude.

A jerk, but a jerk she had to deal with now that Hugh was gone. Her breath caught in her throat. She swallowed the lump.

This guy didn't give off any kind or concerned vibes. Belligerence pumped from every pore. But since talking to him was unavoidable, she might as well get this done. She rose to her feet and held out a hand. "I'm Jayne Sullivan."

Standing eye to eye with Jayne, the cop frowned at her. He ignored her hand and fished a notebook and pen from his pocket. "Have a seat, Miss Sullivan. I'm Acting Chief Doug Lang. I'm here to take your statement."

Reed pulled the mask from his face. It dangled around his neck by the elastic straps. "Acting Chief? Give me a break, Doug. Can't her statement wait until Doc checks her out?"

"I don't have all day, Reed. In case you haven't noticed, the police station burned down, and the chief was killed." He yanked down his jacket zipper. The fabric parted around a flat abdomen clearly displayed in a uniform shirt one size too small. "I'll need a statement from you too."

"No shit, Doug." Reed coughed. "*I'm* the one covered in soot. I didn't see you in there. Were you out directing traffic?"

Doug flushed. Piggish eyes turned small and mean in a face that was just a little too fleshy for Jayne's comfort. He yanked off his coat and tossed it onto a nearby chair. His forearms were thick and corded, with basketball-sized biceps pumped up enough to make face-washing a challenge.

OK. So Reed and Doug had issues, and Reed was on an emotional edge. But couldn't Reed wait until after she'd given the cop her statement to tick him off?

Doc returned from the back room with a tray of first-aid supplies. He barely spared the cop a glance as he replaced the mask on Reed's face. "Do you really have to do this now, Doug?"

The cop went rigid. His face pinched. "Yes, I do."

Jayne nodded and shrank a little in her skin. Her abraded knees throbbed in rhythm with the pain that spiked though her temple. "Let's just get it over with. What do you want to hear about first?"

The cop glanced toward a closed door. "I'd prefer to do this in private."

Reed pulled the mask two inches from his face. "No way." He coughed. "She's not leaving my sight."

Jayne's throat tightened. Did Reed suspect the cop of being her abductor? Doug had blue eyes. He was a little short, but she could be wrong with her height estimate. Her recall wasn't 100 percent on either attack. Jayne's heart quickened. Could it be Doug? Could the man who had kidnapped her really be standing just a few feet away and she didn't recognize him? A wave of nausea rolled through her as the cop paced toward her.

What had Doug been doing during the fire?

Crimson crept up the cop's throat. A vein bulged. "You have nothing to say about it."

"But I do." Doc set the tray on a wheeled cart and began to clean a small burn on Reed's jaw. "She's my patient. You don't get to ask her questions unless I say it's OK. So if you want to talk to her, stop being an ass." The doctor applied a whitish cream to the angry mark and covered it with a bandage.

The cop huffed but didn't ignore the doctor's threat. He faced Jayne. "OK. Start at the beginning. You came into town on Thursday."

Jayne shifted in the hard plastic chair. She pulled the borrowed parka tighter around her shoulders and gave him the CliffsNotes version of the last three days. Had it only been four days since she'd arrived in Huntsville? It felt more like four weeks.

Doug leveled a skeptical look at Jayne. "Let me get this straight. Somebody abducted you and chained you up in a basement. You fought with this man and escaped. Then Reed found you on Route 27. He took you home and kept you there until the roads were cleared this morning. When you arrived in town to meet former Chief Bailey, the municipal building was on fire. *Then* you were attacked again?"

Jayne nodded.

"Do you think it was the same man?"

Jayne squeezed her eyes shut and tried to recall as many details as possible. The attacks blended in a violent collage of images and sensation that brought her sweat glands to life despite the freezing room. "I don't know." Her voice was as weak as her description.

Doug's huff conveyed his opinion of her statement. "Can you give me a physical description?"

"Not really. He was wearing a ski mask. He has blue eyes, and he was at least as tall as me."

"Well, that really narrows it down." The cop didn't roll his eyes, but Jayne could tell he wanted to. "An average-to-tall man with blue eyes."

Not much to go on, she admitted, but it wasn't her fault the kidnapper had worn a ski mask. But the cop was right. Her captor could be anybody. He could be walking down Main Street right now.

Or standing right in front of her.

The cop jotted something down in a small notebook. "What about the house? With zero description of your attacker, I have a better chance of finding the farmhouse. If Reed gives me the exact location he picked you up, I'll map possible places as soon as I get a chance."

"I took a statement from Jayne as soon as she woke up Friday evening. My notes are in the Yukon. Her story is exactly the same," Reed offered. "And she remembered more details when the incident was fresh."

Doc shushed him and concentrated on the stethoscope pressed to Reed's back.

Doug held up a hand, crossing-guard-style, toward Reed. "Excuse me, but you're not a cop."

"You know damned well that I was."

"*Was* is the key word there. You'll have to leave this to a real professional. I don't like civilian interference." The cop gave Reed his back and faced Jayne. "Pardon me, Miss Sullivan, but this all seems a bit far-fetched, don't you think? Especially since you reported an attempted abduction in Philadelphia four years ago. I don't know a single person who's been kidnapped, yet you've reported three attempts, all in broad daylight with no witnesses."

"What the fuck are you saying, Doug?" Reed yelled, and then burst into a coughing fit. Behind him, the doctor yanked out his earbuds and shook his head in disgust. He moved around the table to inspect a row of cuts on Reed's arm.

"You have to admit that Miss Sullivan either has the worst luck in the entire universe or she does something to incite violence. What kind of photographer are you, anyway?"

Bile rose in Jayne's throat as she groped for a response. If she said she was paparazzi, he'd definitely blame her job. His investigation would stop before it started. Her eyes shifted to Reed. She should tell him what she really did for a living, but not with the cop around. Instead of answering directly, she ripped the bandages off her wrists. The two-day-old scabs were dark and raw-looking, slightly puckered around the edges. "You think I *asked* for this?"

Doug crossed his juiced-up arms and puffed out his chest.

"For your information, there was a witness to the attack in Philly," Jayne said. "If he hadn't been there, I'd be dead."

The doctor turned his head to frown at Jayne's wounds. His gaze drifted to the scar on her cheek. His mouth went tight before he turned back to Reed's arm.

"I'm just saying you might not be as innocent as you seem," Doug sneered.

Reed's face purpled. "You—"

"Easy, Reed," Doc cut in and glared at the cop. "Consider this your only warning, Doug. I will not tolerate you upsetting my patients again."

Doug lowered his voice. "Did you know Miss Sullivan has a sealed juvenile record? Wonder what that's all about."

Over the clear plastic mask, Reed's gaze darted to Jayne. His bloodshot eyes were filled with anger. He opened his mouth but erupted in a series of hacking coughs.

Doug's verbal barrage continued. "Ever use drugs, Miss Sullivan? Because drug use would explain a lot."

"Never." Jayne glared at Doug. Her pulse pounded through her temples. Her peripheral vision reddened. She didn't trust her temper enough to say any more.

"Stick around town, Miss Sullivan. I'm going to have more questions for you."

Reed wheezed, "Unless you arrest her for something, you don't have the authority to hold—" Coughing interrupted his statement.

"How the hell is she going to identify the house or her attacker if she's not here? Either you want me to investigate or you don't. Make up your mind." The cop glared at Reed. "I didn't ask for this job, Kimball. If anything it's *her* fault. None of this would've happened if she hadn't come to town." Despite all his protests, Doug's cold blue eyes were glittering. He might not have asked for his new authority, but he was enjoying every minute.

Doc tore off his latex gloves with a loud snap. "All right. That's enough, all of you. Reed, shut up and breathe. Miss Sullivan, it's your turn. Doug, get out." He jerked a thumb toward the exit.

But the cop was right about one thing. The whole situation was all her fault. If Jayne hadn't come to Huntsville to spy on R. S. Morgan, the police chief would still be alive. Reed wouldn't be suffering from smoke inhalation and burns. She wouldn't have been kidnapped. Jayne pressed a hand to her stomach. Nausea churned.

The cop shot Reed a pointed glare. "If you're interested, there'll be a press conference later today. News crews are on the way. Be here in a couple hours. And they just might be interested in a certain piece of information about Jefferson Kimball. Miss Sullivan isn't the only one who isn't as innocent as she pretends to be." Doug stormed out. The door slammed behind him.

Who is Jefferson Kimball?

Jayne caught Reed's eye. Beneath the grime and soot, Reed's face drained. He looked away, his Adam's apple moving with a hard swallow.

Now was obviously not the time to ask him.

The doctor guided Jayne to the exam table. "Reed, you should talk to Nathan. Maybe he'll put a leash on Doug."

"Good idea," Reed said, his tone tight as his bloodless lips. "But I'm not holding my breath. Nathan has his own agenda."

Reed had a secret. Something to do with Jefferson Kimball. Would he share it with her? She studied his face as his expressionless mask slid back into place.

Guess not.

The one man who'd managed to gain her confidence was pulling away. The trust and connection that had been in his eyes minutes before the interview had vanished.

Doug's statement must have hit home. Reed had nearly lost his life because of her. My God, she'd nearly orphaned Scott. This morning's incidents had proved her assailant wasn't going to let her go. Just being near her put Reed and his son in jeopardy. If Reed was smart, he'd keep his distance from her.

And he was a very intelligent man.

The doctor selected a pair of scissors and began enlarging one of the rips in Jayne's jeans. Antiseptic followed with a sharp sting that brought tears to Jayne's eyes. She told herself it was the antiseptic fumes, not Reed's justified withdrawal, that caused her next breath to rattle in her chest.

The doctor bandaged her skinned knees and turned his attention to her wrists. "I'm sorry, Miss Sullivan, but these look like they're going to leave scars."

"I know." Hardly mattered at this point. She'd finally warmed up to a man and look how that had turned out. She'd nearly gotten him killed.

CHAPTER TWENTY

How much does Doug know?

Reed stared through the plate glass window. Outside the closed diner, firemen milled. Across the chrome-edged table, Nathan sat back in the tattered booth. "I'm sorry about Doug. He's just upset about Hugh. We all are."

Reed bit back his response. The only thing that was upsetting Doug was the fact that he hadn't officially been made chief yet.

Does Nathan know? Chances were the cop had run panting to the mayor the second he'd uncovered Reed's past. Reed studied the mayor. Nathan was a hard person to read. He always looked earnest. He probably practiced expressions in the mirror.

The mayor turned his attention to Jayne, who was sitting on Reed's right. "Miss Sullivan, can I get you something to eat or drink? It's lunchtime. I sent the cook home, but I can still heat something up for you. Soup maybe? You look cold." Nathan took Jayne's hand between his palms and held it a few seconds too long.

Reed doused the unexpected spark of anger. He had no claim on Jayne. As soon as they were finished with Nathan, Reed would take her to collect her stuff and her Jeep. Then he had to figure out how to get her home safe. She couldn't drive all the way to Philadelphia by herself. But if Hugh had made other arrangements, he hadn't shared them with his staff or Reed. Hugh's death had left Jayne's fate hanging.

But Doug's threat underscored the reason Reed had avoided relationships all this time.

Because it was the right thing to do.

Jayne had to be long gone before the press arrived and his past turned into a ratings boost for the local media. Wouldn't take them long to discover his identity. Camp outside his house, cameras and mics in hand, ready to attack. The pit of Reed's stomach went sour as he pictured TV vans parked at the curb beside Scott's school, waiting to snap a picture of the child of tragedy.

Again.

"No, thank you." Jayne extracted her hand and shifted a hair closer to Reed. Their shoulders touched. He wanted to put his arm around her but didn't. The fire, Hugh's death, Doug's callous questioning, and yet another attempt on her life added up to a hell of a day.

Reed still hadn't fully processed the day's events. Freaking out over Doug's announcement had been stupid with a capital S, though. Of course the press was coming. A kidnap victim had escaped her abductor and the municipal building had burned to the ground. The police chief had been killed. That was a lot of news for a small town. Doug's statement shouldn't have been a surprise. The cop's use of Reed's real name had, however, been a real shocker.

Reed was still choking on it.

After he removed Jayne to safety, he and Scott could lie low. They could drive down to Bangor and hole up in a hotel for a couple of days while Reed kept an eye on the news.

But running felt cowardly. He hadn't done anything wrong. He didn't feel he could trust Doug to adequately investigate

Hugh's death or Jayne's abduction. Without a proper investigation, a psycho would continue to roam Huntsville or go after Jayne in Philadelphia.

"I'm so sorry about everything that's happened to you." Nathan's voice interrupted Reed's mental debate. The mayor was staring into Jayne's eyes. Sincerity slid from the mayor like grease from a plate of bacon. How could he resist, though? Those eyes of hers could pull a man under, which was why Reed was avoiding all contact with them.

Irritation burned more than Reed's throat. He needed information from Nathan. The sooner he got it, the sooner he could make a plan. "Doug said something about a press conference."

Nathan nodded. "Five o'clock. In front of the municipal building."

"Do you really think letting Doug talk to the press is a good idea?"

"I'll handle the press conference. Doug will read a very short statement and answer any questions with 'I can't comment on an ongoing investigation.' A state investigator is taking over the case anyway. Doug isn't qualified to run this show." Something flickered in the cool blue of Nathan's eyes. "Don't worry, Reed. Doug won't be giving away any information."

He knew something about Reed's past. But how much?

Reed coughed as fresh tension gripped his throat. Nathan wasn't the kind of man to trust with secrets.

Nathan rose from the opposite side of the table and walked back into the kitchen. When he returned, he held a tall glass of ice water in each hand.

"Thank you." Jayne sipped her drink. Reed followed her gaze to the windows as she swallowed. No news vans yet. Outside the glass, firemen worked as the town rallied. People would stick together here. Natives were shy of tourists and newcomers, but once you were in, you were golden. If only Reed could be sure the town wouldn't turn on him like the city of Atlanta. The backing of the community would help him make a stand.

He shouldn't have hidden his identity all these years. The townspeople were sure to resent being lied to. Hugh had known all the details, and he'd supported Reed. But Hugh was dead. There was no one to stand behind Reed now.

Help wasn't going to come from Doug; that was for sure.

"I'm going to clean out one of the back storage rooms for a temporary office for Doug." Nathan was a control freak, so the idea of having Doug right here under his thumb would appeal to him.

The cool water soothed Reed's throat. His coughing subsided but his gut still burned. "Any idea what started the fire?"

Nathan glanced at Jayne. "The fire chief thinks it may have been the space heater in Hugh's office. He must've left the heater on by mistake. We had a power surge when the electricity came back on during the night. It's speculation at this point, though. Nothing's been substantiated except that Hugh's office seems to be the point of origin. We'll have to wait for a full report from the state arson investigators." Nathan sighed and gave his head a sad shake. "I don't know how many times I told Hugh that thing was a fire hazard."

Reed didn't comment. If Nathan had made sure Hugh's office was adequately heated, there'd have been no need for Hugh to use a space heater at all. There was no point in saying it. Nathan's conscience was coated in Teflon. Nothing ever stuck.

Could the fire have been an accident? Cops weren't big believers in coincidence.

"One thing's been buggin' me, Nathan." Ashen dryness rose in Reed's throat and he took a swallow of water. "Hugh didn't have his key in his hand when he was standing in front of the door. Why wouldn't the office have been locked if Evan wasn't in yet?"

Nathan's eyes dropped to the table. He lowered his voice, although the diner was empty. "Who knows? I didn't want to say anything before, but I think Hugh was starting to get forgetful."

"Really?"

Nathan nodded emphatically. "Just little things, but he was getting up there. He'd been talking about retiring for the past year or so, but something was holding him back. Maybe he was afraid he'd be bored."

"Hmmm. Never thought of Hugh as *that* old, but you could be right," Reed said.

"It's a shame he never got a chance to enjoy his golden years."

"How's Doris holding up?"

At the mention of Hugh's wife, Nathan's expression turned stony. Reed would bet Doris had had a few choice words for the mayor. "She's a tough old bird. She'll be OK, but it's going to be hard to fill his shoes."

Typical Nathan. Only worried about what affected him.

"You're not seriously considering Doug, are you?" Reed gave Nathan a pointed stare, which the mayor avoided.

"Well, he's the only candidate so far."

Jayne opened her mouth. Under the table, Reed covered her hand with his and squeezed lightly. She took the hint but pulled her hand out from under his palm. Reed's fingers twitched. He missed both the contact with Jayne's smooth skin and the deeper connection with the courageous woman. But it was better to keep his distance. Really.

"I have some serious objections to the way he treated Jayne during the interview. He was downright rude, Nathan." Reed paused before dropping the bomb. "It'd be a real shame if she sued the town."

Nathan's gaze shot to Jayne. She met his stare with pure blue ice. "You should stick around. The reporters are going to want to talk to you. You could be famous."

Jayne didn't answer, but her fair skin blanched a shade paler. Reed stood, his hand under Jayne's elbow lifting her with him.

"Well, we'd better go collect Jayne's things from the inn." Reed ushered Jayne from the booth, leaving Nathan to stew.

On the sidewalk, Jayne spun him around. "Why'd we run out of there? I wanted to give him a piece of my mind."

"Don't worry. We gave the mayor a few things to think about. You can bet he'll chew out Doug's ass within the hour. Yelling at Nathan only gets his back up." Reed turned her and steered her toward his truck. "What Nathan said about Hugh is a total crock, though. Hugh never forgot a thing. Something else is going on."

Jayne's arm brushed Reed's. Heat radiated from the contact. Reed wanted to get closer. He wanted to bury his head in her hair and forget all about the fire and Hugh's death. But if he took her in his arms, he'd never be able to let her go.

"Are you sure it wasn't that you just didn't see it because you liked him so much?" Jayne asked as she climbed into the vehicle.

Good question. Another good reason to avoid personal relationships. They destroyed objectivity.

Reed stepped into the driver's seat and started the engine. "Let's go get your stuff."

Moments later, wind blasted Reed's back as he jumped out of the Yukon and followed Jayne up the steps of the Black Bear Inn. From the walkway that led to the rear parking area, a parka-clad Bill stopped shoveling. His gaze fell on Jayne. He took a step back, dropped his shovel, and bolted around the corner of the house.

"Bill," Jayne called after him.

Reed cupped her elbow and steered her toward the front door. "Don't worry about it. It's not you. He's just like that around strangers."

The lobby was as stifling as usual. "Mae?" He tapped the bell on the registration desk.

"Keep your pants on," Mae yelled from the back room. She ducked through the doorway from the family quarters. Her puffy eyes, devoid of makeup, lit on Reed and went soft. "Reed, honey. Come sit down. I heard what happened this morning. Are you all right?" She embraced him in a fierce hug and led him to the sofa. The heat from the woodstove seared the burns on his face right through the bandage.

"I'm fine, Mae. Thanks."

Mae turned her motherly charm on Jayne. "I can't tell you how glad I am to see you alive and well. I told Hugh—" Her voice caught on a sob, quickly stifled with Yankee fortitude.

Reed patted her shoulder. "Hugh was a good man."

"That he was. He served this town for thirty years." Mae nodded and sniffed hard. She turned to Jayne. "You'll want to collect your things."

"Yes, ma'am." Jayne's voice quivered. "But I don't know what happened to the key."

"Not a problem. I'll get you the master."

After Jayne retrieved her belongings, then what? She'd pick up her Jeep and drive off? Alone? That idea gave Reed an empty ache in the center of his chest. But what were her options? She couldn't stay in town. Doug sure as hell wouldn't protect her.

Christ, her kidnapper could be anybody. Doug and Nathan both had blue eyes. So did a quarter of the men in town.

Three minutes later, Reed unlocked the door to Jayne's room. One lone piece of crime scene tape dangled from the jamb. Jayne tried to push ahead, but Reed held her back. "Let me go in first, please."

She stepped back and gestured him forward, but she was only two steps behind him when he crossed the threshold. She stood in the corner and rocked back and forth on Scott's big boots as Reed gave the room a quick sweep.

"OK."

Jayne made a beeline for the armoire and threw it open. Her face paled. "My equipment's not here. The compact camera was in my purse, but I left my digital SLR and all my lenses in here."

"Get the rest of your stuff and we'll talk to Mae again. Maybe she locked up the valuable things."

Jayne took one minute to shove her clothes into a duffel bag. She opened the bathroom kit and emptied it on the counter.

"What are you doing?"

"I always keep emergency cash hidden in two places when I travel. In my car and in my makeup bag. Just in case something gets stolen." She opened a cosmetic compact of some kind and lifted the mirror out. Underneath were folded bills. "I'm going to call Pat while I'm here. Now that I've given my statement to the police, I can leave, right? I mean, he can't really make me stay here, can he?"

"No. He can't." But Reed wished *he* could.

Jayne began pushing buttons on the phone. After everything that had happened today, it was natural that she'd be anxious to get away from Huntsville. He should want her to go. It wasn't safe here. But her stalker could easily follow her when she left. It would be better if she waited for one of her brothers to come and get her. She couldn't leave by herself. Not after Hugh had died. Not after someone had tried to abduct her a second time.

He had to find another way to get her home, even if it meant risking exposure.

Her mouth tightened as she held the receiver to her ear. "No answer at the bar." She glanced at the digital clock on the night-stand. "I'll try him at home." Another series of numbers. She shook her head. "No connection there. The phone must be out. And the call won't go through on his cell. The wireless company is saying the system is experiencing unusually heavy volume."

They trooped downstairs. Mae had the local news on the TV in the small parlor off the lobby. Jayne's eyes were riveted on the reporter as she detailed the impact of the storm on the Mid-Atlantic region. Nearly four feet of snow had accumulated back home. Airports were just opening. Millions were without power. Phone lines were down. Many major roads had yet to be plowed.

"You can try your brother again later," Reed said. "Looks like it may take a day to get Philadelphia straightened out."

Jayne nodded but concern was etched in her face. "We're not used to this. We normally don't get more than six inches or so a couple of times each winter."

Reed turned to Mae. "Jayne's camera equipment isn't in her room. Any idea where it might be?"

Mae nodded. "Sure. Hugh took it. He was going to lock it up as possible evidence."

"Thanks, Mae." Reed accepted another hug before leading Jayne out the front door.

He climbed behind the wheel of the truck and closed his door. In the passenger seat, Jayne huddled against the cold.

Reed hesitated, key an inch from the ignition. "Jayne, tell me again what you did when you arrived in Huntsville on Thursday. Don't leave anything out, no matter how trivial it seems."

Jayne shivered. "You think the fire was set to destroy something in my bags?"

He started the engine and cranked on the heater. "Let's just say I'm skeptical of coincidences."

"OK. I stopped at the Quickie Mart for gas, and then took some pictures around town." In the middle of changing Scott's oversize boots for her own sneakers, she tapped her forehead. "Pictures. Could it be that simple?"

"I don't know. It's awfully convenient that everything in Hugh's office was destroyed, including your camera equipment." Reed gripped the wheel. "But if all he wanted was your pictures, why did he try to grab you today?"

Because there was another reason this man wanted Jayne. And Reed's gut instinct told him the reason was personal.

– – –

Jayne jumped out of the Yukon and followed Reed into Huntsville Auto Repair. In her pocket was the new disposable cell phone Reed had just purchased for her at the drugstore. She scanned the garage. Her Jeep sat in the rear bay, ready to go.

Jayne's freezing palms dampened with sweat as she contemplated heading out of town alone. But what was her choice? Staying in Huntsville?

Not gonna happen.

Her stalker had burned down the municipal building and killed Hugh because of her. The shock settled low in Jayne's belly. Her insides turned icy.

Reed and Scott were in danger every second she was with them. Reed had probably realized the risk she brought to his son. Otherwise why would he be acting so strange, so distant? She couldn't imagine he'd really be that upset about her juvie record. Jefferson Kimball maybe? Had one of Reed's relatives done something bad? It wouldn't matter to her. A man couldn't pick his family. The chill spread to the center of her chest as she realized how deep her feelings ran for Reed.

But she'd let him go rather than risk his life or bring him more pain.

She had to get as far away from Huntsville as possible.

This guy could follow her to Philadelphia or grab her anywhere along the way. But that was a risk she had to take. She would not put other lives in danger to protect herself. She stuck her hands in her pockets to conceal the trembling of her fingers as she walked to her vehicle. She tried the door. It wasn't locked. She bent down and reached under the driver's seat. Yes! Her fingers encountered the plastic sandwich bag. She peeled the tape free and pulled out her second emergency stash. All in all, three hundred bucks would get her back to Philly.

A thin man in his twenties walked across the concrete garage floor. Wavy blond hair, parted in the middle, hung down to his shoulders, rock-star style.

"Put on two brand-new tires. Rotated the rest." The mechanic stopped to degrease his hands with orange Zep. Then he led the way to his office in the corner of the garage. A metal desk and filing cabinet were the only furniture in the small but spotless room. "I'll get the bill and your keys for you, ma'am."

He handed her an invoice. The total would eat up most of her funds. "I'm sorry. My purse was stolen. I don't even have a credit card. Is there any way I could send you a check?"

The mechanic sighed. "I can't afford to let a few hundred bucks slide, especially since you're out of state. I'm sorry."

Jayne's stomach clenched. She'd never get out of here. If something happened to Reed or Scott because of her...

Reed drew his wallet from his back pocket. "I'll cover it."

"I'll send you a check," Jayne promised. She would've promised him anything to get her Jeep back.

"Don't worry about it." Reed shot her a suspicious look and Jayne averted her eyes. She wasn't telling him she was leaving until the last possible minute.

"I *will* send you a check."

Jayne collected her keys. Outside, Reed stood oddly still while she transferred her duffel from his Yukon to the Jeep. "What are you doing?"

Jayne glanced at the display on her phone. "It's only three o'clock. I can get as far as New Hampshire tonight." She forced a smile on her stiff lips. The cold rose from the asphalt into her sneakers. The garage blocked the sun, and without its rays, the winter chill seeped right into her bones.

Reed's expression was strained, the shadow of the building casting his chiseled features in stark relief. "You can't just leave."

Jayne took a step back. "I have to."

"You're alone and vulnerable. Someone is stalking you. You have no credit cards. No driver's license. Three hundred bucks isn't going to get you far if you factor in a hotel room. You haven't been able to get in touch with your family." Reed ticked the items off on his fingers. "What will you do if he follows you? There's a lot of empty space between here and Philadelphia, and at the moment, much of it is buried under several feet of snow. You don't even know that all the roads are clear."

Jayne had no idea what she would do. But she had to break away from Reed before she drew the killer to his door.

"He still wants you."

Her head ached with fatigue as she held back tears. She raised her chin. "We don't know that. Maybe he destroyed everything important in the fire."

"Then why did he try to grab you again? The fire had already been set."

Good point. *Shit*. Moisture gathered hot in the corners of her eyes and she blinked away from Reed's piercing gaze.

"I'll be safer anywhere but here." More accurately, she wasn't going to be safe anywhere, but Reed and Scott wouldn't be in danger once she was gone.

"I can't let you just drive away all alone." Reed's voice softened. "Let me call Becca Griffin. Get her to keep Scott for the night. Then I'll drive you to the airport in Bangor. You can wait there for the next available seat on a flight to Philadelphia. With all the heightened security, you'll be safe at the airport. Hopefully, we'll able to contact your brothers by then. Surely one of them would come get your Jeep."

Jayne hesitated. It actually sounded like a rational plan.

"OK." Her eyes grew hot, filling with tears. She looked away from the man she'd grown to trust in a very short time. "I'll start calling airlines. I'd have to borrow more money."

"Not a problem." Reed pulled his cell from his pocket as he opened the door to the SUV. "May as well sit in here where it's warm. I'll start at the back of the alphabet. You take the front."

"All right." Jayne climbed in the passenger seat. The leather was cold on the backs of her jeans-clad legs, but Reed switched the heat on full blast. Before she could dial, a tap on the window made her jump. Doug Lang stood outside the passenger side of Reed's truck, breath fogging in the damp air. Jayne lowered the window.

Doug's face compressed into a piggish scowl. He handed Jayne a manila envelope. "Read this before you decide you're safe with *him*."

Reed didn't speak, but his knuckles turned white on the steering wheel as Jayne opened the clasp and slid a few stapled pieces of paper from the envelope.

Doug jerked his gaze to Reed. "Nathan won't let me make this public. Thinks it makes the town look bad, but you and I both know it's only a matter of time before the reporters figure out who you really are. And why you're hiding behind your middle name. Your whole life here has been a lie, hasn't it?"

Jayne looked at a computer printout of a newspaper article. Reed's picture stared back at her. The headline sent the blood rushing from her head. No. This couldn't be. She couldn't trust the wrong man twice.

Did Atlanta Homicide Detective Jefferson Kimball Get Away with Murder?

CHAPTER TWENTY-ONE

Reed stared at Jayne's back. His gut twisted. Pressure built inside his chest. "It's not what you think." He turned toward her. Jayne opened the door and jumped out of the truck. Reed climbed down from the cab and rounded the hood. As he stepped toward her, her posture went defensive, one hand extended in front of her, palm out.

She backed away, turquoise eyes open wide and brimming with betrayal.

Reed halted and lifted both hands in surrender. "Jayne, I didn't kill my wife. The case dragged on, and the press wanted someone arrested so they skewered me. They wouldn't leave us alone. Christ, they even parked outside Scott's elementary school. That's why we moved here. That's why I use my middle name now. I can't stomach the thought of Scott getting hammered by the media again."

No doubt Jayne was thinking about another man she'd once trusted, the fellow student who'd attacked her.

"I'm sorry, Reed." She slid behind the wheel of her Jeep. Her voice shook. "I need to think."

"Where are you going?"

She didn't answer as she slammed her door. The locks clicked with a finality that made the ache in Reed's chest swell. She'd trusted him, and now she thought he was a killer.

Reed's raw throat clogged as she pulled away.

"Better start packing, Kimball." Doug's mouth twisted as he spat out the words. "This town will turn on you once everyone finds out you've been lying all this time. But you'll have to hang around for the investigation. I'm sure the state police detective will want to speak to—"

Reed turned his back on the cop midthreat. The cop's voice faded under the weight of Reed's thoughts.

Jayne was alone. Vulnerable.

But what could he do? *She'd* left *him*. Because he'd hidden his past. Doug was an asshole, but he was right. Reed had been living a lie for years.

He reached for his vehicle door handle and jerked it open. He drove away without a backward glance. His fingers were numb as he punched in the number for Jayne's new cell. He'd programmed his cell number into the new phone. She'd know it was him. The sick, helpless feeling in his gut intensified as the line rang.

Jayne didn't answer.

– – –

He ducked behind the dashboard of his vehicle as Jayne passed by. Her Jeep stopped at the corner, then pulled out onto Main Street.

He glanced at the digital clock. He'd give her five minutes so he didn't frighten her before she was out of town. Then he'd "happen upon" her and offer roadside assistance. The Taser was in the console, ready to subdue her if necessary. There was no reason to engage in a physical confrontation. No doubt Brigid had spiritual powers. She possessed unusual strength of body and soul befitting a Celtic goddess. His balls and jaw still ached from the blows she'd landed.

His goddess had proven herself worthy once again.

He bit his lip and checked the time. Her five minutes were up. By now her Jeep had likely died. He started his engine and turned onto Main. Jayne wouldn't be able to drive more than a few miles before breaking down. Not with a load of bleach in her engine oil. She wouldn't make it to the highway.

He'd get her this time. He had to. The solstice approached.

Time was running out.

– – –

Jayne stopped at the last intersection on Main Street. Her Jeep coughed as she accelerated through the turn onto the country road that led to the highway. A thick mixture of loneliness and fear crushed her chest. Tears blurred her vision, and she swiped an angry hand across her eyes.

Despite the half hour she'd sat in front of the park, stewing over Doug's revelation and trying to get her head on straight, a course of action eluded her.

She wasn't sure whom she was angry with—Reed, Doug, or Ty Jennings. All three deserved a portion. Maybe she wasn't meant to have a normal relationship. She could get a dog. Dogs were faithful. Dogs didn't lie.

But a dog couldn't make her insides melt like Velveeta in the microwave.

She checked her rearview mirror for the twentieth time as she left the town behind. Nothing but white, asphalt, and trees stretched out behind her. A sense of isolation crept up her spine.

She was on her own.

A shiver passed through her bones. She cranked the heat a notch higher and pushed the Jeep past the speed limit. The engine wheezed in protest, so she backed off the accelerator.

Snow blanketed the countryside. Its frozen surface reflected sunlight like frosted glass. With the turbulence of her emotions, she expected dark clouds to gather overhead. But the sun shone with a vengeance, illuminating all that had been concealed by the storm in harsh, brilliant light.

Had she been a fool? Was Reed really dangerous?

Her instincts said she could trust him. He'd saved her life, hadn't he? So he hadn't told her everything about his past. They'd only been together for few days. Hardly enough time for complete soul-baring. But she'd trusted Ty and hadn't seen any sign of his violent, angry side until it was too late.

Jayne hadn't exactly been honest about her job. The whole tabloid thing had failed to come up in a single conversation. She knew from her self-defense classes that stranger attacks were rare. Most women who suffered violence were assaulted by someone they knew.

The landscape passed by in a white blur. Where was she going? She needed a plan. Something proactive to block out the grief wringing her insides dry.

She slipped a hand into the pocket of the borrowed coat. The disposable cell phone Reed had bought her was heavy in her palm as she drew it out. There was only one person who'd have the real scoop on Jefferson Kimball's story. She punched the numbers for the *Daily Scoop*, feeling slimy before the line even connected.

A few minutes and a truckload of lies later, Jayne disconnected the call and crossed her fingers. Her plan was sketchy, but not bad considering she'd had all of five minutes to come up with it. Jason had agreed to wire her some money as soon as she hit the next town. He'd also spring for a hotel room. Apparently, her firsthand account of the kidnapping was worth serious coin. And the inquiry into Reed's background had set off her editor's vulturish instincts.

Like a good scavenger, Jason had smelled blood.

When Jayne was settled, safely hidden in a room under the corporate name, she'd wait for Jason to call with the information about Reed. She wasn't making any decisions until she knew the truth.

Had her request put Reed in danger of exposure? Yes, but with news crews already en route to Huntsville, that was a given regardless of what she did.

She'd read the article the cop had given her. The piece was light on facts and heavy on speculation. Jayne knew that newspapers lied. The *Daily Scoop* twisted the truth into its evil stepsister every single day, which made Jason the perfect person to ferret out the real story.

According to Jason, the next town was about thirty minutes down the interstate. Jayne was fishing in the center console for her GPS when the engine sputtered and the Jeep began to slow. Was that smoke coming from under the hood?

Jayne eased off the gas pedal and scanned the dashboard. Her temperature gauge waved way into the red. A few agonizing seconds later, the engine died out with a final shudder and wheeze. Smoke and steam poured from the engine. With no power steering, Jayne hauled on the wheel to guide the Jeep as far to the side of the road as possible. The plows hadn't cleared the entire shoulder. Her tires crunched on the icy snowpack.

Shit. Shit. *Shit.*

Her forehead dropped onto the steering wheel, and she smacked a palm on the dashboard. "I know you're old and I haven't always treated you right. But did you have to die on me *today*?" Unless her car had been sabotaged. Could someone have broken into the garage and tampered with it?

Regardless, her plan had just been erased.

Jayne raised her head and looked out the windshield. A green highway marker rose from the roadside about a quarter mile away. She squinted. Did it say the ramp was two miles ahead? That put her maybe three miles from town. Walking distance. She scanned the ice-covered landscape. In the summer. In this weather, the distance would feel like an eternity.

A quick call to the auto shop netted her a promise that the tow truck, out on another call, would retrieve her car in an hour or so.

This was what she got for working for a tabloid paper, her just desserts served up as a long walk in dirty roadside slush.

She kicked open the door and retrieved her duffel bag from the backseat. The bright winter sun glared at her from over the trees. She could call Reed. He would come and get her. No. Not until she heard from Jason.

She'd better move it if she wanted to be in town before dark. She zipped up her borrowed jacket and started walking. Icy water invaded her mesh running shoes in the first ten strides. She tucked her hands inside the coat pockets.

She'd walked for ten minutes when an engine purred. Jayne stopped; her heart bumped. A small speck appeared on the horizon, coming from the direction of town.

Jayne scanned her surroundings. The forest edge was about twenty yards away. Should she run for the woods and hide? She'd have to slog through several feet of snow. She'd never make it. And her trail would be too visible for her to hide anyway.

What were the chances that was her stalker? It could be any-body. Huntsville had over a thousand residents. Unless, of course, he'd followed her.

The vehicle sped closer. It was a truck, a large dark SUV.

It slowed as it approached.

Jayne held her breath. She removed the shoulder strap of her duffel and gripped the hand straps to make the bag easier to drop if she needed both hands free. Or if she needed to run. The truck pulled over. Sunlight glittered off the windshield. The door opened.

Nathan Hall climbed out.

Jayne's breath whooshed out in one quick exhalation.

"Having some car trouble?"

"It overheated. Can you believe my luck?" Jayne waved a hand at the disabled Jeep. "Do you know anything about cars?"

"A little."

"Could you take a look? Maybe it's something minor."

His eyes widened at the mushroom cloud issuing from under the Jeep's hood. "That's not something minor. And you shouldn't open the hood until the engine cools. I could drive you back into town."

Jayne chewed her lip.

Nathan tilted his head and flashed a smile. His clothes were rumpled but clean. No sign of the soot that had streaked Reed from head to toe. Nathan hadn't run into a burning building to save a friend.

"It's a long walk," he said.

How many options did she have? It would take her a half hour to walk to town. A lot could happen to a girl in that span of time, especially in an isolated spot like this one. The road wasn't highly traveled. Nathan's was the only car she'd seen so far. Once again, Jayne was smack between a rock and a slab of granite. But could she trust him? And if she didn't, who might come along next?

"OK."

Her cell phone rang as Nathan reached for her bag. She reached into her pocket. "Excuse me for a minute."

– – –

Reed shifted into park and looked up. He was sitting in front of his house. Numb, he climbed from the vehicle. The phone pealed just as he opened the front door. A tiny spark of hope was immediately extinguished when he read the display. Scott. Not Jayne. His next breath was a lonely shudder.

"Dad?" Scott's voice came over the line. "Can I stay at Brandon's tonight? School's closed tomorrow. Some issue with the heat or something."

Perfect. "It's fine with me. Is Mrs. Griffin OK with that?"

"Yeah. She has to work at the bar tonight. You're feelin' OK and all, right?"

"Right." Reed had talked to Scott shortly after the fire. "I'll drop off a change of clothes."

"Cool. Me and Brandon are taking the boys sledding, and we still need to dig out her back porch."

"All right," Reed said. "I'll bring pizza, too." Becca worked two jobs and still could barely feed her boys, let alone an extra mouth.

"'Kay." Scott's tone perked up. "I'll tell Mrs. Griffin."

Numb, Reed fed Sheba and called in a pickup order at Tony's. He peeled off his smoky clothes and tossed them directly into the washer before walking into the bathroom to wash off the soot. As he turned on the shower, the flowery scent of the hotel shampoo Jayne had used smacked him in the face. He closed his eyes and leaned on the vanity while the scent of her overwhelmed him.

How could he have let her go? How could he have stopped her?

Damn Doug. Reed's head dropped forward. Hell, it was his own fault. He'd been living a lie for years. The truth was bound to come out eventually.

Reed went through the motions of washing and dressing in slow motion. His body moved heavily, as if he were underwater. Grabbing his keys, he left the empty house. He coughed as the cold night air hit his abused lungs. Sheba trotted behind him to the Yukon.

"Come on." Glad for the company, he opened the door for her. "You can ride shotgun. The seat happens to be empty."

Because Jayne was on her way to Philadelphia.

Alone.

She consumed all his thoughts as he stopped at the restaurant and drove to the Griffins'. The aroma of hot pizza filled the truck, yet Reed wasn't even tempted to steal a slice. He hadn't eaten since breakfast but had no appetite.

Jayne hadn't eaten lunch either. The empty space in Reed's chest swelled.

When Rebecca Griffin opened her door, Reed had to shake himself to be polite.

"Reed, thank you." Becca was obviously getting ready to head out to her second shift of the day. Instead of the white waitress uniform, she was dressed in black slacks and a white blouse. She'd applied makeup with a heavy hand, but nothing could conceal her perpetual dark circles. "You didn't have to bring food."

"Becca, Scott will eat you out of house and home."

"He and Brandon chopped a lot of wood for me today. He's a good kid." Her face cracked into a weary smile.

Reed's heart squeezed. This woman was trying to be nice, and all he could think about was a tall redhead. Under the exhaustion, Becca was an attractive woman. Reed just had never felt any spark around her. But maybe fireworks were overrated.

Amicable companionship wouldn't leave a crater the size of the Grand Canyon in his heart. What would Becca think of his past? They'd known each other for years instead of the few days he'd spent with Jayne.

"Come in." Becca stepped back. Her eyes lingered on his bandaged cheek. "We heard about the fire—and Hugh. I'm sorry."

Reed crossed the threshold and passed close to Becca in the narrow hall. She smelled like coconut. Reed continued straight through to the kitchen. The house was cold and Reed wondered if she was rationing her woodpile. He set the pizza boxes on the counter.

Becca pulled a few chipped dishes from the cabinet. She looked as tired as he felt. "You brought dinner. Why don't you stay and eat with us?"

He and Becca had a lot in common. They were the same age. Their lives revolved around their kids. They'd both had shitty days. Hell, they'd both had shitty lives. If anyone would understand how he'd gotten the shaft, Becca would.

CHAPTER TWENTY-TWO

John stuck his head outside the cabin door and listened. No engine. He scanned the clearing. Nothing. A deep breath of winter air stung his lungs. He inhaled again, relieved to feel the cold burn after an eternity of numbness.

One step outside the door, the chain around his ankle snapped taut. He knelt and extended his arm to scoop snow into the plastic cup. With his other hand, he grabbed a log from the pile. The cold burrowed through his filthy sweater. Back inside, he stacked the log with the small pile he'd accumulated that day. The cup went near the fire.

He glanced at the bottled water stacked in the corner. No chance. He'd wait for the snow to melt. He hadn't consumed any of the water since last night. By morning his vision had cleared and his limbs no longer felt as if they were weighted. By mid-afternoon he could stand and walk without weaving. Weakness persisted but that was to be expected after so many weeks of limited movement. His guess had been correct. The water had been drugged. He'd eaten several protein bars and still felt OK.

How long had he been held captive? Weeks? Months? He had no recollection of time. In the old house, days and nights had passed in a fluid blur. But now, his world was clear and sharp again.

The change wasn't 100 percent positive. He could think about his family now. Had his parents given up hope? Did they think he was dead? His gut ached when he imagined their grief—and guilt. They'd moved to Maine just to keep him safe.

But the worst thing about being clearheaded was the ability to project his future. He had no idea why he'd been imprisoned, but he was going to die unless he escaped. No one was coming for him. No doubt his family thought him dead already.

He squatted five times. His quadriceps burned, but this morning he'd only been able to do one.

He needed a plan. He needed to get the manacle off his ankle. He needed a weapon.

John stuck another log in the potbellied stove. With no matches to be found in the cabin, he'd been careful not to let the fire go out. He sat on the sleeping bag and extended his sock-clad feet toward the fire. Heat infused his toes. He tensed and released all his muscles. Blood flowed with reassuring pinpricks.

His reality was dim. The cabin was empty. Even if he managed to free himself, he wouldn't make it very far without shoes or a coat and no idea which way to run. He was in the middle of nowhere, and his survival skills ran more toward spotting trouble in the subway.

His best bet would be to take his captor by surprise and steal his vehicle. His gaze was drawn to the woodpile. He reached over and broke a long sliver off the cut side of the closest log. He touched the pointy end with his forefinger. Was it sharp enough to do some damage?

John sorted through the logs until he found one narrow enough to curl his hand around. His arm trembled when he lifted it high, but with a two-handed grip, he managed to swing it in a wide arc. A crude club.

He needed every advantage he could find. There would only be one opportunity for escape.

John shifted his feet. Something caught on his sock. He crawled closer and ran his forefinger over the rough wood floor. A nail head poked out an eighth of an inch. John picked at it with his fingernails.

– – –

Reed turned off Main Street and urged his truck way past the speed limit. Jayne had a good head start on him, but her Jeep was old. If he pushed it, he might be able to catch up with her. She'd be on the state highway for at least thirty miles before she hit the next town. It was the only main route south.

Becca Griffin had looked disappointed when he'd declined dinner. But she knew there wasn't any attraction on his part. And Scott's comment had pierced Reed to the heart.

Why'd she leave? She didn't have any money or anything. Aren't you worried about her?

Why had he let her go so easily? Why hadn't he tried harder to make her listen? Seeing that old headline had shocked the hell out of him. The black print had looked so bold above the full-color glossy of him exiting the police station after identifying his wife's body. He'd been transported back to that afternoon. The warm Southern sun shining on his head had felt like an abomination with Madeline's body lying cold on a stainless-steel table in the morgue. The whirring and clicking of cameras had followed him to his car, his house, Scott's school, even his wife's funeral. Reporters had stalked him for months. When the case remained unsolved, and he hadn't been arrested, the press had screamed corruption. He'd quit the force. Hell, he'd quit living—until this week.

So the real reason he'd let Jayne leave was fear. He was afraid of the feelings she drew from him. Things he hadn't felt in a long time, maybe ever. He wanted to live again. But allowing himself to hope he could have a second chance was opening his scarred soul to another potential wound.

The snowy landscape rolled by, monotonous and endless and bleak, until two vehicles on the side of the road caught his attention. Nathan's SUV was parked behind Jayne's Jeep. Smoke seeped from under the Jeep's hood. Nathan was throwing Jayne's duffel in the back of his truck.

Jayne turned. Her gaze settled on him through the windshield, and she lowered the cell phone from her ear. Her hair caught the sunlight like a halo. Relief bubbled up in his chest, and his heart jumped for joy. She was safe. How could he have let her take that risk?

Sheba caught sight of Jayne and whined. The dog put both front paws on the dashboard and wagged her tail. *Exactly.*

He pulled over to the side of the road and jumped to the ground. "What happened?"

Jayne froze. Something hard flashed in Nathan's eyes. Was he jealous? Did he have designs on Jayne? Well, too fucking bad for him. Reed was not letting her endanger herself a second time.

Nathan smoothed his expression. "Jayne's car overheated. I was giving her a lift into town."

"I'm here now. You can get home to Aaron and Evan." Reed stepped forward.

"Jayne. Would you rather go with Reed?" Nathan asked. His words and tone were amicable, but his jaw clenched as if he had to bite the words off.

Jayne hesitated.

Reed caught Jayne's gaze. "Please," he said. "I'll explain everything."

Her eyes searched his. She turned to Nathan. "Thank you for the offer, but I'll go with Reed."

Reed would've preferred Jayne be more excited at the prospect of coming home with him, but he'd take what he could get. Once they were alone, he'd explain that he hadn't meant to be a total ass—and he'd tell her all about the disaster of his life in Atlanta.

Reed stepped forward and tugged her duffel from Nathan's grip. The mayor held on for a split second too long. Nathan definitely wanted Jayne for himself. He didn't move as Reed steered Jayne toward the Yukon.

On the passenger side, Reed tossed her bag in the backseat and opened her door. "Sheba, in the backseat."

The dog hopped over the console. Reed climbed behind the wheel. "Do you need anything else from your Jeep?"

"No. It's all in the bag."

Jayne reached over the seat and gave Sheba a head rub.

Reed K-turned back onto the road and headed toward home. In the rearview mirror, Nathan was still standing on the shoulder as Reed pulled away.

With his eyes back on the road, he felt Jayne's stare on his face. "I need to apologize and explain about that article."

"I know what happened in Atlanta." Jayne held up a hand. "It's OK."

Shock burst through Reed. "You know?"

Jayne lifted a shoulder and turned toward the passenger window. "I called a friend and asked him to check out the article."

"I'd still like to explain. There was a lot of information that didn't make it to the press."

"It doesn't matter," Jayne said. "I know enough. I should've trusted you, but I had a bad track record. I was naïve once before, and I almost died."

"It matters to me." Reed exhaled and lowered his voice. "I don't want any more secrets between us."

Reed glanced sideways. Her chin was up, her jaw tight, and her face pink from the cold as she stared out the window.

"OK."

Reed turned into the driveway and parked. Dusk was an hour off, but the sun had dipped behind the trees. Shadows reached for the house.

Reed grabbed her bag and led the way up to the door. Ice and rock salt crunched under their shoes on the porch. Sheba pushed past their legs and trotted into the house.

In the kitchen, Reed made a quick call to the auto shop. "The mechanic said he'd call later tonight, after he's had a chance to look at your engine."

The house wasn't cold, but she shivered as she followed him into the kitchen. Her arms hugged her stiff body. Wet socks left footprints on the floor. She looked lost, like she didn't want to be there. He couldn't blame her. She'd wanted to leave town. He rubbed at the pressure building in the center of his chest. She'd wanted to leave him.

"OK." Jayne toed off sodden sneakers in the mudroom and hung her coat on a peg. "Where's Scott?"

"He's staying at Brandon's tonight."

Jayne's posture remained stiff. Did she not want to be alone with him?

"Do you want to try and call your brother?"

She nodded. "Soon as we hear from the auto shop. If the Jeep is repairable, I'll get one of them to fly up and drive back with me. If it's toast, I'll just fly home."

If that turned out to be the case, Reed would go with her and deliver her safely to her brother.

"I didn't kill my wife."

She turned and met his gaze, head-on. "I know."

"Scott and I were camping with his Boy Scout troop that night." Words crowded Reed's chest, scrambled free. "Madeline had moved out a couple months before. She said she couldn't be a cop's wife anymore. Too much stress." He swallowed the guilt.

Jayne moved a step closer. "It's not your fault."

"But I knew from the beginning she wasn't cut out for that life. Madeline wasn't good with pressure. If I'd have left the force like she wanted, she'd still be alive."

"You know it's not that simple." Her hand found his forearm. The solid weight of it grounded him. "What happened to your wife was horrible. But you can't take the blame."

Jayne squeezed his arm, but Reed pulled away. He took a few steps and focused on the window. Outside, darkness had fallen. He flipped on the exterior lights. Snow reflected the brightness, illuminating the yard in stark black and white.

"One of her friends testified that Madeline suspected she was being followed. She hoped it was me. That I wanted her back. That I was ready to leave the force for her."

Jayne took a step toward him. "Reed, you don't have to—"

Raising a hand, he cut her off. The truth had been festering inside him for years. As painful as the process was, he needed to let it out. "But I didn't want to reconcile. Honestly, I was relieved the day she walked out the door. No more bickering 24/7. She died because I was selfish. I just wanted some peace and quiet." And there it was. The real source of all his guilt. Something he'd never allowed himself to admit. When Madeline moved out, an incredible, blissful silence had filled his house. No more coming home from a long shift to a longer argument. Even though he had to share custody, Reed enjoyed his time with Scott so much more without all the stress Madeline had added to the equation.

"Your wife was killed by the superintendent of her building. It had nothing to do with you."

The twenty-year-old super had stalked Madeline from the day she moved in. His hidey-hole in the basement had been covered with photos, notes on her day-to-day activities, small things he'd stolen from her apartment when she wasn't home. He'd been arrested for stalking in Richmond the year before, but no one had ever pressed charges. He had no official record for anyone to check. The only person to blame was the murderer. None of that stopped Reed from carrying the guilt of her death.

"The police never considered me a suspect. But it took them a while to accumulate enough evidence to arrest the real killer. The press had months to speculate on my guilt. Not only did they have the statement from Madeline's friend claiming she thought I was following her, they had the money I inherited. Madeline came from a wealthy family. Even though we'd separated, she hadn't taken me out of her will. I was never interested in the money. I put it all in trust for Scott." He turned to Jayne, searching her eyes for any sign that she was now repulsed by him.

But Jayne's eyes only reflected his pain. She eased closer and reached for his hand. Her fingers were cold and Reed enveloped her hand between his palms. "Thank God he was with you that night."

A wave of goose bumps passed over the exposed flesh of Reed's forearms. If Madeline's killer had picked the next weekend…"I do that every single day."

Dark semicircles underscored her eyes, reminding Reed someone had tried to kill her a few days before. His chest tightened again, the relief from purging his soul evaporating as he contemplated the danger surrounding her. Nothing could happen to Jayne. "You should eat something."

"I'd rather shower first, if that's OK. I'm freezing."

"Sure." But all Reed could think of was the last time he'd warmed her up. Body-to-body, tucked into his sleeping bag. And how much he wanted to do it again. Her long limbs would surround him, hold him close enough to feel the beat of her heart against his chest. He'd give her warmth, and she'd give him sanity.

Instead, he carried her duffel bag through the master bedroom to the bath and set it on the vanity, keeping a few feet of empty space between them. "Do you remember where everything is?"

She brushed past him. Their arms rubbed. The contact sent a wave of electricity through his body, even through the soft wool of his sweater and her thick sweatshirt. Jayne glanced over her shoulder. Her blue eyes widened, darkened, mirrored his desire. The pulse that thrummed in his temple began to echo in his loins. Primal urges to possess, protect, and claim her rushed through him.

"Yeah. Thanks." The bright bathroom light illuminated purple smudges of exhaustion under her eyes and the pallor of her smooth skin. The oversized sweatshirt hung off one pale shoulder, the exposed patch of skin so smooth, so soft he could taste it. She'd smell like his soap, from her shower that morning. His body imagined how her long legs would encircle his waist as he sank into her tight heat. A yearning that was more than physical took root in his gut, pulled him toward her like a divining rod to an underground stream. It took every reserve of Reed's willpower to turn around and step toward the bedroom.

Behind him, the faucet squeaked. The shower started up with a rush. Water splattered on tile.

Reed glanced over his shoulder.

Jayne hugged her arms. His eyes locked with hers. Need swam in their turquoise depths. Reed was dragged under by the wave of desire that flooded him. Blood surged to his groin and hunger unfurled deep in his chest. His need to hold her, to mark her, to become part of her, was primitive, as demanding as the need to take his next breath.

He couldn't walk away. His feet turned toward her, controlled by instinct.

He stepped closer. Jayne's pupils widened. Her body leaned toward him, just a fraction of an inch, but enough to tell him he wouldn't be denied. He wanted one night with her, one night to be needed and wanted, one night to feel complete.

– – –

Jayne's heart stammered. Reed's eyes darkened as something was unleashed inside of them. In one swift stride he was in front of her. An inch of emptiness still separated them, but the heat from his body crossed the space. He reached out and cupped her face with both hands. Callused fingertips brushed her cheek. A shiver of anticipation shot down Jayne's spine. Regret followed right behind it. She shouldn't be here.

Her very presence was putting Reed's life in jeopardy.

She pulled back. "I shouldn't be here."

Reed held on. His hands tensed on her jaw. "You could've been in that fire. Or *he* could've caught up with you before me or Nathan."

He kissed the corner of her mouth.

"Reed—"

He silenced her with a finger on her lips. "Please don't go off on your own again. I couldn't take it if something happened to you." His eyes speared hers. "Promise me."

Jayne shook her head.

He bent over her. His lips brushed against her mouth, just a tease, a taste of what was to come. His mouth trailed along the line of her jaw. As her brain protested, her head tilted back to give him more room. Teeth scraped up the side of her neck and Jayne quivered. Hot breath caressed her ear.

"Promise me, Jayne."

"I can't." Hot tears gathered in her eyes. "I shouldn't even be here. Hugh died because of me. Just me being here is dangerous for you and Scott. You *were* in that fire. You could've died right along with Hugh."

He leaned back to meet her eyes. "But I didn't, and Scott's not here. So far, your attacker hasn't taken many risks. He's only stalked you when you were alone. He probably set that fire when the municipal building was empty overnight. I doubt he'll come after you while you're with me."

"But what if he does? Scott needs you."

"I was a cop, Jayne. I can protect us both. What would Scott think of me if I abandoned you? His dad's a coward? Willing to let a woman face a stalker alone to save his own skin?"

Anger heated her cheeks. She jerked her chin out of his hands and stepped away. "This guy's dangerous. He killed Hugh and probably those college boys, too."

"I know." Reed's hands settled on her shoulders. He turned her to face him. His thumbs caressed her collarbones, the calluses rough against her tender skin. "That's why I'm not letting you go until I know you're safe. Really, Jayne, even if you leave, I have to find out who he is. I have to stop him before he hurts someone else."

He inched closer. His mouth pressed against her lips. At the contact, heat blazed through Jayne's belly. The kiss was too much to resist. *He* was too much to resist. Something gave inside of her. She opened her mouth and let his tongue sweep in, hot and demanding.

A burning hand settled on her lower back and pulled her against the hard length of his body. Jayne's hands unclenched, releasing the wool of his sweater from her grasp. Her hands splayed on the firm muscles of his chest. Blood pulsed in her temples, rushed in her ears, and gathered hot between her legs. Unyielding need built like a symphony's crescendo. She hooked a leg around his thigh, hauled him closer, and pressed her center against the ridge in his jeans. His answering groan made her increase the sweet pressure.

"Wait." Reed's request was barely a whisper. His cheek rested against her forehead. "I can't do this. I need to show you something first."

Jayne froze. "Right now? Seriously?"

"Right now." Reed stepped back.

Jayne lowered her foot to the floor. "But…"

"It'll just take a minute. And it's important." After turning off the shower, he took her hand in his and pulled her through the house toward the back door. "Put on your coat and boots."

"OK."

Reed tugged her across the yard to his workshop. Jayne was surprised steam didn't rise off her skin as the cold hit her heated face. Inside, he continued through the first room and opened the door to the storage room. Except it wasn't used for storage. In the center, on a long, low workbench, lay a section of raw wood that resembled a log stripped of its bark. Slender, at least seven feet long, and roughly shaped like a person. A woman. Black dots marked features not yet carved into the pale wood.

Holy—

"I'm R. S. Morgan." Reed stepped toward the table. His hand settled on the wood.

Oh my God. Reed was R. S. Morgan. If the media found out that R. S. Morgan was a man once fingered by the press for murdering his wife, he'd never have a moment's peace. No wonder he kept a low profile. He'd already been skewered by reporters once.

"I didn't want any more secrets between us." Reed turned and pressed his body against hers again. Blood rushed in her ears, drowning out both her shock and her conscience. She should tell him that she'd come here to expose him. But did it matter? Jason could go scratch. There was no way she was outing Reed.

In fact, she was never going to take tabloid pictures again. Seeing what the media had done to Reed's life hammered the offensiveness of her occupation home. She was exactly what he despised the most.

Since she was done with all that, what did it matter?

No secrets.

But would he forgive hers? Could she take the risk? What if the fact that she'd come here on a tabloid assignment to uncover his identity ruined everything?

Regret passed through her like a tremor.

"I'm sorry. It's cold in here. Let's go back in the house." He tugged her back through the door and across the frozen yard. All the way back to the master bathroom. They shed their outerwear en route, leaving a trail of coats and boots on the hardwood. The bathroom was still steamy and it only took seconds for hot water to pour from the showerhead. Reed took that brief span of time to step closer. His hand slid up her arm.

Jayne's heart thudded against her breastbone. Hunger shot through her belly. Her hands clenched in the loose knit of his sweater and pulled him closer. Heat from his body rose through the wool. Jayne leaned closer and breathed him in. He smelled like soap and man. The hint of smoke reminded her of the panic she'd felt when she'd thought he had died in the fire.

But here he was. Alive. Breathing. Touching her. Being touched.

Everything else faded before the wonder of the moment.

His hands slid to her shoulders, smoothed her biceps and forearms, and settled on her hips. He grasped the hem of her sweatshirt and slowly raised it over her head, dropping it to the floor at her feet. She wasn't wearing anything underneath. She hadn't had a chance to change into her own clothes since they'd retrieved her things at the inn.

His eyes roamed over her breasts. Her nipples puckered as if he'd touched them.

But he didn't. Not yet.

He unbuttoned her jeans, dropped to one knee, and drew them down her thighs. A breath hissed out of his mouth. Since she'd drawn the line at borrowing boxers, she'd gone commando there as well.

Inches from her sensitive skin, he inhaled and closed his eyes as if the smell of her was intoxicating, irresistible, and delicious. He exhaled, the breath hot on her thighs as he licked his lips.

"I wanted to worship you the first time I saw you." Green eyes, dark and intense with desire, looked up at her. "I'd never seen anything so beautiful."

Reed moved down, sliding the jeans to her ankles. He cupped each foot and gently worked the fabric over her heel. The jeans joined the rest of Jayne's clothes on the floor.

Reed's eyes caressed her from her feet up, sliding up her legs, pausing on the juncture of her thighs, before roaming up to her breasts.

Steam filled the room as he stripped off his shirt and pants without the finesse he'd shown disrobing Jayne. He stood naked in front of her in seconds, all sleek muscles and smooth skin on display for her. But he gave her no time to savor the view. He reached under the vanity for a condom and set it on the top of the shower door. His hand settled on her waist and he steered her into the shower.

Jayne ducked under the spray. Hot water cascaded over their bodies as Reed pulled her close. His hard body pressed against her breasts, belly, and thighs. She pressed a kiss to his chest and tasted smoke. Her hand closed around a bar of soap. She leaned back a few inches and slid it across his chest. With soapy hands, she explored his body, washing away all traces of the morning's horrors from his skin. Reed's head tipped back, and a low rumble of pleasure came from deep in his chest.

When she brought the bar to her own body, his hand closed over her hand. "Let me." Hoarseness invaded his voice.

Callused hands lathered every inch of her body. He knelt to massage her arches and slide his fingers between her toes. Then he worked his way up her legs, kneading her calves, sliding up the inside of her thighs and around to cup her buttocks. A moan bubbled from her throat.

Jayne's legs parted for him, hot and aching for his touch.

The heat and his hands mesmerized her. She could think of nothing but the feel of his fingers on her skin, anticipating where he'd touch her next. Every beat of her heart pushed desire through her veins like a drug. She couldn't see. She couldn't hear anything but her own blood pounding in her head, pulsing between her thighs. Only he could make her blood hum, her body turn limp and helpless with need. For him. Only him.

His hands slid around her hips to her belly and moved up to cup her breasts. His fingers teased her already hard nipples. She splayed her hands on his pectorals. His heart pounded against her palms. She slid her hand down his flat stomach.

A low groan sounded from his throat as she closed her hand around the hard length of him. Reed trembled against her. "Jayne."

He backed her against the shower wall, the tile cool against her heated skin.

Jayne's palms sought his shoulders for balance as he pulled one of her legs around his hip. Thickly muscled thighs pressed against the inside of Jayne's legs. Her fingers dug into the hard muscles of his back as he worked himself slowly inside her. Too slowly. Jayne arched. "More. Now. Please, Reed. I need you."

"Easy," he whispered along the cord of her neck and rested his head against her temple.

With a sharp intake of breath he grasped her hips and moved against her, thrusting deep. He filled her completely, and they both groaned at the exquisite sensations.

Reed set a slow, teasing pace. Pleasure pierced her with each deliberate thrust. She clutched him harder to her, unable to get close enough. Tension mounted, grew, and swelled inside her, dragging another guttural moan from her lips.

"Come for me, Jayne," Reed breathed against her ear, his voice throaty, raw with need. He buried his face in the crook of her neck. His fingers dug into her hips as he pounded into her.

Jayne's heart raced forward. Her lungs heaved, and she rocked into him. The orgasm built from her toes and ripped through her entire body. It subsided in waves as Reed surged.

His body jerked, and a spasm ripped through his muscles. With a mighty animal-like growl, he sagged against her. The shower spray beat down on their still-joined bodies. Jayne rested her head on his shoulder as her breathing and heart rate slowed.

A hand brushed strands of wet hair from her forehead. Reed tilted her chin upward. His green eyes were filled with tenderness as he planted a soft kiss on her lips. The gesture moved her more than the orgasm. The combination was overpowering.

Jayne shook her spinning head. She felt wrung out, loose, and spent. And freezing cold.

A shiver began at her feet, where the shower pounded on them. His body blocked most of the spray.

"Reed?"

"Hmmm." Two fingers stroked along her hip bone. The rest of him hadn't moved.

"The water's cold."

"Ugh. Sorry." He reached around his back and twisted the knob. Opening the shower door, he stepped out onto the mat and grabbed two thick towels from the rack. He wrapped one around her shoulders and used the other to buff her dry, starting at her feet and ending by gently squeezing water from her hair. After wrapping her in his warm robe, he rubbed a towel briskly over his own skin.

"You're shivering." He wrapped a towel around his lean hips.

Chills that had started in the shower hadn't let up. Her skin erupted in goose bumps.

"I have an idea." He stepped into a pair of sweatpants, scooped her off her feet, and carried her to the living room. He set her on the sofa and with a quick flip of his wrists snapped a blanket from the back of the couch and spread it on the floor in front of the woodstove. A second blanket and a couple of pillows followed. The stove door opened with a squeak. Reed added wood and stoked the fire.

Jayne relocated to the blanket and stretched her fingers toward the stove. Heat soaked into her skin.

Reed latched the door before disappearing into the kitchen. Minutes later he returned with a tray loaded with sandwiches and milk.

Jayne scarfed down half of a turkey-and-cheese on wheat. The sadness and fear from the events of the day still lurked, but making love with Reed had released long-buried tension. Four years' worth. Four years of not trusting anyone enough to get close.

Reed hammered back a sandwich. The phone rang and he reached for it.

"Hello." His eyes narrowed. "Really? Well, that sucks. Yeah, it is weird. I'll tell her. Thanks for calling."

Dread curled up in Jayne's stomach. "How bad is it?"

"Your engine burned up. It's done." Reed took her hand and squeezed gently. "The mechanic thinks something caustic was added to the oil. Maybe bleach. He said the underside of the hood had these strange symbols drawn all over it."

"I don't know why I'm shocked." Jayne set down the remainder of her sandwich. "He did it to keep me here. Just like he cut my tires."

"He still wants you."

"But why? And who is he?" Frustration and fresh fear coiled inside her. "I want to try Pat again."

Reed handed her the phone and retreated to the kitchen.

The call went through on Pat's cell. Her brother's deep voice brought tears to her eyes. Her story came out in a bubbling, incoherent rush, but Pat understood. Pat always understood.

"It couldn't be Jennings, could it?" she asked.

"Nope. Phones here have been wonky for days or I would've called you. Conor saw Jennings hanging around the bar. The cops picked him up for violating the terms of his parole. He had a knife on him. He's back in prison, Jaynie. For as long as they can possibly keep him there."

"I didn't really think it could be him. But I thought I'd ask."

Pat's frustration came through the line. "You don't have to worry about him. Here I thought you were safe."

"I'm sorry, Pat. I'm such a pain in the ass."

"Jaynie, honey, there's nothing to be sorry about. There are a lot of scumbags out there." The angry edge in Pat's voice softened. "I love you, and I'm coming to get you. I'm going to try to get a flight right now. I'll call you back."

Jayne ended the call and stared through the glass door of the woodstove. An ember popped. Logs shifted. Another man coming to her rescue. When was she going to be able to fend for herself? Ever?

"You OK?" Reed sat down next to her, first-aid kit in hand.

"Yeah. Pat's coming." Pressure built in Jayne's chest. "Ty Jennings is back in prison. He broke parole trying to stalk me."

Reed snipped wet bandages off her wrists. Jayne stared at the scabbed-over wounds. Two more reminders of her weakness. "Well, that's good, right? That means you'll be safe at home."

"Unless my kidnapper follows me there. I don't even know what he looks like, Reed. He could be any blue-eyed stranger who walks into the bar." How would she live? She'd never be able to go anywhere alone. She'd be looking over her shoulder, thinking every newcomer was out to get her. She'd go crazy.

"If I hadn't run away, if I'd have stayed home and faced Jennings, none of this would've happened. Hugh would still be alive. You and Scott wouldn't be in danger. I shouldn't have run away. I'm a coward."

"Or Jennings would've hurt you before they caught him." Reed applied fresh bandages, then reached up to stroke the scar on her cheek with the pad of his thumb. "These are battle scars. Cowards don't fight back. Cowards roll over. You're a warrior."

Jayne focused on the clean, white gauze. She bet he wouldn't have said that if he'd known she'd originally come to Huntsville to reveal his identity to the world. Warriors were honest.

No secrets.

CHAPTER TWENTY-THREE

Reed cupped her cheek and lifted her chin. Her eyes avoided contact with his. Was she regretting her decision?

"I know you can't wait to go home. I can't blame you, not with all you've been through here. I'll call you. Visit you in Philadelphia. If that's OK?"

Jayne only nodded. She'd been quiet since they'd made love. Did she think this was a one-night stand?

"Good. I don't do casual sex. I care about you." More than he could verbalize.

The past suddenly seemed so long ago. For the first time in years, he had hope that he could move on with his life, experience happiness without the side of guilt. But hope was an emotional double agent that could turn on him at any time and betray the very heart it bolstered.

Didn't matter. What was done was done. He'd been dragged out into the sunlight. Once he'd experienced its warmth, there was no shoving his soul back underground. All because of the beautiful woman in front of him. The woman who'd lost so much, yet still had something to give to him.

He sunk to the blanket next to her. "Still hungry?"

"No."

Reed moved the dinner tray aside. A feral longing to claim her, to *show* her how he felt, passed through him. He rose onto his knees and crawled over her body.

Jayne fell back onto the blankets. Her robe parted and a pink nipple peeked out from between the lapels. Reed's blood surged to his groin.

Heat from the stove washed over them as his body covered hers. "Well, I am. I barely got a taste of what I wanted."

He pressed his lips to her temple. The scent of his soap on her skin was like a brand. His lips traveled down the side of her face and paused to kiss the scar on her cheek.

He worked his way down her neck to run his tongue along her collarbone. Beneath him, Jayne shivered.

"Are you cold?"

She shook her head.

"Good." Reed nuzzled the robe open, exposing a breast. Soft and full, it fit perfectly in his palm. He plumped it with his hand and licked her nipple into a stiff bead. He went hard as a tire iron in one heartbeat.

She arched toward him. "More."

"No rush." He had one night to show Jayne what she meant to him. She kept saying that he'd rescued her, but in reality she'd saved him from a lifetime of darkness. "We have all night."

He uncovered her other breast and laved it with his tongue. Jayne's fingers twined in his hair, pulling him harder to her. He opened wide and sucked her nipple into his mouth. Jayne groaned, a deep and throaty sound that made his erection throb.

Her warm hand slid down his abs toward the waistband of his pants. Said erection practically crawled toward it.

Much to its dismay, Reed moved lower down her body before she could touch him.

"Come back here." She pouted.

"No way. This time you're going to be the one who loses control."

Jayne's turquoise eyes went wide, then darkened.

Reed sat back on his haunches and untied the sash on the robe. "I feel like I'm opening an early Christmas present." He folded the flannel back to expose her smooth, creamy skin.

"Well, do it faster." Her skin was flushed with heat and excitement. Jayne shifted her legs restlessly. They were long and lean, and Reed's mouth watered.

"I'm going to taste every inch of you." He looked up at her. She sucked her lower lip into her mouth and bit down on it. Watching, a shudder coursed through him.

He started at her ankle and ran his tongue up the length of her calf. His hands followed, stroking up her soft skin. When his mouth found the sensitive spot behind her knee, the breath rasped from her mouth. Blood hummed through Reed's veins, pulsing, throbbing harder in his groin every time she moaned.

Reed's pulse pounded as he cruised up the inside of her thigh. She groaned and scissored her legs. But he continued up to her hip bone and teased her, licking at the dent next to it.

He couldn't hold back any longer. He kissed his way across her pelvis and settled between her legs, pushing her thighs open wider until she was spread out before him like dessert.

Their eyes met. Hers were dark and unfocused.

Perfect.

He explored every inch of softness, paying attention to her whimpers and moans to find just the right spot until Jayne's body quaked with a violent orgasm. Her limbs went pliant and sank back to the floor.

"Jayne, look at me."

Blue eyes opened, dazed.

Reed moved over her and slid inside. She was wet, still tight and throbbing. She bowed back as he thrust forward. His body took over, finally where it wanted to be, so deep inside her he no longer could feel where he ended and she began.

"Reed." Her nails dug into his back, and she clamped around him.

Reed tried to hold back, but her response wrung him out in just a few hard thrusts. The pressure built from his spine. His heart jackhammered. His lungs heaved. He had no choice but to follow her over the edge. It would be like this always. He collapsed on top of her. His limbs twitched as he shuddered with aftershocks.

So much for maintaining control. Jayne made him feel things he'd never before experienced.

He levered onto his side and watched her recover. Her body was limp and damp, flushed all over, tempting him to start again. He would never have enough of her.

The phone rang and Reed reluctantly picked it up. The caller ID screen displayed a Philadelphia exchange. Not trusting his voice, he handed the receiver to Jayne. She answered in a sleepy voice Reed hoped her brother would attribute to actual sleep.

Two minutes later she tossed the phone aside, rolled over, and draped an arm across his chest. Her eyes flickered with regret. "No flights tonight. My brothers are driving up. They'll be here midday tomorrow."

Reed stood and scooped her off the floor. He carried her to his bed and crawled in with her. The sheets were cold. Jayne curled up against his body for warmth. He had only one night to hold her close. He was going to savor every second of it. Regardless of his intentions or the fullness of his heart right now, Jayne had a life halfway down the East Coast, one that didn't include a stalker. Her brother's call confirmed that she'd be much safer at home.

It would be wrong to ask her to stay. He brushed a hand over her hair. But his heart was a selfish bastard. That's exactly what it wanted.

– – –

He descended into the bowels of his house. Even through the soles of his boots, a chill settled into his feet as they hit the concrete.

With skeletal fingers he set a Tupperware bowl containing oatmeal cakes in the box next to a Ziploc baggie of mistletoe pollen. His hands were gnarled, bone-thin from weight loss, and his grip weaker than it should be for a large man.

He retrieved the wooden bowl and set it in the box with the other things for the ceremony. And the note he'd carefully written for his loved ones. If he wasn't saved by the ritual, he didn't want to go on.

No question. No hesitation. No indecision.

He knew what was coming. He'd seen other members of his family waste away. If this didn't work, there'd be no more living for him, just a slow torturous death. Better to die on his own terms, with a shred of dignity. He could start over in the afterlife. Not so awful for him. He was tired of it all, anyway.

He needed to think about his family here on Earth, though. His salvation would be theirs as well. This disease had plagued his kin for generations. There was no reason to think it would end with his death. More hinged on this upcoming ceremony than his own wretched existence. Much more. His bloodline. The suffering of future generations.

A few minutes later he climbed the stairs and closed the basement door. The hinges squeaked. He winced at the noise and shot a look to the recliner in front of the TV. The body sleeping in the comfortable chair didn't stir.

His body ached to sink into blessed unconsciousness. He could no longer remember when he'd last even dozed. Yesterday? The day before?

Would death be a relief? Would he be rid of this disease when he moved on to the afterlife? He could only hope.

He tucked the package under his arm and crept into the mudroom. His heavy outerwear hung neatly on pegs, dry and ready. He shrugged into the parka, ski mask, boots, and gloves. The storm had abated, but he was not so foolish as to ignore winter conditions. His life was in its last season, his time as limited as the remaining days of winter.

He slipped out into the night. Above him, moonlight filtered through blowing clouds. The weather would be cold and clear for the solstice. Tonight he'd check on Jayne, make sure she was safe, and present her with a gift befitting a goddess.

A goddess whose sacrifice could save him. As befitting her station, he must pay homage to her with an offering.

Then he had to get rid of the man who stood in his way, Reed Kimball. As soon as Kimball was dead, Jayne was his.

He opened the shed and started up the snowmobile. The shed was far enough from the house that the engine noise wouldn't wake anyone.

Hopefully, he'd be finished with his quest and back in the house before the rest of the household woke. He turned the machine in the direction of the woods and the game trail that led north, toward Reed Kimball's house.

CHAPTER TWENTY-FOUR

A noise jerked Reed out of a light sleep. In his arms, a sated and exhausted Jayne slept on. Her sleek limbs were curled up, her smooth back pressed into his chest. Reed glanced at the digital clock on the nightstand. Two hours remained until dawn. He listened for a few seconds, then pressed a kiss to her soft shoulder and rested his head on the pillow.

A low growl came from the other room. Where was the dog?

Reed eased away from Jayne and slid out from under the thick comforter into the cold of his bedroom. He stepped into a pair of jeans on his way into the hall. At the threshold to the living room, he paused, eyes searching the dim room.

Sheba stood facing the window. The dog growled again, deep in her throat. She took a stiff-legged step toward the back of the house. Keeping to the shadows, Reed moved to the side of the window and peered through the gap between the blinds and the wall. Behind the glass, darkness shrouded the yard.

His gaze scanned the tree-ringed clearing. Reed could just make out the dark shapes of trees and outbuildings on the all-white background. Something flashed in his peripheral vision. The hairs on the back of his neck tingled as he shifted his line of sight to the corner of his workshop. A dark shape faded into the shadows. Then it was gone.

Reed blinked. Had he imagined it? No. He'd seen something out there. He glanced down at the dog. And so had Sheba. Her ears were still pricked toward the window; her hackles stood on end. But what was outside?

An animal?

He eyed the doorframe above his workshop entrance and estimated the height of the shape was within a foot of the top trim. Deer, elk, moose, and bear were all tall enough.

So was a man.

Tension vibrated down Reed's spine.

Could be nothing. Could be a moose. Hell, it could be his closest neighbor Jim, chasing after his kid's pain-in-the-ass pony again.

But on the other hand...

Reed slipped back into the bedroom and glanced at Jayne, sleeping soundly, her face a perfect, pale oval in the darkness. One slim, bandaged hand poked out of the covers. Resolve solidified in his gut. He wouldn't take the chance that a threat lurked outside. She'd been through enough.

Better safe than sorry.

"Jayne. Wake up," he whispered on his way past the bed.

"Ugh."

He entered the closet and sought the safe on the top shelf. For the first time in five years, he welcomed the weight of the nine-millimeter Glock in his hand. He curled his fingers around the familiar grip and removed the trigger lock before loading the weapon. The magazine slid smoothly into its well and clicked into place. Though he hadn't carried the weapon, he'd practiced regularly and kept the gun clean.

Tucking the gun into his waistband, Reed ducked back into the bedroom and tapped Jayne on the shoulder. The metal was cold on his belly as he leaned over.

Reed tapped her again. "Come on, Jayne. Wake up. It's important."

Reed's sharp whisper caught her awakening attention. She rolled over and blinked up at him. "What?"

"I saw something outside. I'm going to check it out."

"No. Wait." Jayne stumbled out of bed and grabbed his robe from the foot of the bed. She nodded at the gun. "Do you have another?"

"Can you shoot?"

Jayne nodded. Her eyes sharpened. "Oh, yeah."

Reed retrieved his backup piece, a subcompact baby Glock, and pressed it and a magazine into Jayne's outstretched hand. While he tugged a sweater over his head, she checked for a round in the chamber and loaded the weapon with reassuring competence.

Jayne followed him into the mudroom. He slid his bare feet into boots and drew on a parka. Then Reed headed for a little-used side door, where there wasn't an overhead light fixture to highlight his presence. Pointing the barrel at the floor, he pulled back on the slide and released it. The bullet entered the chamber with a comforting *snick*.

The dog butted her head against the closed door and growled. Reed pushed her back. He didn't need her getting in the way, tangling with a bear or whatever else was out there. If he needed to pull the trigger, he didn't want to worry about hitting his dog. Nor did he want her to spoil any element of surprise. In the house, Sheba could protect Jayne. "Stay."

Jayne grabbed her collar and tugged the dog away from the doorway. "Be careful."

Sheba whined. Whatever was out there, she wanted a piece of it.

"Lock this behind me and stay out of sight." Reed stepped off the small stoop. Ice crunched underfoot where the top layer had melted and refrozen. There was no way to walk silently, but he stayed in the shadows as he circled around the house. He stopped at the corner and peered around. Ice pellets blew off the roof and barraged his face.

His workshop sat on the rear of the yard, right at the edge of the trees. A man could move in the thick woods with less difficulty than out in the open, where the drifts were thigh-high. In his dark jacket, he'd be an optimal target against the backdrop of pure white. Reed scanned the area, looking for a place to cross the open space and come up behind the workshop.

He chose a line of shrubs. Adrenaline pumped hot through his veins as he crossed to the trees. Ice crunched underfoot. He exhaled as he stepped behind a mature oak. An intruder would have to be stone deaf not to hear him coming. He, however, didn't hear any indication of a trespasser. Maybe it had been just an animal. Leaning against the fat trunk, he scanned the perimeter. The area behind the workshop was clear.

Reed's eyes moved across the landscape. The yard was empty. Nothing moved in the trees. He approached the workshop from the rear. One glance down at the ground had him ducking behind the building.

A trail of human footprints led from the rear of the outbuilding and disappeared into the forest. As Reed inspected the tracks, the high-pitched whine of a snowmobile engine cut through the night air and faded rapidly.

Shit.

Reed turned and stared back at the house. The ground was elevated slightly behind the shop. From his position, he had a clear view of the entire rear of the house. How long had the man been out here?

The urge to go after Jayne's stalker surged in Reed's veins. The tracks would be easy to follow, but the guy had a whopping head start. Then there was the possibility that the man would double back and ambush Reed.

Or return to the house.

Jayne would be unprotected. She'd be alone, vulnerable. As Madeline had been. Drawing Reed away could be the plan if Jayne's captor really wanted her back—which he obviously did.

The man pursued her with terrifying determination.

Reed's gut clenched as a cold wind blew ice crystals off the workshop roof and dumped them onto his head. Cold water invaded the neck of his coat and slid down his spine. A shiver rode behind it. He circled the house but found no other signs of the trespasser. He listened. Nothing but the wind.

Had he scared the man off for the night?

Reed pivoted and surveyed the yard once more. The clouds shifted and a beam of moonlight fell across the yard. In the tree next to his workshop, something glittered.

Reed backtracked. About six feet up on the tree trunk, something hung. It was circular and shiny. He ducked into his workshop for a flashlight. Hanging on a nail driven into the tree trunk, the object was twisted metal, about eight to ten inches in diameter and open on one end. Reed jogged back to the house. Jayne met him at the side door. The gun was in her hand, ready. He stomped his boots on the porch.

"Well?" She slid the dead bolt home.

"Somebody was out there."

"He knows where I am." Jayne's face went grim.

"Everyone in town knows where you are." Reed clumped into the living room and pulled his digital camera from his desk drawer. "There's something outside, in the tree. I'm going to take a few pictures before I bring it in. Can you find a clean pillowcase in the linen closet and lay it on the kitchen table?"

Jayne shot him a confused look but nodded. "Is he gone?"

"Yeah. I'll be right back." On his way through the kitchen, he snagged the barbeque tongs from the drawer. Reed photographed the strange object before using the tongs to lift it from the tree. It was heavier than he'd expected.

In the kitchen, he laid it carefully on the pillowcase. The gold shone dully against the chocolate-brown cotton. The metal had a lack of definition, a smoothness that suggested centuries of wear.

Like the Celtic coin that had been found under the teenager's remains.

Reed stripped off his coat and tossed it over the nearest chair back. "What do you think it is?"

"I don't know. Looks like something that should be in a museum. Some kind of artifact. Necklace maybe?" Her nose wrinkled as she concentrated on the odd engravings that adorned the dull gold. Small spirals decorated the flattened ends. "These engravings look like those symbols that were all over the basement walls. The same ones he wrote on my car and on the door at the inn."

"What's this?" Reed pointed to the vine wrapped around the metal. Clumps of white berries hung on the greenery. Tucked in the vine were three long black feathers and something that looked like burnt bread or cake. "Except for the feathers and food, it looks Christmasy."

"That's because it's mistletoe." Jayne circled the table to look at the piece from another angle. "So what do we do with it?"

Reed hated his answer before he gave it. "We call Doug Lang." *Unfortunately.*

Jayne's eyes shifted from the metal to Reed. "No, really. What do we do? Doug doesn't like you very much."

"I know. He's afraid I want the chief's job, but we don't have much of a choice. It's evidence. We have to call him. He's the only cop around. He'll at least dust it for prints and call the state police. They have a lot more resources than the small municipality of Huntsville." Reed tilted his head and stared at the object. She was right. It looked as if it belonged in a museum. He glanced at Jayne, who was giving him a you've-got-to-be-kidding look. "But first we take a whole bunch of pictures and measurements so we can find out what the hell this thing is in case Doug sits on it for any length of time."

"That I can do." Jayne took possession of Reed's camera and adjusted the kitchen light. While Reed left a message for Doug, she walked around the table and snapped shots from every conceivable angle while Reed closed the blinds. "What do you think this thing means? Do you think *he* left it for me?" A quiver edged into Jayne's voice. Her eyes looked wet for just a second; then she blinked.

"Yeah. I do. I think this psycho left you a damned present." He quickly told her about the ancient coin.

"That's. Just. Too. Freaky." She sucked in air as if it were courage and pounded a fist against her thigh. "I wish we could figure out who he is. I can't spend my life wondering if every person I meet is going to try to abduct me."

"I know. But 'tall white guy with blue eyes' isn't much to go on." Reed closed the blinds in the kitchen. "With all the Norwegian blood around here, he could be almost anybody."

"I should've ripped off his mask."

"And taken the chance that he'd get a nice, firm hold on you?"

"No." Jayne sighed. "But I wish I'd have gotten one good look at his face."

"Me, too. One thing, though. He's a better woodsman than me, not that that's any great feat. I sounded like a moose crashing through the trees. He didn't make any noise." Reed switched on the light. "I'm going to review Hugh's file on that dead teenager again. Maybe something'll pop out at me."

Jayne turned the lens on Reed and snapped a picture as he turned. He flinched at the click of the shutter.

She lowered the camera. "I'm sorry."

"It's OK. I don't like having my picture taken."

"Understandable." She set the camera on the table. "I'm going to get dressed, then make coffee."

Reed wanted to follow her, to peel the robe from her body and forget all about the outside world for a few more hours. But it was too late. He needed to put some distance between himself and his lovely houseguest in order for his brain cells to reactivate.

Jayne's stalker had been right outside. Less than a hundred feet away while they slept inside—totally helpless. If Reed had been thinking with his brain instead of his hormones, he'd have been awake and standing guard all night instead of curled up with Jayne's naked body. But he'd allowed his emotions and libido to make the call.

That couldn't happen again.

– – –

Jayne set her toilet case on the vanity. Toothbrush. Deodorant. Hygiene basics had become luxury items. She set her makeup case aside and settled for a quick face wash, rinsing with cold water in the hope it would wake her up.

She dug through her duffel bag for a change of clothes, inordinately thrilled to have her own things. Socks and underwear. Squee!

She yanked a T-shirt and sweater over her head and wriggled into her jeans. Sticking her hand into her front pocket to smooth a bulge, she encountered a small rectangle.

Oh my God. She drew it out and stared. *Duh.*

Why hadn't she remembered she'd shoved it in her pocket? Usually she stored memory cards in the zippered pouch of her camera case, but she'd been in a rush to change out of her wet jeans. She'd totally forgotten.

She hurried out of the bathroom. "Reed?"

"Yeah." At the kitchen table, he raised his head from the file. He swept the photos he'd been studying back into the manila folder. What didn't he want her to see?

Jayne held up the digital memory card.

He removed his reading glasses and set them on the table. Interest lit his eyes. "Is that what I think it is?"

"Uh-huh. It was in the pocket of my jeans. I totally forgot about changing them after I fell in that puddle." Jayne froze, realization hitting home. "He killed Hugh for no reason. The camera Hugh took was empty."

Reed absorbed that information for a few seconds in silence. "Do you know what's on it?"

"All the pictures I took in town," Jayne said. "I can't imagine any of them being incriminating or scandalizing in any way. Most of them were just old buildings and scenery."

"Cross your fingers. This could be our first real break." He retrieved the laptop from the living room and booted it up. Jayne stuck the memory card into the SD slot. The computer's media viewer opened at Reed's click. "If we're right, Hugh was killed for something on this card."

Jayne's eyes filled. She blinked hard to clear them. Hugh had died for no reason.

"Three hundred pictures?"

"That's about right," Jayne said. "No reason to limit myself with digital media."

Reed clicked the Download button. "I wouldn't think there were three hundred things to photograph in town."

"If I like a subject I might take a few dozen pictures of it. Multiple angles, shutter speeds, apertures. There are filters and effects to play with. Light and shadow. Different types of focus."

While the computer chugged away, Reed poured her a cup of coffee. "Are you hungry?"

"No, thanks." Jayne's stomach was doing somersaults. No way could she eat anything until she found out what was on that memory card. "Anything in the file?"

"Not yet." Reed moved back to the page he'd been reviewing when Jayne entered the kitchen. He froze, frowned, then flipped back a few pages. His finger tapped a photocopied report. "Wait a minute. That cannot be a coincidence."

Reed's eyes darted back and forth between the folder and the gold circle laid out in the center of the table. "In addition to the two-thousand-year-old coin, crow feathers were found around and under the body. Normally that wouldn't be unusual. Birds are scavengers. The body was found in the woods. Stranger things turn up at outdoor crime scenes. But..." They both looked at the odd metal circle, with its mistletoe and feather adornments. "There's nothing normal about this case."

The computer emitted a soft chime.

"The pictures are ready to view." Jayne sank into a chair and opened the folder.

CHAPTER TWENTY-FIVE

"I don't see anything exciting." Reed sighed and scrolled through another set of pictures. "Lots of old buildings. Trees. Maybe we're on the wrong track. These pictures are as boring as the town. No offense."

"None taken." Jayne reached for the laptop. "Let me have another go through."

"Wait." Reed squinted at the screen. A small dark shape lingered in a stretch of woods. "What's this?"

Jayne leaned over his arm. Her hair brushed his face. "When I took it, I thought it was an animal. Let me blow it up."

Reed rubbed a soft tendril between his fingers. Intent on her photos, Jayne didn't notice. A sexy furrow popped up between her eyebrows as she frowned at the image. She tapped the keyboard. "It's a man, I think."

Reed reminded himself to back off and released her soft curl. He needed to focus on her case. He needed to put some space between them. But he wanted her to stay.

Shit. This wasn't going well.

He blinked hard and concentrated on the image. Jayne's life could be at stake. "Do you remember where you were when you took it?"

"Yeah. I was pumping gas. These trees are across the field behind the station near the edge of town." She clicked the mouse a few more times, zooming and centering. "OK. This is weird. He's wearing an ankle-length hooded coat. Does that look like fur to you?"

"It does. And he's carrying something." Reed stood and circled behind her. He rested his palm on her shoulder and leaned closer to the screen. Close enough to get a sweet whiff of the floral scent in her hair.

He studied the strange man in the picture. Odd. It seemed he was wearing a robe rather than a coat. Reed pointed to the man's head. "Can you lighten this part here? His face is shadowed by the hood."

"Not with this software. I had a more powerful program on my laptop." Jayne went quiet and slouched in the chair. Her hand went to the back of her neck and she winced.

Unable to resist, Reed rubbed her nape and shoulders with one hand. The muscles were knotted under his fingertips. Her laptop was likely a very expensive piece of melted plastic, but he had no doubt Jayne was thinking about Hugh, not her computer. "Can you download something that'll do the trick?"

"Probably." She rolled her neck on her shoulders, switched to the browser window, and opened Google.

Reed stepped away from the table—away from Jayne—and refilled his coffee cup. The first sip burned all the way down. His stomach was on fire from too much coffee, and not enough sleep or food. He chewed four Tums and washed them down with another swallow. Sleep wasn't going to happen anytime soon. Cooking would give his hands something to do besides touch Jayne. "I need breakfast. Eggs?"

"Fine." Jayne gave him an absent nod without taking her eyes off the screen. "This'll take a few minutes to download."

The phone rang as Reed poured a half-dozen beaten eggs into the frying pan. He glanced at the caller ID display. "Doug."

"Blech."

"I know he's a jerk but we need his help."

"Hey, I wasn't the one who royally pissed him off in Doc's office." Jayne crossed her arms over her chest and leaned back in the chair. "And thanks for that, by the way."

"Sorry. I was a little strung out," Reed said. "But you weren't exactly Miss Congeniality."

Jayne huffed. "I tried, but he is a serious button-pusher. It's a shame because the whole victim process is easier if the cops don't hate you."

Reed's heart squeezed at the reminder of her past. No matter how many times karma knocked her down, Jayne got to her feet and forged ahead.

Reed punched the Talk key and gave Doug the rundown on what they'd found. To his surprise, Doug responded, "Fine. I'll pick it up in ten minutes." The phone went dead in Reed's ear.

"Doug's on his way." Reed whipped a few more eggs and added them to the pan. Then he slapped four pieces of bread in the toaster and threw some bacon in the microwave. By the time Sheba announced the cop's arrival, breakfast was ready. Maybe a meal would make Doug more amenable. Reed had been a cop long enough to know that as much as Doug wanted to be chief, this wasn't what he'd planned. Doug's personality made it difficult to pity him, but the cop's life was going to suck for quite some time.

Reed swung the door open. Doug stood on the step. His snug uniform was wrinkled. Dark circles underscored his eyes. The smudges on his face and the smoky scent that wafted off him indicated he'd likely been at the scene all night and hadn't been home since the fire.

"OK, Reed. Let's see it. I don't have all day."

Reed breathed and bit off a response. He couldn't expect Doug to be in a good mood, not after the last twenty-four hours. Still, this was going to be harder than he'd thought. "Come on in."

Doug stepped through the doorway.

Reed led him back into the kitchen. "Hungry?"

Surprise, then suspicion, crossed Doug's face. "Uh. Sure. Thanks. I was just on my way home to shower and grab some clean clothes. Been at the scene and on the phone with the state and county police most of the night."

"Good." Reed poured coffee and set a plate of food on the kitchen table across from Jayne. "Don't be afraid to ask them for help."

"Thanks, but I know what I'm doing." Doug gave Jayne a cool nod. "Miss Sullivan."

"Officer Lang." Jayne's response was polite but chilly enough to frost a beer mug. She returned to her software download, leaving Reed to make nice.

Doug pulled out the chair and sank into it. He two-handed the mug and Reed nearly felt sorry for him.

Be careful what you wish for…

Reed set a glass of orange juice in front of the cop.

"Thanks." Doug forked eggs into his mouth with an appreciative grunt. Reed waited the entire three minutes it took Doug to clean his plate, then Reed refilled the cop's coffee cup.

"Is that it?" At Reed's nod, the cop leaned forward to study the metal object. "Any idea what it is?"

"None," Reed said. "Looks like it belongs in a museum to me."

Doug used his fork to point to the engravings on the flattened end pieces. "What are those symbols?"

"No idea. That looks like a spiral."

"How about this one?" Doug indicated a spot nearly worn smooth. The shape was barely visible.

"I didn't see that one." Reed squinted at the faint mark and reached for his reading glasses. He glanced over at Jayne. She was focused on the computer screen, her chin rested in her hand. "Jayne, what do you think?"

She looked up from the laptop. Her eyes darted to Reed, then Doug. "What?"

"Take a look at this symbol," Reed prodded. "What do you think it is?"

Jayne adjusted the light over the table. Dull gold gleamed. "Could it be a pentagram?"

Doug's brow wrinkled. "And it had the mistletoe wrapped around it with the feathers and cake when you found it in your tree?"

"Yeah. I have pictures." Reed braced himself for the criticism.

"You shouldn't have moved it." And there it was.

"I didn't know what it was."

"You knew it didn't belong there."

Reed swallowed his irritation. "This thing reminds me of the ancient Celtic coin found under that teenager's body."

"Shit. I hope you're wrong." Doug lifted a tired shoulder. His eyes shifted to the metal circle and worry creased his face. "I don't like this at all. Looks like some freaky occult thing. I'm going to send this to the state lab. Maybe they have experts who can make some sense of it. I don't even have a friggin' office. At minimum they can tell us what it is and take prints from it."

Jayne reached for a piece of toast. "Any word on what started the fire?"

Doug's mouth went tight. "Point of origin was Hugh's space heater. So far it looks accidental."

"You don't really believe that, do you?" Reed asked.

"I won't believe anything until I get the final report." Doug's head shot up. His face was flushed with red spots. "But if it looks like a horse and smells like a horse, I don't have time to go lookin' for a zebra."

A bonfire flared in Reed's gut. "Jayne was attacked twice. Her photographic equipment and purse were in Hugh's office. Don't you think the fire was a pretty big coincidence?"

"Coincidences do happen."

My ass, thought Reed. "You're going to blow off the similarity between this thing"—he nodded at the gold object—"and an artifact recently found under a corpse?"

"I will not ignore it once it's been corroborated by an expert. Look, I'll pass your concerns on to the fire marshal, Reed. But there isn't much else I can do if there's no evidence of arson." Doug folded the pillowcase over the objects and slid the whole package into a paper evidence bag. He stopped and turned toward Reed with a tight-ass frown. "Look. If you want to do some research, there's this occult store down on Route 31 in Greenville. Maybe the lady who runs it would know what this all means." He waved a hand over the bag. "I don't have the time."

Reed drew back in surprise. Doug offering information? Was there hope for him? "Jayne and I can run down there this morning."

Doug nodded stiffly. "Let me know if you come up with anything. If I hear anything on the prints, I'll give you a call. Are you going home, Miss Sullivan? Or shacking up with Reed indefinitely?"

Jayne bristled. Reed touched her shoulder. Any hope that Doug's attitude could change went down the drain.

"My brothers are coming to get me later today." Although her jaw was clenched, Jayne's tone was miraculously civil. "Have you found the farmhouse where I was held?"

"No. With the fire and Hugh's death, I haven't had two minutes to spare." Doug stood. "Well, I guess that's that. I'll contact you if we get any leads on your case."

But don't hold your breath.

"You know, Doug." Reed pointed at the evidence bag. "Crow feathers were found at the crime scene with that teenager's body."

Doug's face flushed. "Don't go into that again. That kid died of exposure unless I get an official statement from the medical examiner saying otherwise. And it's hardly unusual to find bird feathers outside. If and when the ME tells me the cases are related, I'll treat them like they're related."

Reed didn't reply as Doug stomped out the front door.

Doug didn't even want to give Jayne's case five minutes, let alone enough time to uncover any leads. Plus, the cop was determined to ignore any link between the crimes. In Reed's experience, coincidences weren't all that common. The kid's death, Jayne's abduction, and the fire were all related. Reed just didn't know how or why. But Doug was right. Occult cases were disturbing.

"Reed," Jayne called from the kitchen.

"Did you get it to work?"

"No. I'm going to e-mail it to a friend of mine and see if she can do something with it. She's a whiz with editing photos and has all the latest software." Jayne tapped the keys much harder than necessary.

Reed stopped next to her chair. He itched to lean down and rest his forehead against her temple. But he didn't. Space was what he needed. And a clear head. Besides, it was going to be hard enough when she walked out his door later that day. If he let her get any more entrenched in his heart, it would crack in two the moment she left. "You OK?"

"Yeah." She breathed out a long sigh. "I don't want to go home without knowing who is after me. It'll never be over."

Reed inhaled the scent of her. He didn't want her to go home period. But, putting his selfishness aside, she'd be safer at home. Even if she could stay, her family ties to Philadelphia were strong. He doubted she'd leave her brothers to live out in the middle of nowhere with him. She'd be miserable. Jayne was a city girl. She'd miss her family, and he couldn't ask that kind of sacrifice from someone he'd known for a weekend.

No matter how much his chest ached at the thought of never seeing her again.

The least he could do was ensure she was safe. Doug could kiss his ass. Reed would continue to work on Jayne's case after she left. With Doug determined to wait on official reports, the case was going stale fast.

Careful not to touch her, Reed reached over and Googled the occult store in Greenville. "Wiccan Ways is about forty minutes away. If we leave now, we can be there when the store opens and get back here well before your brothers arrive."

"OK. Pat said he'd call my cell when they were a couple hours away." Jayne stood and stretched her long, lean body. Reed's hand twitched to stroke her torso, but he resisted. He could make love to her every day and never be sated. Better to make a clean break.

She was leaving in a matter of hours.

A few minutes later Jayne stepped out onto the salt-dusted stoop. The sky was a clear winter blue, the air thin and brisk as it chilled her nose and cheeks. Reed followed a few feet behind her as they walked on the path to the truck.

As Jayne reached for the car door, Reed slipped on a patch of ice. The loud crack of a rifle shot snapped through the air. Splinters of wood exploded from the cedar siding behind him.

CHAPTER TWENTY-SIX

Jayne's heart vaulted into her throat. Before the shot's echo faded into the woods, Reed launched his body at her. The air hissed out of her lungs as his shoulder slammed into her midsection. Her martial arts training kicked in and she executed a sloppy forward fall, slapping the frozen ground and spreading the impact evenly from her hands to her elbows. The move saved her from broken wrists, but her forearms still stung.

Reed crawled up her body and pressed her down next to the driveway.

"What was that?" she breathed over her shoulder. His breath warmed her ear as cold seeped into her body from underneath.

"Rifle shot." Reed's weight on her back shifted.

Black metal flashed in Jayne's peripheral vision. *Reed is armed.*

He whispered in her ear. "We're in a bad spot here. I can't see anything over those banks. We're going to move forward so we're between the truck and the house. Stay low." Reed lifted himself into a crouch. "Get behind the engine block."

Jayne crawled to the paved drive. Reed followed closely, his back pressed to hers, obviously using his own body as a human shield. Annoyance warred with gratitude at the gesture. Jayne knelt behind the front end of the Yukon. Reed rose on his knees and peered over the hood.

Another shot rang out. The bullet hit the house behind his head with a spray of cedar chips.

Reed ducked. "Son of a bitch!"

He leveled his gun over the hood and squeezed off two rounds into the woods. Though she knew it was coming, the quick *pop pop*, loud as firecrackers, still made Jayne flinch.

"See how the bastard likes return fire."

They listened for several long minutes. No sound came from the woods except the occasional plop of melting snow dropping from sun-warmed tree limbs. Then the distant whir of an engine turning over broke the silence. The rumbling faded fast.

"Sounds like he doesn't like it very much." Reed scanned the trees. "I'm pretty sure he's gone, but just in case, stay in front of me. We'll run up to the house. Don't run in a straight line."

Jayne hoped he was gone, too. She estimated the distance from the truck to the house as approximately twenty feet, a flipping marathon if someone was pointing a rifle at you.

"Let's go." Reed shoved her in a jagged line toward the front door, keeping his body between Jayne and the threat in the woods. "Move."

The few seconds it took them to run up the front walk seemed to pass in slow motion. Reed pinned her against the house and then behind the storm door until he unlocked the door, and they both stumbled across the threshold. He reached back and clicked the dead bolt into place.

"Stay down," he ordered as he pushed her onto her hands and knees. They crawled into the kitchen and sat down with their backs against the refrigerator while Reed called the police.

Someone had shot at her! Just when she thought she'd been through it all, *wham*, something new bulldozed into her life to scare the bejesus out of her.

Her lungs expanded in short, fast pants like a bellows. Her ears rang. Dark spots appeared around the edges of her vision. A few seconds later she was breathing into a paper bag Reed was holding over her nose and mouth.

"Slow breaths." His hand moved in a circle between her shoulder blades.

It took several deep breaths into the bag before Jayne's head cleared. She pushed it away from her face. "I'm sorry. That was the first time I've been shot at."

"Nothing to be sorry about. Only an idiot wouldn't be scared."

Jayne's stomach was still on the Tilt-A-Whirl, but her head had stopped spinning.

"What now?"

"Now we wait for Doug." The cordless phone on the floor shrilled and they both jumped.

Reed picked up the handset. "Yeah." His mouth went flat. "That's exactly what happened. Yes, I'm sure. In the driveway. No, we didn't see anybody. No, it's not like the other times. This one came within a foot of my head." He caught Jayne's eye and sighed before he hung up. "Doug'll be here in twenty."

"This has happened before?" Jayne lived in the big bad city, and no one had ever shot at her.

"Not like this. We've had people hunting too close to the house," Reed admitted. "But we've never had anyone shoot *at* the house."

"Oh." She sighed. Her chest collapsed as reality cut through hope like a serrated knife through a rare rib-eye. "For a second I thought maybe it was a coincidence."

Reed took her hands. His palms heated her numb flesh as he spoke the words that needed to be said, the ones that clarified the situation to the last remaining shred of denial.

"Looks like your stalker's changed his mind. He doesn't want to kidnap you. He wants you dead."

– – –

Jayne crossed her arms over her chest. "I still can't believe Doug blew off the shooting."

"He didn't blow it off," Reed corrected. "He dug the bullet out of the house. It's not his fault there wasn't any other evidence."

"He could've done more." She turned her head to watch the white landscape roll by the passenger window. They passed a green highway sign that indicated Exit 31 for Greenville was two miles ahead.

"Like?"

"I don't know. I'm not a cop. But believing you would be a start."

"The fact is I've had poacher problems for years." A heavy sigh escaped Reed's broad chest. "Doesn't really matter. The ground in the woods was frozen solid. No tire tracks or footprints." He glanced over at her for a second before returning his gaze to the windshield. "I know you're frustrated, and I can't stand the guy either. But honestly, there isn't much else Doug could've done. The shooter was long gone before he arrived, and we didn't see a thing."

"I know." Didn't mean she wasn't annoyed, though. She did not want to go home with this threat hanging over her head. How would she live? Her brothers would escort her everywhere. She'd escaped her kidnapper only to be a virtual prisoner. Unless this guy abducted someone else and was caught, something she couldn't wish for with a clear conscience, she was SOL.

She already knew what it was like to have this kind of threat hanging over her head for an extended period. The six months she'd waited to testify had been brutal. She'd been unable to let her guard down for a second. She'd given up her apartment, her independence, and her privacy to move in with Pat. With his wife and three kids, Jayne was lucky to sneak into the bathroom alone.

She couldn't live like that again. She'd hoped to move out of Pat's house at some point. Despair ripped through her chest; her anguish was compounded by the thought of leaving Reed. After tonight, who knew if they'd ever see each other again? With the danger and upheaval she'd brought to him and Scott, she had no place in their lives—unless they could find her stalker.

Reed slowed the truck and navigated the exit. Jayne snapped out of her mood before the SUV hit the local road. Self-pity was a waste of time. Her energy was better spent trying to figure out who was after her.

A few miles later, they turned into a strip center. Wiccan Ways occupied the end unit in a row of half a dozen stores. With a brick front and sign scripted in Old English type, it matched all the others in the row and could've easily been a gift or clothing shop instead of a shop for freaky Halloweeny stuff.

A digital chime announced their entry. Inside, the store wasn't as exciting as Jayne had expected. Instead of a smoky haze and chanting, the store was bright. An instrumental flute piece floated softly from overhead speakers. Most of the stock ran to candles, incense, and crystals, lined up on neat displays. The cacophony of scents assaulting her nasal passages reminded her of the candle store in the mall. Bookcases brimmed with volumes on the occult. There was a definite focus on nature, healing, and divination, along with an entire section for almanacs and books on astral projection.

"May I help you?" A short sixtyish woman hurried from a back room, brushing her hands onto her jeans as she spoke. She looked entirely too normal to be running a Wicca supply store. No black robe, no pointy hat, no warts. She tucked a hunk of her limp beige pageboy hair behind her ear. Instead of old-lady perfume, she smelled like lemon and rosemary. "I'm Ellen Dean."

"Are you really a witch?" The words popped out of Jayne's mouth like a rude burp as curiosity hijacked her common sense. In her peripheral vision, Reed's eyes did an exasperated roll.

Ellen cocked her head and indulged Jayne with the tolerant smile of a nursery-school teacher. "Not in the fly-on-a-broom, turn-people-into-toads sense. But my sister and I have been practicing the Craft all our lives. Our coven meets at the senior center. I used to be a high-school librarian. Glenda and I opened this shop when I retired. This is so much more fun than shushing teenagers and shelving books all day."

"We're trying to identify a couple of symbols. We thought an expert on the occult might be able to help." Reed smoothed over Jayne's flub with a Southern-gentleman routine. His accent thickened and his manners went to antebellum formal. The old lady practically simpered as he introduced them, turning his masculine charm on full blast and clasping her fragile, blue-veined hand between his strong palms.

Flattery will get you everywhere, Jayne thought as Ellen blinked up at his handsome, significantly younger face. There was no denying Reed's hottie factor. For the AARP set, he'd be a boy toy.

He drew the five photos from his pocket and laid them on the glass counter.

"Sure, let me take a look." Ellen picked up the first picture and tapped on the image.

"What is it?" Jayne asked.

"A torc." The storekeeper pointed to the metal circle with her forefinger.

"Huh?"

"A necklace of sorts. The Celts wore them, so did a few other European cultures in the same time period." In full librarian mode, Ellen pulled a pair of glasses from her pocket, set them on her face, and snapped on a light next to the register. She squinted at the photo. "This looks real. Where did you find it?"

"It was a gift." Reed smiled. Ellen smiled back.

"Does it have any meaning?" Jayne asked.

"It was a sign of nobility. Warriors also wore them. This one looks like gold. If it is, it would have belonged to a person of high social rank."

"Does mistletoe have any significance?" Reed flashed her the pearly whites one more time.

Ellen responded with a flush, as any normal woman with a beating heart would have. "Mistletoe was sacred to the Celts' priests, the Druids. It stood for life and fertility. Our custom of decorating with mistletoe at Christmas comes from the Druid tradition of cutting mistletoe at the winter solstice. It's still used in many pagan ceremonies."

"Wow." Reed beamed. "It looks like we came to the right place."

A blush spread across Ellen's crepe-paper cheeks as she pointed at the photo. "The winter solstice ceremony isn't as nice as the summer celebration. The weather in June is much kinder to these old bones. We do the whole ritual sky-clad." She leaned closer to Reed and lowered her voice to a whisper. "That's in the buff."

"Errr." Reed coughed. "Really?"

Ellen's penciled-in eyebrows did a little shimmy. "It's liberating."

"I bet it is. Sounds like fun." Jayne swallowed a snicker. "Doesn't it, Reed?"

Reed shook his head like an overturned Etch A Sketch, no doubt trying to erase the image of a baker's dozen Social Security recipients dancing around the woods in their birthday suits.

"Don't get me wrong, tonight's ceremony will be lovely. You're welcome to join us." Ellen directed her invitation to Reed, of course.

Reed's smile was noncommittal. "I thought tomorrow was the solstice?"

"We actually start the celebration tonight at sunset." Ellen's mauve-tipped finger lingered on a close-up of the torc. "What's this?"

Reed leaned sideways to view the picture with her. Their shoulders brushed. Behind the horn-rims, Ellen batted her frigging eyes. Jayne fought the urge to roll hers. But Reed was in full get-information mode, working the old lady with shameless and, Jayne supposed, harmless flirting. Ellen was going to have quite a story to tell ol' Sis over supper.

"Hmmm." Reed flattened his lips thoughtfully and gave the storekeeper the undivided attention of those intense green eyes. "We're not sure. Some kind of bread or cake. It was very grainy and a little burned. These black feathers were stuck in there, too."

Ellen ripped her gaze off Reed's eyes and concentrated on the picture. "Crows and ravens are omens to modern Wiccans. Dark omens. To the ancient Celts, a crow or raven foreshadowed death."

Reed's face flickered with brief alarm. "What about the bread?"

"I imagine it's oatcake, or bannock, a traditional celebratory dish. The torc, the cake, and the mistletoe all point toward a Christmas or winter solstice holiday celebration, likely Wicca or Druid. But the crow feathers. I don't know how they fit in with the rest. Doesn't make sense. The winter solstice is a time of rebirth, of coming from the darkest day into the light. Crows signify the opposite, darkness, misfortune, bad luck." Ellen turned her palms up in logical defeat. "Who knows?"

"You don't see a dark, sinister meaning behind all this?" Reed waved a hand over the photos.

"Look, paganism gets a lot of bad press, but all the term really means is one of the primitive non-Christian religions. There are many different religions within paganism, including Wicca, Druidism, Native American shamanism, and voodoo. Satanism is one very small sect within the large group. Wiccans and Druids are peaceful. Their gods are tied to the natural world. They worship water and forest deities. Celebrate the seasonal changes. It's all very organic."

"How about these engravings?" Jayne butted in. Reed shot her an annoyed look. Ellen didn't spare her a glance, but Jayne insisted. "That looks like a pentagram."

Ellen's eyes stayed on Reed as she gave Jayne's comment an indulgent head-shake-and-sigh combination. "The pentagram also gets a bad rap. It has nothing to do with evil spells. It's a symbol of protection for Wiccans. The points represent the four natural elements plus one more spiritual one." She paused. One blue-veined finger traced the repeated spiral pattern. "The spiral is a symbol for power and the natural cycle of the world, for life, death, and rebirth. Mother, maiden, and crone. All of these markings are common for the time. There's nothing inherently evil about them." Ellen hesitated. "But the crow feathers…They make me uncomfortable. Did you know that a group of crows is called a murder?"

– – –

Reed opened his laptop. "Great. There's a wireless signal here."

Jayne's phone vibrated on the chrome-edged table. She pressed the OK button. Her eyes swept the display.

"Pat says he won't be here until evening. A bridge washed out in New York State. Big detour." Jayne set the cell down between their place settings.

Reed turned the computer to face her. He'd have her a few more hours. A heavy ache settled in his chest. He was torn at the prospect of Jayne's leaving. On one hand, while she was in his sight he was positive she was OK. On the other, there was the strong likelihood she'd be safer in Philadelphia. No promises there, though. The bastard seemed determined to have her. What would keep him from following her back home?

Not a damned thing.

He had no way to keep her safe no matter where she lived. The pressure against the inside of his rib cage amplified. He reached into his pocket for a roll of Tums and popped three into his mouth. Despite his broken promises to his son, Reed wouldn't, couldn't stop until he found her tormentor. He doubted he'd sleep again until the guy was caught and Jayne was safe.

"Reed, you OK?"

His response dried up in his tight throat as he chewed the antacids. Ice water didn't improve the nasty fake mint taste in his mouth. All he managed was a nod as he swallowed his fear along with the chalky wash.

"OK then." Her eyes lit up like aquamarines in the sunlight. "I'm online. Thanks to our favorite old witch, at least we've confirmed my personal weirdo has a fixation on the ancient Celts or Druids or both and is probably planning some sort of ceremony."

Reed peered over the screen as she two-finger-typed the words *Celt*, *bannock*, and *mistletoe* into a Google search and tapped the Enter key. "What came up?"

Her face creased into a studious frown. "A couple articles on winter solstice ceremonies and some links on bog bodies, whatever they are."

Reed paused. A memory flickered. "Why does that sound familiar?" He turned the laptop sideways for a better view.

"You're familiar with bog bodies?" Jayne's eyes widened.

"I think I saw a documentary on bodies found in peat bogs in Great Britain." Reed scrolled down the list for a site that looked legit. He glanced up at Jayne's amused expression. "What? The winter is long and cold up here."

"If you say so."

"Aha. I knew it. I saw this on TV." Reed gave himself a mental head smack. "I guess I just verified my geek status."

"Don't worry about it." Jayne's hand landed on his shoulder.

Contact with her palm felt solid and right, as if she was what he'd been missing all his life. Reed's hand moved toward hers, automatically wanting to confirm the physical connection. He stopped the movement halfway. His fingers curled and he lowered his fist to the table. Wrong time. Wrong place. Wrong everything. It wasn't meant to be.

Hurt flashed in Jayne's eyes, dropping another brick onto the load on Reed's chest. But separation was necessary. She needed to get away from Huntsville, at least until this guy was caught. Her safety had to be the top priority. But the pain in her gaze nearly shattered his resolve. He wanted nothing more than to gather her in his arms and keep her there forever.

He tore his gaze away and turned back to the computer. The screen blurred. Reed squeezed his lids tight for a second to clear his vision, then clicked the link. The computer chugged for a few more seconds before the window opened.

He scanned the article, the details of the TV special flooding back. "There it is. Every once in a while, an ancient body turns up in a peat bog in England or Ireland. The most famous recent one is Lindow Man. Scientists found mistletoe pollen and charred bread in his stomach. Some historians think he was a nobleman sacrificed to ward off the Roman invasion."

When he looked up at Jayne, sadness had been replaced with stoic determination. Her eyes shifted over his shoulder as the waitress set down their order. Reed's ham and Swiss on rye didn't look as appealing as it had sounded five minutes ago.

She turned the laptop around to get a better view of the screen. "Ewww. His skull was crushed, he was strangled, *and* his throat was cut. Overkill, I think."

"Apparently, the Celts thought they'd get the favor of three gods if they killed him three times," Reed said.

"Interesting logic."

"Efficient anyway. I guess they didn't want to knock off all the noblemen."

"What do you think it means?" Jayne yanked the toothpicks out of her club sandwich. "To my kidnapper, I mean."

"I don't know. Mrs. Dean said mistletoe and bannock were used in a lot of ceremonies. Could be something as simple as a gift to the object of his obsession."

"Well *that* creeps me out just as much." Jayne picked at her potato chips.

"Me too."

Reed's phone buzzed and skittered across the speckled Formica. He flipped it open. The digital readout told him that school was just letting out. "Just Scott reminding me to pick him up at the Youth Center tonight at six. He's finishing his community service for his college applications." Reed texted back. *R the apps done?*

Scott's answer came back in the blink of an eye. *Yeah :)*

"They need to get mailed out this week." Reed crossed mental fingers and set the phone on the table. He tried a bite of the sandwich. Being empty wasn't going make his stomach feel any better. "I don't understand why he waits until the last minute for everything."

Jayne laughed. "At least he's doin' it."

"Good point." Scott's college applications were the least of his worries at the moment. A killer was loose in Huntsville. At least his son was safe with the crowd that would be at the Youth Center today. But the ham and rye bread still landed in Reed's stomach like a cannonball. "Any e-mails from your photo-magical friend?"

Jayne clicked the e-mail icon. "No. Not yet."

Reed reached up and scratched the tingle riding up the back of his neck. Jayne was with him. She was fine. So why the impending-doom itch? Whatever the reason, he was too twitchy to sit still.

Jayne's plate was nearly clean.

Reed signaled for the waitress. "Let's head back."

The bad feeling stuck with him, and it wasn't just all this strange Celtic stuff Jayne's assailant was apparently into. Reed's gut had been very reliable during his years on the force. No matter how he rearranged the clues in his head, the puzzle wouldn't take shape. Something was missing. Something vital. Something that meant the difference between life and death.

If only Reed could figure out what it was before it was too late.

CHAPTER TWENTY-SEVEN

Jayne grabbed the armrest as the truck careened into a sharp turn on the outskirts of town. "Where're we going?"

"We're going to make a stop at Jed Garrett's place on the way home." Reed slowed the Yukon and stopped at a four-way intersection. "I want to show him where I picked you up. If anyone can tell us every landmark in the area, it's Jed. I don't know why I didn't think of Jed before."

Jayne's gaze lingered on his chiseled profile. Probably he hadn't thought to tap Jed as a resource because he'd been busy keeping her alive. And while Jed seemed to be the town's go-to man for tracking game and other wilderness-related stuff, no one would sculpt him out of bronze deep in thought.

The bisecting road was clear, but Reed didn't depress the gas pedal. "Unless Jed was the one who kidnapped you. He lives alone. He's single. Jed knows his way around the woods. He's young and strong. But I'm not sure he has the gray matter or the malice to pull all this off."

Jayne closed her eyes for two seconds, trying to summon up an image of her attacker's eyes. Her glimpse had been so brief. With her adrenaline roaring like a raging river, she'd barely taken note of blazing blue tightly framed by the black knit of a bala-clava. Not enough to ID anybody. Her assailant could be sitting right next to her and she'd never know it. "What color are his eyes?"

"Brown. Right, it wasn't Jed." His relief was tangible in the confines of the truck. "Good. I'd hate to think Jed would hurt anyone. And if Jed had taken a shot at you this morning, he wouldn't have missed."

That thought should've been more comforting than it was.

A mile down the rutted dirt road, Reed pulled off into a gravel parking area. Jed's cabin sat in the center of a large clearing. Next to the house, half a dozen dogs barked and wagged feathered tails from the runs of their chain-link kennels.

Jed was standing on the porch in jeans and a wool sweater. A yellow Lab sat at his feet. The dog leaned on his legs.

"Hey, Reed. You looking for another dog?" Jed extended a hand.

Reed shook his hand. "No, but if I were, this is where I'd come." He gave the dog a pat on the head. "Good morning, Honey."

The dog shuffled forward to sit in front of Jayne with a paw raised. Her tail thumped on the porch floorboards. Jayne sank to her knees and stroked the pale head. Soft brown eyes gazed up at her as she dropped her hand to scratch Honey's chest.

"I was wondering if you'd do me a big favor, Jed." Reed's voice drew her gaze to his face. He might have been talking to Jed, but his eyes were locked on Jayne as her fingers threaded through the dog's soft fur. Concern shone in his gaze, and warmth settled deep in Jayne's belly.

"What is it?" Jed's question broke the spell.

Reed blinked away. "I'd like to show you where I found Jayne and see if you can figure out where she was held."

"Sure. I got maps inside." Heavy boots clomped across the porch to the door. He held the door open for them. "Coffee?"

"No, thanks." Reed stepped aside to let Jayne through first. Their arms brushed, and an empty ache throbbed through her chest. She wanted to lose herself in his arms again, which was a shame, because in a few hours she'd be with her brothers. Tomorrow she'd be back home.

Her time with Reed would be just a memory. Her old life felt as if it belonged to someone else. How could she have changed so much in only a few days?

"I'm good." Jayne swallowed the emotion thick in her throat as she crossed the threshold. In the middle of Jed's log cabin's decor sat a computer desk and a heap of modern electronics. Surprisingly quiet in his thick-soled boots, Jed moved across the wide-planked floor to a filing cabinet and opened a drawer. He selected a map and spread it out on the thick oak kitchen table.

Reed measured the mile markers and tapped a forefinger on the approximate location. "Right about here. What's within two or three miles?"

Jed rattled off a couple of names Jayne didn't recognize. "And Aaron McCree's place is over here."

Surprise flashed across Reed's face. "Really?"

Jayne stopped in front of the glass-fronted fireplace. "Who's Aaron McCree?"

"Nathan's uncle," Reed said.

"Aaron has cancer. He's living with Nathan while he gets chemo, so the place has been empty for a while." Jed pulled a heavy coat off a wooden peg. "I'm gonna take a ride over and check it out. I'd like to let Nathan know if somebody is squatting in Aaron's place."

Reed nodded. "Good idea. We'll ride along to see if Jayne recognizes the place."

Unease skimmed up Jayne's spine on the drive over. In the passenger seat, she picked at her bandages. Reed reached over and grasped her hand, stilling it. "I won't let anything happen to you."

His palm was warm and solid, tempting her to latch on and never let go. But she didn't. She lifted her gaze to his face. The fresh burns on his jaw reminded her that he'd already taken enough risks for her safety. She had to stand on her own two feet. No more relying on Reed's strength to get her through. After tonight, she would likely never see him again. He pulled his hand away as if thinking the same thing.

"I know." But, along with the skein of sadness, fear wormed its way into her belly. "But if this is the place, it's going to be creepy to go back into it."

If Jed's truck hadn't been in the lead, they would have missed the narrow private road. The entrance was tucked behind a thick stand of evergreens. The Yukon fishtailed with the turn. The road had been plowed but not scraped down to the base, indicating the road was dirt- or gravel-based.

"Who plowed the road?"

"Good question." Reed straightened the SUV.

Without the haze of swirling snowflakes, the surrounding woods hardly resembled the nightmarish landscape of her desperate, panic-stricken flight. She scanned the ground ahead of the truck, but no footprints marred the snow's smooth surface to indicate that she'd run down this road. The storm, and a plow, had erased all evidence of her escape.

The house appeared as they rounded a gentle bend. The square structure hunched against the winter wind in a large cleared area. Gooseflesh rippled up Jayne's arms. She hugged her torso and waited for Reed to park the SUV next to Jed's pickup.

Reed glanced down at the odometer in his truck. "You ran almost two miles in that storm."

Jayne knew it wasn't athletic conditioning or courage that had gotten her through. Sheer terror had carried her such an incredible distance.

"Does it look familiar?"

"Yeah." Might as well get this over with. She reached for the door handle, her resolve collapsing like a Jenga tower.

Reed's voice stopped her movement. "I'm right here with you. OK?"

Words wouldn't form around the salty lump in her throat. All she could manage was a nod as she jumped out of the SUV.

Jed walked ahead, scrutinizing the ground. "Somebody's been here."

Jayne sucked in a breath of bitter wind. The bite deep in her lungs grounded her. In the approaching dusk, the shadow of the house stretched toward her. Oh, this was the right place. Three stories of malevolence were ready to reach out and touch someone.

Her.

"You OK?" Reed stepped up beside her.

The movement jarred her back from her horrific sense of déjà vu. She shook it off. "I'm fine. Let's get this done."

Logically she knew nothing bad was going to happen, but her heart banged against her rib cage as if it wanted out of the crazy body it was trapped in. She approached the door to her prison, the place where she had almost died in a most awful and terrifying way. Her thighs quivered as she paused at the bottom of the porch steps and looked up. Above the porch roof, a large branch had fallen, breaking several windows and ripping away a portion of the gutter like a jagged wound.

Jed tried the door. "Locked. I'll go round back."

"Try not to touch anything," Reed said.

"'Kay." Jed waved over his shoulder.

Jayne stood back. Her feet were rooted to the shoveled walk. She would not be unhappy if the place was locked up tight. She wasn't exactly excited to get back in.

Several minutes passed with no sound from Jed. Boots crunching, Reed started around the back of the building. "I'm going to check on Jed. I'll be right back."

Jayne had no intention of staying out front alone. Bad things happened to the chicks in horror films when they stayed behind while their boyfriends checked things out. She followed Reed, sticking her sneakers in the trench made by his boots. Moisture invaded, but cold feet were way better than having a masked guy with a machete jump out from behind a tree. "Wait up."

Reed paused at the rear corner of the property. "Jed?"

Jayne balanced in his last footprints and peered around his body. Jed stood twenty feet away, facing the house behind them. His eyes and jaw hung open. His face was a mime-white mask.

Reed turned his head to track Jed's gaze. Surprise and horror lit his eyes. Despite the leakage factor of her sneakers, curiosity drew Jayne from the trench. She pivoted for a better view.

"No." Reed's hand shot out to grab Jayne's arm. "Don't look."

He tried to push her behind him, but the damage was already done. Her gaze locked on the grisly sight. In Jayne's belly, her lunch cartwheeled.

Secured to the top of a six-foot post near the back door was a rotting human head. On top of the skull, a crow pecked at a loose flap of dangling scalp.

CHAPTER TWENTY-EIGHT

Jayne stood up and wiped her mouth with the back of her hand. Her confused body poured sweat and shivered simultaneously as her panicked thermostat went berserk.

Strong hands grasped her shoulders and propelled her around the side of the house. Her feet followed the momentum. Leaning against Reed's truck, Jayne gulped cold, damp air. "Is that what I think it is?"

Reed hesitated, then sighed. "Yeah. It is."

Tremors passed over her like a wave, nearly sweeping her feet out from under her shaking body.

A firm hand on her back bent her at the waist, and held her upright while she leaned both hands on her thighs for balance.

"Head down. Take slow breaths."

The ground tilted under her feet. Reed wrapped strong arms around her, holding her against his solid body. Jayne leaned in. The hell with independence. Her forehead rested against his broad chest. Her scalp tingled where his fingers threaded through her hair and stroked the back of her head. Closing her eyes, she inhaled and brought the smell of Reed's soap deep into her nose. The scent steadied her.

Were those his lips against her hair?

She lifted her head. Her knees were barely knocking.

"You OK?" Reed tucked a loose strand of hair behind her ear.

"Yeah." Jayne raised her chin, fortified by his intimate caress.

"I wish you hadn't seen that." His green eyes held regret. "Hell, I wish I hadn't seen that."

"Me too." Jayne tried to step away, but her legs weren't at steady as she'd hoped. She stumbled.

"I've got you." Reed's firm grip on her elbow kept her on her feet. He steered her around the front end of the truck, opened the passenger door, and boosted her into the seat. Reaching across her trembling body, he started the engine and turned the heat on full. He produced a bottle of water from the pocket behind her seat. "I'll be right back."

Jayne took a small sip of cold water as Reed disappeared around the house. He wasn't going to swoon at the horrible thing in the yard. Neither had Jed, although the hunter had looked shocked as hell. But Reed, he'd acted like it was business as usual.

For an ex-cop it probably was.

He slid into the driver's seat and shifted into reverse. "We're going to call Doug. Jed'll wait here."

Jayne closed her eyes. A vision of the head immediately popped into her mind. Better to concentrate on the pebbled gray dashboard.

Wonderful. Her kidnapper was a deranged killer—only deranged killers, ancient Romans, and barbarian hordes left decapitated heads on poles—and they were going to call Doug. While he halfheartedly conducted a half-assed investigation into her abduction, the murderer roamed free in Huntsville, possibly preparing to hunt down another victim.

Or come looking for Jayne in Philadelphia.

Reed K-turned onto the main road. "He'll have to call the state police in now."

But was it too late?

Would she ever really feel safe again?

– – –

Nathan's eyes shot to his office window. Outside, dusk encroached on the overcast sky with none of the usual sunset colors. The gradual loss of daylight reminded him of the increasing dimness in Uncle Aaron's eyes, a clouded confusion that made Nathan's chest ache. His uncle's illness was progressing. Traditional medicine had failed. His uncle was turning to desperate measures. Nathan dropped his chin into his hands. The gloom and doom felt right on par with the rest of his life.

Accounting spreadsheets blurred as he stared at the computer screen. He set his drugstore reading glasses on the desk and rubbed his eyes with both fists. The phone in the next room pealed, only slightly muffled by the thin wall between Nathan's office and the storage room where Doug's temporary office was set up. Nathan could hear everything that went on in there.

Handy.

"Doug Lang." Doug didn't notice he was working in an auditory fishbowl. His voice rang through the Sheetrock clear as music from Evan's iPod through a set of Bose speakers. "A head? At Aaron McCree's old place? Are you sure it's human?"

Nathan concentrated harder on Doug's voice as the cop promised to check out the find and call for state police support. Merry fucking Christmas. What was he going to do now? He'd made a promise to do everything in his power to help his uncle.

But this did complicate things.

"You're not going to believe this." Doug poked his head around Nathan's doorway and repeated the news.

Nathan feigned shock, complete with a slack jaw and an open mouth. His acting skills were getting quite the workout this week. "Oh my God! No. Are you sure?"

"I'm only relaying what Reed Kimball said." Doug's chest expanded. "I'm going out there now to investigate before I call anyone else. Wouldn't want to bother the state police if it's just a deer or something. Kimball's a city boy. Probably wouldn't recognize an animal skull."

"Good thinking." Nathan pushed to his feet. Reed Kimball was no fool. He knew exactly what he'd found. And Jed certainly knew an animal head when he saw one, but Doug needed his ego stroked. "Hugh's death was such a loss to the community, but it comforts me to know you're in charge. The rest of the town council feels the same way." Actually, most of the members thought Doug was an incompetent moron, but Nathan liked having a cop in his pocket, so to speak.

Doug gave him a serious nod. "You need to come out and have a look at your uncle's place. I'll need you to go through the place and see if anything's missing. If Reed's right, somebody must've broke in and used Aaron's house. Transient or squatter or something."

"I was at Uncle Aaron's just the other day. I didn't see anything unusual, but then I was mostly concerned with plowing the road and making sure the house was still standing. I was in a rush to get back here. Didn't even go inside." Nathan reached for his coat. "I just never imagined anyone would be interested in the place. Nothing worth stealing. The place is a mess. Uncle Aaron really let it go over the past couple of years. I should've known something was wrong with him."

"Give yourself a break. You couldn't have known."

"Thanks, Doug. I'll meet you out there. God, I'm so sorry I didn't properly inspect the property. There's no excuse, really. I hate to think a killer was using the house to hurt people."

"You have an awful lot on your plate right now with taking care of Aaron and all." Doug waved off Nathan's apology. "I'm sure this is just an animal or something."

"You go on ahead. I'll be right behind you." Nathan shrugged into his coat. "I want to call home real quick and see if Uncle Aaron is OK."

Doug turned. "See you out there."

– – –

"How many more bags of stuff?" Scott snagged another slice of pizza from the box and tilted the box toward Brandon. "Another?"

"Thanks." Brandon grabbed a cheesy wedge, folded it lengthwise, and took a huge bite. Half the slice disappeared. "Not too many. We may finish up earlier than we thought."

"Cool." Scott chewed through his crust and wiped his mouth on his sleeve. He reached behind him for another black trash bag, dumping the contents on the buffet table. An assortment of gloves, hats, and coats hit the table with a rustle of nylon. "I gotta finish that history paper for Miss Seacrest. It's due tomorrow."

"You're still workin' on that?" Brandon grinned at him. "Dude, she assigned that weeks ago. No wonder you drive your old man nuts."

"I'll get it done." Scott laughed. "Always do. Have to mail my college apps this week, too."

"Christ, nothing like sliding them in under the wire." Brandon shook his head. "Mine went in a month ago. Not that it'll matter."

"Hey, man. Don't say that."

Brandon tossed a pair of faded pink mittens into a plastic bin marked Girls' Gloves & Mittens. "No scholarships for me. I'm not a straight-A student or a great athlete."

Hard to be either with two jobs, Scott thought. Brandon had been filling the shoes of his worthless old man since he was in grade school. "What about financial aid?"

"Even with, the only school I can possible afford is community college."

"Nothing wrong with community college."

Brandon snorted. "Sure, says you. Where'd your old man go?"

"Georgetown. Man, he's gonna be pissed if I don't get in." Scott threw a pair of rubber boots into the appropriate plastic tub. "And he's gonna be even more pissed if I do and back out."

"Why don't you just tell him you don't want to go there?"

"My dad has wanted me to go to Georgetown since I was born."

"He'll deal." Brandon dumped another garbage bag of clothing on the table, pulled out a ripped jacket, and tossed it into the discard pile. "Just tell him you want to go somewhere else."

"That's the thing. I don't know where I want to go." Scott sighed. "What I really want is to take a year off and travel. Take my time and figure out where my head's at. But I'd have to get the old man to approve a withdrawal from my trust. I doubt he'll agree."

"You never know until you ask."

"True." Scott turned for another bag, but the space behind them was empty. "Yo, was that the last one?"

"Seems like."

"Cool. I should call my dad to come and get me." Scott reached into his pocket and drew out his cell when a voice called from the kitchen entrance.

"Hello, boys. Could I ask a favor of you both?"

– – –

"Doug and Nathan are on their way to the house." Reed set a cup of steaming tea in front of Jayne. She was still pale, but her spine was straight and her jaw set as she booted up his laptop on the kitchen island. She'd tough it out, but the memory would haunt her forever. An unpreserved head was a nasty sight for a jaded professional. Even in winter, a sunny day warmed things up enough for decomposition to occur, albeit at a slower rate than in warmer seasons. Then there were the animals. Hungry scavengers did not differentiate between a human head and a roadkill squirrel.

Although the fact that it had been a crow picking on that head was just plain bizarre.

Reed glanced over Jayne's shoulder at the dark glass. Before he clicked on any lights, Reed toured the windows and closed all the blinds. Darkness had overtaken the yard. "I have to go pick up Scott."

"OK." Jayne opened the browser. "Ooh. E-mail. Here's the picture back."

She clicked Download. "Holy. Shit."

"What is it?" Reed leaned in closer.

Mute, she turned the laptop around to face him. The screen displayed the image of the robe-clad man in the woods. Reed's eyes were drawn to the grisly object held in the man's huge hand like a bowling ball, now lightened to the point of recognition.

"Do you think that's the same head?"

"I sure as hell hope so." Reed also prayed it was the rest of Zack Miller's remains. Otherwise there was another headless body out there somewhere. Another victim. Reed leaned in closer for a better look, but IDing the head on a visual wasn't possible. Dental records or DNA would be required to identify the remains.

"Do you know the guy in the robe?"

Reed shifted his gaze to the face, formerly obscured by the robe's shadow. Stunned silence hung over the kitchen. *It couldn't be.*

He squinted at the picture again.

"Do you know him?" Jayne repeated her question impatiently.

"Yeah. I know him."

CHAPTER TWENTY-NINE

John's legs wobbled. The grating of tires on packed snow ceased. Cold sweat leaked into his filthy wool sweater as he crouched behind the door hinges. His arms trembled under the weight of the log in his hands. One day without drugs wasn't enough to restore his balance or strength after more than a month of imprisonment and malnourishment, but it was all he was going to get.

On the other side of the closed door, boots crunched on ice, then rang on wooden steps.

Fear slipped through John's bowels. He tensed, lifting the wood above his shoulder in a two-handed grip.

The door opened. Through the gap at the hinge, John waited for a masked face to appear. When a gray head moved into view, John hesitated. The white head was bare.

Could this be the wrong guy?

Who else would be here?

The head turned. Clouded blue eyes scanned the room. Recognition and fury flared simultaneously. In the precious seconds it took John to swing the log, the old man registered the threat and ducked.

John missed. Momentum carried him forward. He fell onto his hands and knees. Over his shoulder, he saw his captor clearly for the first time. A thin face topped with a shock of wild, white hair.

Fists rained down on his shoulders and back. John's arms folded like a cheap TV tray. Fresh pain shot through his face as his chin hit the wood floor. A boot connected with his temple.

His last conscious thought was that he'd been right. He wasn't getting out of this alive. This time his captor hadn't bothered to cover his face. Obviously the old man was no longer concerned with concealing his identity.

– – –

Reed repeated his internal mantra as he rolled through a stop sign. Scott was safe. He was at the Youth Center with a whole bunch of other teens and responsible adults. There was no way Nathan's Uncle Aaron could get to him. He couldn't believe Aaron was the killer. Brain cancer must have eroded his sanity.

In the passenger seat, Jayne chewed on her thumbnail. "Maybe his cell didn't have a signal."

"Our cell phones always work in town." Reed gunned the engine. The truck roared forward. Stark, bare trees whipped by in the darkness.

"Or he didn't hear it ring."

Reed didn't respond. His parental radar was beeping away, telling him Scott was in danger. Reed shifted his weight and pressed the gas pedal harder. The Yukon responded with a surge of speed.

Jayne grabbed the chick strap as they sped into town. Three turns later, he pulled up at the curb in front of the old clapboard house that housed the Youth Center. Lights illuminated the bare windows.

Reed took the walk at a jog, his heart pumping with the sickening panic of helplessness. The front door was unlocked and he pushed it open with a quick rap on the door frame. He stepped into the foyer and held the door for Jayne as he called out, "Hello?"

The house was way too quiet to be filled with teenagers. Reed's chest clenched tighter.

Two girls emerged from the kitchen.

"Can I help you, Mr. Kimball?" the taller one asked. Reed recognized her as one of Scott's classmates, Emily something.

"I'm looking for Scott." But Reed knew his son wasn't in the house before she answered.

Emily smiled. "I don't know where Scott and Brandon went. We were upstairs. When we came down, they were gone."

– – –

The Druid added logs to the bonfire that roared at his feet. He moved to check on the initial sacrifice. A young man in his prime. Two more were necessary. Brigid plus another healthy specimen. He sent a prayer to the gods that his apprentice would not fail in his quest. Great salvation could not be achieved without great sacrifice. The balance must be maintained.

An engine approached. Minutes later, boots crunched on frozen snow.

His apprentice carried a young man over his shoulders like a fireman.

"I'm sorry. I couldn't obtain the woman. I brought a substitute. I have no excuse." The apprentice carefully lowered his burden to the ground in front of the second pillar, then knelt in the snow at his master's feet. "I failed."

The Druid placed a gentle hand on the beloved blond head. "I failed in that task as well. The situation is not ideal, but we will make do. We have little choice. Now be quick and bring me the final sacrifice. The hour nears."

– – –

"Becca doesn't have any idea where they went."

Reed snapped his cell phone closed. Next to him, Jayne flinched.

"She thought the boys were still here." Reed's eyes flickered to the driver's window. The two teenage girls exited the Youth Center, locking the door before giggling their way down the walk. Scott should be hanging around, chatting up the pretty girls while he waited for Reed. The pressure inside his chest increased until he thought his ribs would crack under the strain.

Jayne reached across the console to grab Reed's hand. He didn't pull away. He didn't respond in any way. Shock had dulled his reflexes. She gave his fingers a light squeeze, but Reed's gaze didn't waver from the window. He dragged in a breath, the muscles of his chest constricting like an ever-tightening vise.

"We'll find him. Maybe they got hungry and went to grab something to eat."

"There were empty pizza boxes inside."

"Oh." Jayne drummed the fingers of her free hand on her thigh. "Anywhere else they might have gone? Is there an arcade or video game store in town?"

Reed shook his head. Jayne's question prodded him into action. She was right. Sitting here wasn't getting Scott back.

"We start looking for Aaron. We'll try Nathan's place. That's where he's been staying."

"Want me to try Scott's cell again?" she asked.

"He didn't answer the last three times, but sure." He tossed her the phone. Reed had already called the state police. Surprisingly, so had Doug. Unfortunately the state cops were coming late to the party and the whole catch-up process would take more time than Reed could spare with his son missing and a resident killer on the loose.

Jayne selected the number from the outgoing-calls list and pressed Send. From the driver's seat, he heard the call flip to voice mail.

"Didn't even ring that time." She left another message.

"I'm gonna stop at the diner. See if anyone saw the boys. We can try to catch Nathan there, too." Reed jerked the gearshift into drive, and the truck roared away from the curb. "I could drop you off with Mae. She and her twenty-gauge would keep you safe."

Part of Reed wished she'd agree, though he hated to let her out of his sight. Rationally, he knew she'd be safer with Mae than actively going after a psycho with him. The other part wanted all the help he could get to save his son. The decision was tearing his soul apart.

Jayne took the choice away. "I'm with you all the way. We *will* get Scott back."

Reed had no doubt Jayne would do anything for Scott. Her face was full of the same fierce determination and strength as when she'd stepped between him and the coyote.

Love, fear, and gratitude continued to play tug-of-war with Reed's heart. "Let's try the diner."

They arrived at the restaurant a few minutes later. Reed jumped down from the cab. Jayne met him around the front of the vehicle. From the sidewalk, they peered through the big plate glass windows. No Scott. No Nathan.

"You go in the front door." Reed started toward the back.

"OK."

Reed jogged around the building, entering through the rear door. He made a quick tour of the storage rooms, Nathan's office, the restrooms, and the kitchen before sweeping into the dining room. He saw Jayne across the room, standing by the entrance. She shook her head.

Shit.

Reed scanned the dining room. Business was slow. Only three tables were occupied. Jed sat in his usual booth. Mandy balanced a tray in the aisle. She stopped at Jed's table.

Reed careened to a stop, his boots squeaking on commercial linoleum. "Has anyone seen my son?"

Mandy slid the tray onto the table and turned to greet Reed. Her smile evaporated as she met Reed's gaze. "No. What's wrong?"

"I can't find him. Is Nathan here?" Reed's voice rose with his frustration, and Mandy backed away. Her baby blues went wide.

"I'm sorry, Mandy." Out of the corner of his eye, Reed saw Jed getting to his feet, ever ready to defend Mandy. Reed exhaled to the count of three. His feet had stopped moving, but his body was strung tight enough to snap. He jumped as a weight settled on his arm. Jayne squeezed hard. Reed drew strength from the contact and wrestled his vocal cords into submission. "It's important."

Jed stepped up behind Mandy. With two hands on her upper arms, he gently moved her to the side so he could plant himself between her and Reed. "I left Doug at Aaron's place. Nathan was supposed to meet him there."

Reed caught Jayne's eye and tilted his head toward the waitress.

Jayne stepped in. "Hey, Mandy, I could use a glass of water."

Mandy backed away with obvious relief. She and Jayne headed for the kitchen. Reed dropped his voice to a whisper and told Jed about the photo.

"Son of a bitch," Jed said. "I can't believe Aaron would do something like that. The cancer must have rotted his brain."

"I'm going to drive out to Nathan's place. I have to find Aaron. Any idea where else he might go?"

Jed concentrated hard enough to make Reed's head hurt. "How about his hunting cabin?"

Reed had no idea what Aaron was up to, but any kind of weird pagan ritual would need seclusion, more seclusion than Nathan's house would afford. And tonight was the solstice. "Is it isolated?"

"Oh, yeah. Nobody goes out there. It's not that far from Aaron's place as the crow flies, but there's no real road. Dumb spot for hunting, if you ask me. He's got some woods right around the cabin, but the rest of the property's too rocky. Not enough forage for game."

A hunting cabin that wasn't in a great spot for hunting. Sounded perfect for other activities that required seclusion. "Will my truck make it?" Reed asked.

"Definitely. But you might have to put her in low."

"OK. Can you give me directions?"

"I can do better than that. I've got trail maps in my truck." It took Jed a minute to fetch the maps from the parking lot. He spread it out on the table and pinpointed the cabin. "I could take you out there."

Reed debated. "No. I need you to call this man." Reed wrote the name and number of the state police investigator on a piece of paper. "The detective's on his way, and he'll need someone to show him where the cabin is."

"Got it."

Reed sure as hell hoped so. A lot of lives depended on it. Like Scott's.

A buzzing sound from the floor caught Reed's attention. Jayne's phone vibrated at his feet. He leaned down and picked it up. The external display indicated a text message from the *Philadelphia Daily Scoop*. Why would Jayne be getting a message from a tabloid? With a small twinge of guilt, he flipped open the phone and pressed OK.

The message was only two words.

Got pics?

She'd lied to him. She wasn't a travel brochure photographer. Jayne was paparazzi.

"Oh. There's my phone." Ice clinked in the glass in Jayne's hand. "Must have fallen out of my pocket."

Reed handed her the phone, still open to the tabloid's message, wordlessly. Jayne's eyes bugged. The color bled from her face. She opened her mouth.

"I don't have time to discuss this now." Reed cut her off.

Jayne swallowed. "But I can explain."

"I said I can't deal with this right now." Reed's teeth ground as he pivoted and headed for the door. "I have to find Scott."

The cab of the truck had cooled in the brief time they'd been inside the diner, but the outside temperature couldn't compare to the chill that had swept over his heart.

"Reed, I can explain." Jayne's voice was strained.

Without looking at her, he shook his head. Had she already sent the photo she'd taken of him to the paper? No point in asking. Her answer couldn't be trusted. After all, she'd offered him an explanation, but she'd never denied her betrayal.

– – –

A moan woke John. Fresh pain blasted through his body, and it wasn't just from the recent beating. His arms were tied behind his back and securely fastened to something behind him.

In a panic he took stock. Sky over his head, ice under his ass. There was cold air at his back, but heat from a bonfire five yards away kept him from completely freezing his nuts off. He kept his eyes off the fire so his pupils wouldn't constrict. His vision focused on the ring of wooden posts.

The tremors that rushed upward from the soles of his feet had nothing to do with the winter night.

He knew exactly where he was. The same clearing where it had all started. Where Zack had died.

Panic ripped through him with a freight train roar.

His weight strained against the ropes that bound him to the post. Rough fibers bit into his wrists. Inside his chest, his heart beat against his ribs like a frantic parakeet, trying to break free of its bone cage. But he was trapped.

An icy crackle had John jerking his head around. The old man circled the clearing, chanting. John couldn't make out the words, but they flowed over him like a hypnotic drum. The old guy was pouring something from a jug just inside the circle. Dark liquid glugged into the snow. It was a replay of that night with Zack.

Hard cold fact: he was going to die tonight.

John's vision went red around the edges. The rushing in his ears drowned out the intonations. His head lolled to his shoulders.

But instincts were a bitch. And survival was the most relentless nag of them all. Even after all he'd been through, he didn't want to let go. Neither did he want to face whatever horrors his captor had planned for tonight.

John lifted his head an inch. The frozen air caressed his bare skin. Another moan brought his head around to the other side. Two more forms were slumped in front of upright poles. His heart did a double take. Two more poor souls were going down with him.

And there wasn't jack shit John could do about it.

He swiveled around at a scraping sound. His captor was arranging a limp body, a young man, on the flat-topped center stone strewn with pillar candles.

"Tonight we seek an ancient power." The old man moved to stand in front of John. His voice was deep and accented as it carried across the clearing. He shoved a few dusty crumbs into John's mouth. John tried to spit them out. The old man backhanded him across the face. Pain slammed through his cheek as the old man continued. "The power that rules all of the universe. The power that has united us all from when we received our first meal of blood in the womb."

There was a rustling of nylon in the frigid night. The old man began to chant as he circled John.

"In blood we find peace. In blood we find nourishment."

The old man moved behind John. A thin cord encircled his neck. His numbed skin pumped a gallon of sweat to its surface.

"In blood we find power." The cord around John's neck tightened. "In blood we are united."

John's neck was jerked back, his wind cut off. In his peripheral vision, silver flashed in the firelight.

— — —

Jayne gripped the door handle as the Yukon lurched to a stop in front of a dark rectangle. Neither she nor Reed spoke as they slipped from the vehicle and drew their weapons. Reed's subcompact Glock felt secure, well balanced in her grip. She followed his instructions, providing cover while he opened the door.

His heart might have been lost to her, but she'd help him save his son.

The single room was empty, but the chain attached to the woodstove was an obvious clue. Someone had been held prisoner here.

Jayne's stomach flip-flopped with pity and fear as memories flooded her. Someone else had suffered as she had, probably more. Her eyes found dark splotches on the rough wooden floor. Blood? Definitely more.

Reed motioned toward the door. On the porch, he stood and listened. Chanting floated on the wind. They both followed the sound to a game trail behind the cabin.

They crept down the dark path. Jayne tried to be as quiet as possible, but she was more accustomed to concrete than to forest. As they drew closer, the crackling of a large fire covered the sounds of their approach.

Two SUVs were parked in a small cleared area next to a stand of thick evergreens. One had a plow attached to the front.

Reed moved around the evergreens, using one hand to hold her behind him. Jayne tiptoed across the icy ground, testing each step and trying to avoid the crunchy spots.

Reed stopped short, reached a hand up, and pushed the branch of a Scotch pine aside. They both sucked in a breath at the scene before them, illuminated by a huge bonfire in the center of the clearing.

Six-foot wooden posts ringed the perimeter. Opposite the fire, three shorter posts formed a triangle around a body on a stone altar. And tied to those three posts were three people. Jayne squinted. The closest figure looked like Scott. From his slumped position, he didn't appear to be conscious. At least she prayed he was only unconscious. The second figure, maybe Brandon, stirred and let out a soft moan.

The third was about to die.

"No shot. They're too close to him," Reed breathed in her ear.

A parka-clad figure stood behind the last captive. Red-and-gold flames flickered on a young, thin face and struggling body. The man looped something around the kid's neck. Murmurs floated across the brittle air. Silver gleamed in the light of the blazing fire.

A knife!

"That's Aaron." Reed's voice was barely a whisper.

Fear gripped Jayne's insides and twisted. Aaron was going to strangle that boy and cut his throat. Her gaze darted to the stone slab. On it, next to yet another body, rested a wooden club.

It was the triple sacrifice, the bog body's fate.

Jayne reached out for Reed. Her hand moved through empty air. She'd been so transfixed by the scene, she hadn't noticed him slip away. Jayne lifted the pistol and took aim. Still no shot.

The boy's head jerked backward.

"No!" The shout leapt from Jayne's throat. Her feet started running toward the doomed boy before she could think.

A shadow burst from the trees and tackled the man with the knife. Reed! The kid slipped to the ground. Still attached to the post by the wrists, his body twisted awkwardly. Behind the boy, the two silhouettes grappled. Jayne's vision tunneled down to the struggling men. Other than their grunts and movements, all sound was muted. In a surreal haze, she flew past Scott and Brandon.

Aaron lunged, weapon extended. Reed evaded. The knife slashed horizontally, level with Reed's midsection. Jayne's heart catapulted into her throat as Reed stumbled, then steadied himself with a palm on a wooden post. He swayed, reaching for the gun on his hip. The crazy man advanced.

Jayne's arms extended. Her gun leveled itself. "Freeze."

Aaron stopped. He turned toward Jayne, knife at the ready.

"Brigid, you came." Cold blue eyes flashed. Forthright. Soulless. Insane. "We are honored. Perhaps you were not meant to die here tonight, but to bear witness to the ritual, to petition the gods for our salvation."

How could she have thought she wouldn't recognize the maniacal gleam in those eyes? The tip of her finger touched the trigger. The blue eyes shifted to look over Jayne's shoulder. Aaron smiled.

Agony slammed through Jayne's skull. Her world inverted as her bones went soft. The gun dropped to the ground next to her head. In her blurry peripheral vision, she watched the kidnapper's gaze move beyond her. She swiveled her head.

Nathan stood behind her, a wooden club clenched in his hand.

"Save Evan. May my sacrifice save you both." Aaron's voice faltered, and Jayne turned back to him. His hand jerked. Silver flashed as he yanked the blade across his own throat. Blood bubbled down his robe and onto the snow in a dark, wet rush. His body tipped forward and crumpled.

"Jayne!" Reed's voice cut through the shock. He was stumbling toward her, way too unsteady on his feet.

Jayne rolled onto her back and heaved her shoulders up. Her stomach tumbled. She gulped night air as she scanned the clearing. Nathan had disappeared. So had the body on the stone. "Where's Nathan?"

"I don't know." Reed lurched toward her, his eyes sweeping the perimeter. "Let's get these kids to the truck before he decides to come back and kill us all."

With a still-spinning head, Jayne scooted to the first boy. His open eyes surprised her. Reed stooped and slashed the rope that bound the kid's wrists. His hands flew to his neck, yanking a thin leather cord away. Thank God. Reed had jumped the old man before the garrote had done its job.

"Can you walk? We have a car at the cabin." Jayne nodded in the direction of the trail.

Beneath the horror and pain, a glimmer of determination shone in the kid's eyes. "I'll get there if I have to crawl." He choked the rough words out in a croak.

No wonder he'd survived.

Jayne glanced up. Reed had managed to rouse Brandon. The kid was on his hands and knees, nodding emphatically to whatever Reed was saying. Brandon pushed to his feet, stumbled, but stayed vertical with the help of the nearby post.

"Scott's still out cold, but his breathing and pulse are steady." Reed squatted and hauled Scott up and over his shoulders. He carried Scott, Jayne half-dragged Brandon, and the other kid staggered back to the Yukon on his own. Once the three boys were safely inside, Jayne jumped into the cab and locked the door.

The landscape tilted as she straightened. Pain pulsed through her skull.

"Are you OK?" Reed leaned on the passenger side of the truck. One hand went under his jacket as he held the keys out in the other. "Because I think you better drive."

Jayne's eyes dropped. Dark droplets stained the white ground at his feet.

CHAPTER THIRTY

As soon as the truck hit pavement, Nathan pressed the gas pedal to the floor. A glance in the backseat told him Evan slept on, medicated and oblivious to the night's disaster.

Gods be damned.

The last image of his uncle was imprinted in his head, stored there like a YouTube clip. Uncle Aaron slicing his own throat, spilling his own blood in the sacred circle.

Grief struck him like a blade to the chest. He knew his uncle was beyond his pain and suffering now. He was starting anew in the afterlife. And that he'd gone on his own terms. As he'd wanted.

Had Nathan been a coward?

No. He'd only followed his uncle's last wishes, made clear the evening before as they'd prepared for the ceremony.

If anything happens, above all, save Evan. I am the past. He is the future.

How like his uncle to make the ultimate sacrifice for his kin. Spill his own blood in hopes the offering of it would sway the gods to cure their family of the genetic affliction that plagued them. He'd died as he'd lived, giving everything he had to save Nathan and his son.

Nathan let up on the gas as he approached town. No going around it. Huntsville stood between him and the highway.

Between him and freedom. He needed to drive through as if nothing had happened.

As he drew even with the diner, Mandy emerged. She drew her knee-length parka tighter around her body and leaned into the wind.

Nathan didn't think. He turned into the alley alongside the diner. She was his light. His hope. His destiny. Why had he pushed her away? He lowered the passenger window. "Mandy, get in."

She jumped and swung around as if she'd been slapped.

Nathan checked the street in both directions. No one in sight. He jumped from the truck and approached Mandy on the sidewalk.

If he could only get her into the truck. He had plenty of tranqs left. Once they were far enough away, he'd explain everything to her. She'd understand. She loved him. Sure he'd broken her heart, but she'd forgive him eventually.

The need to take her with him pulsed through his veins with every beat of his heart. His hands reached for her arms. She pulled away, but Nathan caught her slender wrist. "I love you. Just get in the truck."

"No." Mandy stared at him, fear tainting her beautiful eyes. "What's wrong with you, Nathan?"

She shouldn't be afraid of him. He loved her.

He tugged. Mandy resisted. Nathan pulled harder, dragging her into the alley. His truck was only a few feet away. She dug her rubber-soled shoes into the asphalt and dropped her ass toward the ground. "Let me go!"

Damn it. He was going to have to pick her up, throw her in the truck, and drive through the night.

Good thing he wasn't the least bit tired.

"Nathan, what are you doing?" Her voice, sharp with apprehension, echoed down the empty street. Someone was going to hear her. She was going to ruin everything. "I said let go of me!"

Rage at the situation and his sense of impotence boiled over. Nathan slapped her without thought. The crack of his hand across her cheek knocked her to her butt. Her eyes went from saucers to dinner plates.

"Shut up and get in the truck."

Jed flew out of the diner. Two strong hands gripped Nathan's lapels as the hunter got in his face. "Don't you touch her!"

The knife jumped from Nathan's pocket into his hand. His honed blade slid into Jed's belly like it was Jell-O.

An agonized scream shrilled in his ear. Not Jed. His mouth was slack with shock. Nathan turned toward Mandy. He needed to shut her up—fast.

– – –

"I can't believe Jaynie wasn't there. Where could she be?"

From the backseat of a Honda Odyssey, Danny Sullivan listened to his oldest brother, Pat, bitch and moan.

Main Street rolled by with Hallmark charm and enough wholesome Christmas decorations to make Norman Rockwell gag.

Riding shotgun, Conor added, "I got a bad feeling about this."

So did Danny. Fear for his sister lay dormant in the pit of his chest like an Iraqi IED, ready to blow Danny's precariously balanced peace of mind to shit at any second. He just couldn't take it if anything happened to Jaynie.

Pat continued to complain. Both his Irish temper and his concern for their sister had peaked when they'd driven up to Reed Kimball's house to find only a supremely pissed-off Siberian husky in residence. No Jaynie. "It's only nine o'clock and the place is a ghost town. Where the fuck is everybody?"

Back home, the nightlife hadn't even hit full swing yet. The bar would be filled up with the tail end of happy hour and the first wave of partiers.

"Just park somewhere. We'll split up," Conor barked.

Pat pulled over. "OK. Try to find someone, anyone who might have a clue as to what's going on. I'm going to drive around and try to find that inn Jaynie said she stayed at. Shouldn't take long. The whole place is only a dozen blocks each way."

Conor climbed from the van and pulled his cell from his pocket. "Hallelujah. I got bars."

Danny checked his display and grunted his assent as his boots hit the sidewalk. Pat affirmed his service had returned as well. "OK then, boys. Text with news or meet back here in twenty."

The brothers parted.

Conor pointed south. "I'll go this way. Toward that strip center. Looks like a drugstore, at least."

"Whatever." Danny was already headed north. A diner sat at the main intersection, across from the burned-out shell of a building. A glance at the rubble brought a horror of a slide show to Danny's brain. With long practice, he shut that fucker down.

He was so not going there tonight.

Jaynie needed him here, not tripping off into flashback land. Helped that the tiny hamlet of Huntsville, Maine, was the polar opposite of Iraq.

Danny walked in a quiet that was simultaneously quaint and creepy.

A woman's scream shattered the silence. Danny sprinted toward the sound, the slapping of his shitkickers on hard pavement painfully reminiscent. A twinge shot up his left arm.

He passed the diner. A man and woman struggled in the shadowed alley next to a midsize SUV. A third figure lay on the ground a few feet away.

"Get in the fucking truck now." The man pulled the resisting woman by the wrist. She shifted her weight back like a stubborn mule. He raised his free hand and cracked her across the face.

Danny launched his body at the guy, breaking his hold on the lady. Danny and the rude dude went heads over asses. Unable to break his fall with his bum hand, Danny landed in a tangle of limbs while the woman-beating asshole sprinted for his truck. Asshole twisted and pointed at the woman. "You're mine."

Danny got his legs under his body and set up for a flying tackle.

Sobbing stopped him cold.

He glanced sideways. The woman knelt at the prone figure's side. "Help him, please." The eyes that turned on him were blue as a desert sky and just as captivating.

Shit.

Danny gave up on grabbing the attacker and hurried to her side. Her assailant's engine faded as fast as taillights in the dark.

Danny ripped open the guy's bloodstained jacket and applied pressure to a deep stab wound to the belly. Two functional hands would've helped.

The stanching of blood threatened to suck him back in time. Imaginary rockets and bullets began to whistle through the silence. *Keep your head in the game.*

"You have 911 service here?" He turned to the woman and was struck fucking dumb. Even with mascara running down her cheeks, swollen eyes, a hand-size slap mark, *and* her friend's blood smeared all over her, she was the most beautiful thing he'd ever seen. An apparition. An angel.

"Yes."

The warm liquid oozing over his fingers brought him back to the guy bleeding out on the pavement—and vivid memories he'd rather not have. "Call them. If you don't have a phone, mine's in my jacket pocket. Right side."

She dug his cell out and made the call while Danny tried to keep his grip on reality. He was in Maine, not Iraq. That was snow on the ground, not sand. "How far's the hospital?"

"Forty minutes."

Danny was no medic, but he had plenty of experience watching guys bleed to death. Which brought him back to his private horror show. The shakes started deep in his gut and radiated outward as the blood kept coming. "He doesn't have forty minutes. Tell them you need a medevac."

Cold sweat broke out in the wake of the tremors. He concentrated on her voice, brave despite her terror. The sound of it washed over him like a rush of warm water. "What's your name?"

"Mandy." Her voice quivered.

Mandy.

"Please keep talking to me, Mandy."

CHAPTER THIRTY-ONE

Reed raised the head of the bed. His eyelids were lead curtains, and the long set of stitches across his ribs pulled. He glanced at the next bed, where Scott slept off the stress and the residual effects of the tranquilizer Nathan had slipped him. The other two boys were down the hall. Like Scott, Brandon was out cold. John was in worse shape, malnourished, dehydrated, and traumatized, but he was alive.

The sound of his son's deep breathing threatened to lull Reed back to sleep. He forced his eyes open. No sleeping as long as Nathan was still on the loose.

Footsteps scraped. Reed tensed. The man who tapped lightly on the door frame was a stranger. Though his hair was black, his eyes were the same striking shade of turquoise as Jayne's.

He stepped into the room and glanced at Reed's sleeping roommate. "I'm Conor Sullivan," he said in a low voice.

"Jayne's not alone, is she?" Reed held out a hand.

Conor shook it. Jayne's brother was tall and lanky like his sister. "Pat's with her. He won't leave her alone."

Reed relaxed. "She's all right?"

"Mild concussion. They're keeping her overnight for observation. Thanks for saving her."

"She saved herself. She's amazing." Reed hadn't meant to blurt that out, but the emergency room doc had shot him full of something before he'd gone to work closing the wound. Plus, Reed had lost more than a few drops of blood. His eyes ached. He blinked hard.

Conor digested Reed's comment for a few seconds. "Why don't you get some sleep, Reed?"

Reed gave his head a quick shake. His eyes were pulled to his son's sleeping form. "Not as long as Nathan is out there."

"Jaynie sent me to watch over you two." Conor crossed his arms and leaned back against the wall. "Go ahead and close your eyes. You rescued my sister. You and your son are with us now, and we take care of our own."

– – –

Danny moved through the hospital corridors. Machines beeped. The bite of antiseptic and the stench of human misery competed for top billing in his nose—and mind. Pain radiated from his injured hand. Images of explosions and shock and blood rushed through his head. Screams echoed in his ears, the inhuman screaming of men who bodies had been blown to pieces. Or whose friends had been blown to pieces.

Danny had been bleeding out too fast to scream, but the horror was clear as a desert day.

The petite brunette was sitting alone in the surgical waiting room.

Mandy.

Danny hesitated at the threshold, just looking at her. What could he possibly do for her? She was wholesome, lovely, and perfect, while he was damaged inside and out.

She was silent, her eyes blank and her body too still. Numb disbelief. That state when the mind cannot process the horrors presented to it.

That Danny could understand.

He stepped into the room. When she didn't move, Danny lowered his body into the chair next to her. "Any word?"

She turned to look at him. The deep blue of her eyes swam with sadness. Danny shifted on the upholstered seat.

"Ms. Brown?" A green-scrubbed surgeon stepped into the room. "He made it out of surgery. You can see him for a few minutes."

Mandy rose, hesitantly, as if afraid of what she was going to see. "Is he going to be all right?"

The doctor stopped and rubbed a hand over a weary face. "Honestly, I don't know. Right now his chances are fifty-fifty. If he makes it till morning, we'll reassess."

Danny tagged along behind the doctor and Mandy. No one challenged his presence. In the intensive care unit, Danny waited outside the glass cubicle while Mandy went inside.

"Five minutes." The doctor stepped out.

At a counter along the wall, a nurse was reading machines and typing into a laptop. In the bed, Jed was fully automated. Tubes, wires, ventilator. The whole shebang. Danny had seen better color on a corpse. A monitor shrieked. Danny and Mandy both jumped.

The nurse adjusted a dial, and the machine went quiet.

Beep, beep, hiss.

Mandy walked to the bedside and reached out. Her hand hovered a few inches over the sheets like she was looking for a place to touch Jed that wasn't connected to something. A sob hitched her breath. She pressed a fist to her mouth.

She must really love that guy.

Danny rubbed a tight spot in the center of his chest.

Pat would stay with Jayne. Conor could look out for Reed and his son. Someone needed to guard Mandy.

You're mine, the knife-wielding lunatic had said.

Like hell, Danny thought. If there was a breath left in his body, crazy-ass Nathan Hall would never get within a mile of Mandy. From Jayne's story, Nathan didn't seem like the type to give himself up quietly. No, eventually, someone was going to have to hunt that crazy-ass down.

– – –

"Are you sure you're up to this, Jaynie?"

"I am." But as they walked to Reed's room, she leaned on her brother's huge chest. Pat wrapped a beefy arm around her and half-carried her through the doorway. He hadn't left her side since her brothers arrived at the hospital.

Inside the room, Conor was leaning on the wall. Scott was snoring from the bed by the window, and the state police detective was standing at Reed's bedside. The policeman was fiftyish, with salt-and-pepper hair and a sharp face that didn't seem to miss much. Pat went to stand with Conor. Danny had gone to check on Jed.

"Still no luck finding Nathan Hall or his son, Evan." Reed's eyes shifted to Jayne.

Nerves fluttered in Jayne's belly.

"Ms. Sullivan." Detective Rossi motioned to a hospital-issue recliner next to him. "Please sit. I was giving Mr. Kimball an update."

Jayne had given her statement to the cop an hour ago. She collapsed into the chair and tried to focus on the state detective's words. But frankly, she was too tired. Aaron had killed himself. Nathan had gotten away. Maybe the details would matter tomorrow, but right now she just wanted to crawl into a quiet bed with Reed and sleep for about a week.

Not likely.

She leaned her aching head against the vinyl. The detective droned on. "A search of the mayor's basement turned up all sorts of books and objects related to pagan religious rituals, specifically human sacrifices. It seems like that was their intention. The collection of Celtic artifacts is extensive. Some of the stuff is museum-worthy."

"Any idea why they did all this?" Reed's face was pale. His green eyes lacked their usual intensity.

"Maybe." The detective gestured with his pen. "An e-mail on the mayor's laptop indicates that his uncle was suffering from an extremely rare genetic disorder called Campbell's Insomnia. Lesions form in the thalamus of the brain, which is the area that regulates sleep. The individual loses the ability to sleep. Dementia and hallucinations develop in the first six months or so, progressing to coma and death within a year or two."

"So they go crazy and then die from *insomnia*?" Reed asked.

"Basically, yes." The detective nodded. "The disease is genetic, so Mayor Hall and his son may very well carry the gene. If so, they'll both eventually develop the disease. There's no treatment and no cure."

"What about the...er..." Reed glanced at the sleeping boy next to him. "Thing on the pole?"

Jayne flinched. Did Scott know about the decapitation? He'd find out eventually. Horrific information, even though the act had been performed postmortem. As if the kid hadn't had enough horror already.

"Ancient Celts thought *that* was the source of power in a person." The detective dropped his voice further. "Dental records confirm that it's Zack Miller."

"Do you have any leads on Nathan's whereabouts?" Reed shifted his position and winced.

"We have some theories, but nothing is substantiated." The detective stuck his pen in his chest pocket. "A thorough investigation is underway. We're just as concerned as you are that Nathan is still on the loose. I assure you an extensive manhunt is being conducted throughout the New England area. We will find him."

What if they didn't?

Reed nodded. "How's Jed?"

Detective Rossi closed his mini notebook. "Just out of surgery. Doctor's giving him even odds."

That could have been Reed. If Aaron's knife had been two inches lower, it wouldn't have been deflected by Reed's ribs.

Jayne closed her eyes. What was she going to do? She didn't want to go home. She didn't want to go anywhere without Reed, let alone eight hundred miles away from him. She could live in this icebox of a state. She could live without Starbucks. She could even live without her brothers. She'd miss them every day, but she'd live.

Watching Reed bleed all over his truck had convinced her she wanted every possible minute with this man.

But did he want her? They hadn't spoken about the message from her editor. They'd barely exchanged two words since arriving at the hospital. His trust in her had been decimated. Could he ever forgive her?

Reed asked a couple more questions and the cop left.

Pat cleared his throat. "You should go back to your bed, Jaynie, and get some rest."

"In a bit." Jayne's eyes found Reed's. He met her gaze, but his mouth tightened.

Pat's gaze ping-ponged from Jayne to Reed and back again. "I'm going for coffee. I'll come back for you. Please don't go back to your room alone." With a suggestive nod to Conor, Pat ducked out of the room.

Conor was at Pat's heels. "Coffee sounds good."

Though Scott was unconscious, Jayne lowered her voice to a whisper. "I'm so sorry, Reed. I should've told you that I worked for the *Scoop*. My editor got a lead that R. S. Morgan lived at your address and sent me to check it out. But I didn't confirm it. I didn't send any shots of you. The paper is running a piece on the kidnappings, though, just like all the rest. Your identity will come out. I don't see how you can escape it." Apparently, the only thing that paid better than celebrity humiliation was murder. The ritual Celtic angle of the killing was the cherry on her editor's sundae. "They're paying me for an interview, then I'm done with them. Back to travel mags. Money isn't worth selling my soul. My brothers and I have been broke before. We'll manage."

Reed's eyes softened. "I can't hide anymore."

A tear blurred Jayne's vision. "I know. I feel like that's all my fault. If I hadn't come here to expose you…"

Reed reached across the bed. His fingers beckoned. Jayne set her palm in his. Her heart swelled as his hand closed around hers. "It wouldn't have changed anything. Aaron would've kidnapped someone else. Maybe someone less resilient. You foiled his plan by fighting back and escaping. If you hadn't come here, he might've gotten away with multiple counts of murder. Who knows where it would've ended." His voice cracked. "Without you, Scott might not be here."

Jayne couldn't believe her ears. Had he really forgiven her? "Your life isn't going to be nice and quiet the way you like it."

"Doesn't matter. I'm done with hiding. R. S. Morgan is coming clean." Reed tugged her closer. "What would you say if I put my house up for sale? I've been thinking of moving south, like maybe to Philadelphia."

Joy bounded through Jayne's heart.

"I love you, Jayne Sullivan."

"I love you too."

"I don't want to live eight hundred miles away from you."

"Me either." Sheesh. She was a blubbering idiot. "But the pictures."

"I don't give a shit about the pictures. All I care about is you and Scott. My son almost died tonight. You risked your life to help me save him. Without you, I'd have nothing left worth living for. I owe you everything. And I know you. You couldn't have gone through with selling me out." Wincing, Reed leaned forward and kissed her.

Jayne pushed him back onto the bed. "You'll tear your stitches." Reed settled back on the pillow. "I assumed the town would ask you to be chief."

"They did. I turned them down." Reed tugged at her hand. "I don't belong here, Jayne. The town council will have to deal with Doug or find someone else for the job. Besides, I want you and Scott far away from Huntsville as quickly as possible."

"Really?"

"Really. I can sculpt anywhere, Jayne. I just need to be with you." Reed pulled her onto the bed. "Come here."

"So, all of a sudden you're Mr. Easygoing?" Jayne stretched out on her side next to him and brushed her lips across his stubbled jaw. "You didn't even choke when Scott told you he didn't want to go to college in the fall."

Reed grimaced. "After seeing him tied to that post in the woods, I wouldn't care if he told me he wanted to go to clown college or become a carny."

"He's an adult. His choices."

"Whatever." Reed pulled her closer. "The moment I met you, my whole life changed direction. Even my work has taken on a new look. No more negativity. No more hiding."

She stretched out next to him, careful not to touch the large bandage. His arm went around her as she leaned against his shoulder and slid her hand over the center of his chest. Reed's heart thudded against her palm.

"I need you, Jayne." Reed covered her hand with his. "Did I tell you the name of my new piece?"

"No."

"*Triumph*." Reed lifted her hand and kissed her knuckles. "And I can't finish it without you."

THE END

ABOUT THE AUTHOR

Melinda Leigh abandoned her career in banking to raise her kids and never looked back. She started writing as a hobby and became addicted to creating characters and stories. Since then, she has won numerous writing awards for her paranormal romance and romantic-suspense fiction. Her debut novel, *She Can Run*, was a number one bestseller in Kindle Romantic Suspense, a 2011 Best Book Finalist (The Romance Reviews), and a nominee for the 2012 International Thriller Award for Best First Book. When she isn't writing, Melinda is an avid martial artist: she holds a second-degree black belt in Kenpo karate and teaches women's self-defense. She lives in a messy house with her husband, two teenagers, a couple of dogs, and two rescue cats.